Leftovers

I0621935

Carson steeled himself and rea
find, heart hammering, palms sweatii
Around him, the fog was thickening
and swells, but he was oblivious, every ounce of watchfulness locked
by the motionless figure. Dozens of pairs of red eyes had joined the
first few, looking on with fevered delight and breathless anticipation.

Gently, ever so gently, Carson shook the man by his shoulder.
"Hey... uh... you want an aspirin or something?"

The body shifted and rolled, slipping from its perch atop a
crumpled box and spilling fully into the narrow shaft of light. The pale
fluorescent beam gleamed off a bald head, glassy staring eyes and a
sticky red carpet of blood that soaked the figure's chest and ran in
rivulets across the clutching cardboard. In that one horrifying instant,
Carson new three things: the man was a customer, the man was a
friend, and the man was definitely, definitely dead...

Graveyard Shift

The Adventures of Carson Dudley

Book One

Midnight Snack

Chris Weedin

A Horror-Comedy Novel
Inspired by
Horror Rules, the Simply Horrible Roleplaying Game

A Crucifiction Games Book

Crucifiction Games
NO PAIN, NO GAME

A Crucifiction Games Book

Copyright © 2009 Chris Weedin

All rights reserved. No part of this book may be reproduced or transmitted in any form or by any means, electronic or otherwise, without permission in writing from the publisher.

ISBN 978-0-9778263-6-0

www.crucifictiongames.com

Special thanks, as always, to God.

Printed in the United States of America

Cover and interior art by Chris Caprile

To Kelly

Who taught me that two of the very best things in life are a good book and a good friend. Thanks for seeing me through some of the worst chapters of my life and for helping to write some of the best. This one's for you.

Viva Silverdale

Chapter One

Munchie Run

"Werewolves, vampires, zombies... what are you up against?"

There was a pause.

"Demons, I think... but I can't be sure. We've only had one brush so far, but all the signs seem to point in that direction."

Carson leaned across the mini-mart counter, peering closely at the boy. He dropped his voice to a murmur. "Signs, eh? Like what?"

The kid leaned in too, giving the mini-mart a cautious, sideways glance. "The usual," he muttered. "Strange noises, strange symbols, strange disappearances, the occasional whiff of sulfur... they're subtle, but when you've been around as long as we have, you learn to pick up on 'em."

"What's your next move?"

The kid's face went hard. "We go in."

"Guns blazing?"

"Damn straight. Hit 'em quick and hit 'em hard."

Carson whistled softly. "Gutsy."

"Messy, too. But somebody's gotta clean up the night. It ain't pretty, but it's the only way."

A loud crash abruptly shattered the tension of the hushed exchange.

Both heads snapped about, eyes hungry for the source of the interruption. It wasn't hard to find. A few feet away another boy stood by a toppled rack of magazines, arms burdened with chips, cookies, candy bars, snack cakes and an impressively unhealthy assortment of dips.

His mouth twitched into a sheepish smile. "Uh... sorry, dude. I'll pick that up..."

"Hey, no worries kid... I'm on it!" Carson ducked under the counter and hurried to the rescue of the *Newsweeks* and *X-Men* comics. "Looks like you got your hands full. Besides, I hear you guys have a game to get back to."

"You got that right! We gotta... whoops!" A few packages slipped from the top of the boy's mountainous, teetering armload and smacked to the floor. "Aw, man, the Twinkies! A little help, Kel?"

The boy at the counter hurried to help. He was nearly a head taller, and with his superior armspan was able to rescue the remaining snacks from further disaster. Together they staggered to the counter and unloaded their booty.

Kelly rifled through the pile with a professional eye. "You got the cheese dip, Kit? I don't see cheese dip..."

Kit adjusted his glasses, then produced a yellow jar from his jacket pocket, cradling it tenderly. "I may forget the cookie dough, but *never* the cheese dip."

Kelly grinned. "Rock on. Got the Dew, too?"

"Got it!" A third boy appeared, his wavy brown hair just visible above a load of sloshing two-liter bottles that would have made a seasoned stock mule shy nervously. He was the shortest of the three by a hair, sturdy, with a friendly smile and confident stride.

"AJ, you're my hero."

The sodas joined the rest of the countertop pile with a sugary thump. The boys stood silently for a moment, surveying the landscape of their sweet desires.

AJ nodded slowly in appreciation. "Where guns and bullets fail..."

"...caffeine and sugar prevail!"

The boys exchanged a resounding series of high fives and knuckle bumps.

Carson slipped behind the counter, surveying the brightly-wrapped, preservative-enriched mountain with a certain measure of pride. "Gentlemen, I'm impressed - and I sell junk food for a living. Last time I saw this many goodies in one place I was unloading the 5 a.m. truck.

What gives?"

"Munchie run. Got an all-nighter going on." Kit began happily stuffing the goodies into plastic bags as Carson slid them over the scanner, a parade of colors, chemicals and additives that nearly dazzled the senses. The rapid, erratic beeping rang through the store in an eery and unheeded parody of a cardiac monitor.

Carson grinned. "Yeah, right... off to do battle with the forces of darkness once again, eh? I hear it's demons this time."

"You got it! And if I know AJ, they'll be the worst of the worst. I swear, sometimes I think he *tries* to kill us..."

Kelly grunted his agreement, digging some bills out of his wallet as the mounting cost of their feast flashed across the cash register in insistent green. "Yeah - he puts us through Hell... *literally.*"

"So what's the game?"

"*Summoner's Song,*" AJ chimed in. He stood beside his friends, making no attempt either to deny their accusations about his sadism nor to conceal a sinister grin. "And tonight's no ordinary night. We're running an *official* playtest of *Nether Regions,* the upcoming supplement for *Song.* It's got new character types, new rules on midget demons, plus a totally revamped system for determining the effects of failed partial incarnations involving deviant spirits from the Fourth Realm of the Underlands." He drew a new but obviously well-loved book out his rumpled army backpack and dropped it on the counter.

Carson flipped through its dog-eared and underlined pages as the other boys pooled their money. "Cool... 'rhyming vs. non-rhyming chants'... 'Satanic rashes'... 'the effects of demonic possession on daily job performance'... looks like they've got it all covered."

"Yup..." AJ's grin broadened into a hungry smile that had nothing to do with junk food. "I can't *wait* to try it out..."

"Can't wait to turn us into demon kibble, you mean." Kelly punched his friend on the arm with good-natured enthusiasm and just a little too much of what he was really feeling.

AJ winced, rubbing his shoulder. "Yeah. That's what I mean."

Kelly laughed.

AJ didn't.

Kelly's grin faded and he flashed Kit an uneasy look.

"Great..." Kit's eyes rolled. "We'll be payin' for that one all night. Thanks. Thanks for that."

Carson passed back the book and a handful of change and closed the till. "Well, have fun. Don't summon anything I wouldn't."

"Hey, man..." through the reflection of the plastic bags on his glasses, Kit fixed the cashier with a steady gaze. "Let's get one thing straight - we don't mess with the Hot Place. Don't get *us* confused with the Hell Huggers."

"'Hell Huggers?'"

"Yeah, you know... Satanists... cultists... robies, hood-heads, goat boys... call 'em what you like, *they're* the ones trying to stir up all the chaos. *We're* here to stop 'em."

"You got *that* right." Kelly piped in. "Bottom line is, you bring it *into* this world... we take it *out*."

"Yeah... that's how we roll..." Another round of hearty high-fives and knuckle bumps followed.

As the others loaded up with bulging bags and continued their animated reverie of impending cultist-thwarting and demon-thrashing, AJ quietly stuffed the rulebook back in his bag. He paused. "Hey... you wanna play some time?"

Carson blinked. "Dude... sure! I'd love to try your... watchacallit again?"

"Roleplaying."

"Yeah, roleplaying. Sweet! Like *World of Warcraft*."

There was a sudden, intense, almost palpable silence, as if someone had sounded the rear advance on the moon trumpet during a crowded church service. Carson became aware that they were all staring at him.

"Ouch."

"Oh, Carson..."

"If only you knew what you said..."

Carson became dimly aware that he had committed some kind of gamer *faux pas* and struggled to sort it out. "Okay, my bad. I'm getting a vibe here... you're telling me *WOW* is not *really* roleplaying...?"

"Only if Wii baseball is *really* baseball," Kit rolled his eyes, sighing. "You have much to learn, my friend."

"But no worries, you're in good hands."

"Yeah, stick with us, we'll show you the ropes!"

"Cool beans, my little amigos. Gimme a shout some time and I'll definitely hook up with the group. I'm looking forward to branching out, actually. I'm a console man myself... FPS mostly... never really tried the roleplaying thing, electronic or otherwise. Not that there's anything wrong with that..."

"First person shooters," Kelly nodded appreciatively. "Not a bad start, but there's nothing to put the fear of God into you like a good old fashioned RPG... especially with AJ at the wheel."

"At the *trigger* you mean," Kit winked. "Hey we better get going or he won't have time to properly murder us. And don't forget, X-Con is only a few months away and we gotta get this playtest turned in."

"Hey, wait a sec..." On impulse, Carson yanked three large plastic cups off a nearby stack and pushed them across the counter. "Have yourselves a Freezie, compliments of the 24/7."

The boys snatched up the cups with glee, dropping their bags and jostling for position at the Freezie machine.

"Wow, thanks, dude!"

"You're the best!"

"Free brain freeze... rock on!"

Carson watched with a smile as the thick icy mixture gushed from the spickets into their cups, curling and coiling in bright rings like a large snake getting ready to strike at their young, healthy teeth and digestive tracts. "Aw, hey, don't mention it! Things have been kinda slow lately, and you guys are gonna help keep me in the black - for tonight, at least. Not to mention the fact that you're defending an innocent, unknowing world from the forces of supernatural evil. You can't do that properly without being jammed full of sugar."

The three lads hoisted their bulging goody bags again, balancing the ice-cold Freezies with difficulty and calling farewells as they wrestled their way out of the store. A faint, sickly chime sounded from the electronic eye on the front door, indicating that the device was in need of repair.

"We'll make you proud, dude!"

"Yeah, rest easy. You're safe as long as we're around!"

"Later, man!"

Carson gave a nod and a wave. "You guys be careful on the way home, too; it's dark out there. No short cuts! And frag a Hell Hugger for me, alright?!"

Behind them, the door bumped closed.

Carson's voice carried faintly through it and out into the warm night air as he continued calling encouragements. "Lock n' load! Fire in the hole! Semper fi!!"

The calls faded quickly behind them as the trio struck out into the city, laughing and joking and taking long pulls on their neon Freezie straws. Leaving the mini-mart behind, they made their way down a side street lined with modest residential housing and mom-and-pop stores. Overhead, street lights flickered and buzzed, spilling their dull yellow haze onto the cracked sidewalk and casting lazy shadows on picket fences, crowded bushes and darkened storefronts.

AJ chuckled. "Cool guy."

"Yub!" Kit grinned and struggled to make words around a giant mouthful of ice-cold Freezie.

"Carsud is da best... tree bags of dude food, free Freedies and a whole nide of *Subboner's Sog*... whad cud be bedder?"

"A +3 Shotgun of Demon Slaying," Kelly offered.

"Dood!" Kit choked down the rest of the mouthful with an eager swallow, wincing as it set fire to his brain. "Or a..."

His words were cut short as shadows shifted from behind a nearby dumpster and a withered hand shot out to clamp down on his neck. Kit screamed, and a splash of red showered the ground at his feet. There was a moment of chaos, of pandemonium and disorientation, when time seemed to freeze and the luminous globes of the street lights spun crazily. Muffled shouts, jostlings and overstuffed bags of junk food filled the air in a mad, thrashing tangle.

Seconds later a tall, pale scarecrow in a battered army jacket lurched back from the trio of kids, his face wearing a wild, startled look that exactly matched that of the three youths. He was old and gaunt, a mat of stringy gray hair stuffed under a battered ball cap, his grizzled face smattered with thin white stubble and underscored by a rolled and soiled red bandanna that clung loosely around his neck. Fingerless gloves and torn, filthy clothing completed the image of *hobo modernis*, made even more indelible by an almost palpable stink that seemed to cling to him as stubbornly as the grime under his fingernails. Now that the frantic motion had subsided, a cloud of black flies settled in around the old man, buzzing about in a comfortable, well-practiced flight pattern.

"Er... uh... hey there, little man..." his raspy voice came unsteadily. "Sorry I startled ya..."

Kit lowered his fists, breathing hard. "*St... startled*?! Try scared! Freaked! Flipped out!"

"Yeah. I gathered. Er... uh... looks like ya dropped yer deal-io..." the hobo gestured toward a broad splash of red beverage decorating the sidewalk.

"Awww, man! I spilled my Freezie!"

"That's not *all* you spilled, dude... check your shorts!" Kelly poked his friend in the ribs, chuckling. AJ stifled a nervous laugh.

"Yeah, yeah... sorry about that, real sorry," Pete dabbed at Kit's

 6

shirt with the sleeve of his jacket, adding to a wide variety of unidentifiable stains. "My opener's usually a lot better - musta dozed off fer a sec, ya surprised me... shoulda said hullo first, I guess... real sorry kid..."

"No prob... " Kit answered weakly. "It was free anyway..." He watched forlornly as the icy mess warmed, melted and seeped slowly into the cracks of the pavement.

Then the smell hit him.

Kit's look melted from chagrin to surprise, then was quickly chased by shock, horror, wonderment, nausea and finally revulsion in rapid succession. It was as if Pete were two people, the first a man of flesh and blood, the other an invisible and unavoidably powerful mountain of the very worst smells that could be generated by the human body. Kit took an involuntary step backwards.

"Watcha say, kid?"

"Nothing! I just... just a little Freezie comin' back up on me... that's all." Kit discretely covered his nose and refocused on breathing through his mouth, which didn't seem to help much.

The old hobo nodded sagely. "Yeah, they'll do that." He seemed completely unaware of his condition.

An awkward moment of silence passed, during which Kit noticed the streetlights and storefronts were starting to spin slowly. "So... uh... did you... did you need something...?"

"Oh! Sorry. Right... forgot my manners. Name's Pete. Just wonderin' if you boys could spare a little somethin' fer a starvin' human?"

"Uhhh... sure, no prob. Look, uh.... here. Have some Twinkies." Kit fished a packet of yellow cakes out of his bag and handed them over, straining his arm to the full extent of its reach.

The dirty creases in Pete's face bent into a smile. "Thanks, kid! I love these things! Soft and sweet, just perfec' fer an elderly gent like myself. My teeth ain't what they used to be. Or *where*, fer that matter..." he grinned, showing the distressed landscape of his dental work. Under the yellow glow of the street lamps, it looked like the checkered floor of some ancient, long-neglected diner.

"Yeah, sure old-timer," Kit's voice was slightly muffled by the hand that was valiantly protecting his nose, but he managed a smile around it. "Don't mention it." The other boys, goaded by the increasingly pungent odor, made their own hasty donations. Pete thanked them profusely.

"You guys are swell Joe's, no mistake. Just swell! They say kids these days are no good, but this is one ol' geezer that's here to say *no way!!* Swell Joe's, alright... just swell..." Pete stashed his treasures carefully in the unsanitary confines of his jacket. Then, suddenly and quite unexpectedly, his brow knit and his face clouded. The old hobo cast a wary, bloodshot eye at the shadows about them. "Say, look... you guys be careful out there, okay? And head right home - no short cuts. There's somethin' weird in the air tonight. Somethin' real weird..."

"Yeah..."

"Sure, sure..."

"We'll be careful..."

Taking the warning as their exit cue, the boys hurried off down the street, casting assurances over their shoulders as they sought fresher air.

Once they'd rounded the corner, Kit sucked in deep breaths through his nose, relishing the freshness of the air. "Wow... harmless old toothless dude, but definitely on the creepy side."

"Definitely on the stinky side, too," AJ grinned, glancing back to make sure they were out of earshot.

Kit laughed, but the sound of it was still more nervous than genuine. "No kidding, I still smell him."

"I think that's you, dude. I told you, you *totally* duked your shorts!" Kelly twisted his face into an exaggerated, straining grimace, prompting AJ to choke with laughter.

"Dude, he got me alright. I didn't know whether to freeze, flee, fight or faint."

"I think you chose well. Freeze is the classic response, and I have to say you really sold it."

Kit grinned. "Jerk."

Navigating a few more blocks of residential streets, the trio crossed through a deserted strip mall, bypassed a gas station parking lot and paused between the dark, silent windows of a laundromat and a video store. The narrow maw of an alley gaped invitingly.

"Short cut?" AJ asked, jerking a thumb toward the valley of darkened bricks.

"Definitely." Kit shifted grips on his load, flexing fingers to restore feeling. "I'm ready to eat these goodies, not just pack 'em around. Let's get where we're goin'!"

The alley swallowed them promptly.

Conversation turned to *Summoner's Song*, the rehashing of old adventures and the promise of new ones. The echoes of their animated chatter trailed them down the long, shadowy path as they moved further from the light and noise of the street. Occasionally, they kicked a discarded can or scuffed against an old crate in the darkness. Otherwise the alley was theirs.

Then the sound came.

Kelly heard it first. "Hey... you guys hear that?" he stopped abruptly, hand up.

All three boys fell silent, straining their ears as they stood side by side in the thick black. Most of the light from the street was choked off, and only a faint glow poked its way over the tops of the tall brooding buildings on either side.

"Hear what?"

Kelly tilted his head, listening hard. After a minute, his jaw relaxed. "Aw, nothin'. Just thought I heard... nothin'. Never mind. C'mon, let's motorvate."

They set off, but hadn't gone more than a dozen steps when they were stopped again. This time it was AJ. "Hang on... I think I heard it. Sounds like... footsteps?"

"Yeah. Only I don't hear 'em now. You catch that, Kit?"

Kit nodded slowly. "I think so. Only they start when we start. And they're light... and... I dunno... sharp, kinda. Like... like..." his voice trailed off.

"High heels?" Kelly offered timidly, as if expecting the others to laugh. No one did.

Kit frowned. "Does that seem weird to anyone else?"

"Yeah, but that's not the weirdest thing," AJ added. "The thing that stumps me is I don't think they're coming from the street. It sounds more like..." he tilted his head back and jabbed a finger into the darkness. "Up there."

Three pairs of eyes stared, straining to make out the distant edge of the rooftop two stories above. Nothing moved. They stood for a moment in silence, as if time and quiet would somehow allow them to penetrate the black curtain of night.

Kit cleared his throat. "Well. Instead of a streetwalker, maybe we're gonna be propositioned by a roof-walker." He grinned weakly. "Anybody got a quarter?"

Nervous chuckles.

"C'mon, let's roll."

Again, they set off into the night. Again, after only a few steps, a sound brought them up short.

This time it was different.

"That was different." Kit fiddled with his glasses nervously.

"I heard a *whoosh*," AJ muttered.

"Yup. A whoosh. Definitely a whoosh."

"There was a *thump*, too. Like..."

"...like something in high heels jumped off a two-story roof and landed in an alley in front of three dumb kids who took a shortcut even after two grown-ups told them they shouldn't." Kelly finished.

AJ nodded fervently. "Yeah. *A lot* like that."

"Dude, you said 'something.'"

"Sorry... *someone*."

"Thanks, that's better." Kit licked his lips. They were suddenly dry. "Maybe it's just that old hobo again."

AJ frowned. "Dude, he could barely pull up his pants, much less climb on top of a two-story building and jump off into an alley. No way!"

"Maybe he fell?"

Kelly leaned forward and sniffed. He shook his head. "Nope. I don't have the desire to ram a red hot poker up my nose - it's definitely not Pete, jumping, falling or otherwise."

"Maybe a friend of his, then? You know... word got out about the grub and all, someone else came looking for a handout..."

Kelly squinted at his friend in the darkness. "They're Twinkies, dude, not hundred dollar bills. I don't think the homeless are lining up for 'em."

"Umm... okay, so... that's weird and all..." AJ cut in. "But now there's... *fog*..." They turned slowly, staring about at the trash-cluttered landscape and crusty brick walls, the faint details of which were rapidly being swallowed by a soupy gray mist. The ominous mass billowed and swirled about them, forming strange, ghostly shapes as it seeped, snakelike, from cracks and fissures and oozed up from the broken pavement. Eddies and swirls drifted across their feet, obscuring the ground, their shoes and the assortment of discarded tin cans, banana peels and other refuse that decorated the alley floor. Above them it drew closed like a hangman's noose, filtering the wan light from the distant streetlamps, strangling it until it was a mere ghostly luminescence somewhere deep within the mist.

Kelly stared up into the murky, impenetrable depths. "Have I just been playing too much *Summoner's Song*, or is this usually what happens just before someone gets ganked?"

"Definitely gonna have to go with the pre-ganking..."

"Oh, nuts..."

Suddenly, Kit stepped forward, calling out into the mist. "Hello! uh... hi... I mean... hey..."

AJ and Kelly made a grab for his shirt but he was already out of range. They whispered fiercely for him to return to the small clearing that remained in the mist, but he pressed on with a brisk step. After a moment, they had to squint their eyes to make out his shape, nearly swallowed by the hungry fog.

"Hey, uh... you hungry? How about a snack, eh? Twinkie, maybe?" Kit rummaged through his bag. "Crap... out of Twinkies... sorry, I gave my last one to some hobo dude named... uh... Pete! His name was Pete. Maybe he's a friend of yours, hunh? You know him? Nice guy, real... memorable." Kit waited hopefully, ears straining. The damp of the mist was seeping into his shirt, making him shiver as its clammy fingers found the sensitive places on his skin.

"No? No problem... uhhh... let's see what else we got..." He dug deeper into his bag. The rustling sounded hollow and overly loud and scraped at the nerves of his watching friends as they looked on, tense and nervous. "Hey, here ya go! Little Debbies!" Kit drew out a cheerful box, splashed with happy colors and smiling children. "They're not as big but there's more in a box..." He thrust the container out into the mist.

Behind him, Kelly and AJ held their breath.

Seconds passed.

Silence.

Fog.

Nothing.

"Well..." Kit turned around, shoulders slumping in relief. "I guess that's..."

And then he was gone, yanked back into the mist so hard that the plastic grocery bag in his hand burst wide open, showering the alley with foil packages and cellophaned treats. A short plaintive cry was abruptly cut off, fading almost instantly into a sick gurgle. Kelly and AJ jumped back in surprise, then surged forward, shouting.

"Kit!"

"Dude!"

"Where are you?!"

"What's goin' on?!"

"You okay?!"

"Answer me, man!"

They plunged into the swirling white curtain and onward, pelting blindly down the alley, hearts hammering, breathing ragged, banging their shins and stumbling over piles of garbage and refuse half-seen on the alley floor, then rising and racing on.

The sudden, brutal sound of ringing metal brought them up short, and it wasn't for several moments until both boys realized they were lying flat on their backs on the cold, dirty pavement. Above them loomed the dim outline of a large, heavy, commercial dumpster, dragged sideways across the alley and blocking it neatly off. The hollow metallic echoes of their collision still hung in the air and rang even louder inside their aching skulls.

"Whoa..." AJ slurred. He rubbed his forehead, tenderly probing the knot that was already forming. "Didn't see that one coming..."

Beside him Kelly drew himself painfully to a sitting position, shaking his head to clear it and rubbing a bruised shoulder. "I'm betting the garbage guys didn't leave this here. I don't know about you, but I'm starting to feel picked on."

They were still shaking their heads when something small and boxy whistled through the air, punched through the mist and slid to a neat stop a foot away.

They blinked.

"Is that what I think it is...?"

Kelly nodded, swallowing hard. "It is if you're thinking it's a box of Little Debbies snack cakes. Guess whoever's out there doesn't have a sweet tooth. We gotta find Kit..." he heaved himself to his feet, weaved a little and grabbed the edge of the dumpster to steady himself.

"Dude!" AJ cried. "Your hand!"

Something coarse and damp brushed Kelly's fingers and he yanked them back with a yelp. A rat sat perched on the metal rim where his hand had been, fat, black and full of contempt; its beady red eyes drilling fierce holes in him as he backpedaled

"Whoa..." Kelly wiped his hand unconsciously on his pants. "He came out of nowhere."

"And brought friends..."

The boys turned slowly, watching with growing unease as more and more slick dark shapes crept to the edge of the ring of fog. In moments, they were surrounded by a floating horde of hot red eyes, unblinking, malicious and fixed hard upon them. The rodents were everywhere, perched on garbage cans, lurking under crates and crumpled cardboard boxes, skulking over rancid trash heaps, noses twitching and whiskers quivering in anticipation. The alley's only two human occupants bumped softly into one another, working themselves unconsciously back-to-back in the center of the furry black ring.

Kelly's mouth pulled down into a frown. "This can't be good."

"It ain't natural... it just ain't natural!" AJ stared back at the red eyes, his voice tinged with awe. Their blatant scrutiny was making him feel exposed and vulnerable and he didn't like it. Not one bit. He shifted nervously. "What are they doin', man?"

"I dunno... but whatever it is, it's almost like they're trained or something. Look at 'em, just watching... waiting. It's like someone *told* 'em to do that. I mean, why else would they?!"

"What... like the rat whisperer?"

"Dude, how should I know?! I'm just spitballing here..." Kel lurched at the nearest rat, waving his arms. "*Shoo!!*"

The creature didn't so much as flinch a single hair, just hunched where it was on a derelict tomato crate, staring up at him with its dead gaze.

"But who could... why would... this ain't natural!"

"I'm sold on that."

"They're *rats,* dude... they aren't supposed to spy!"

Kelly narrowed his eyes, staring back at the filthy creature he had tried to spook. On impulse he stepped forward and kicked, his heavy boot catching the thing square on and launching it out into the mist with a squeal of surprise. There was a satisfying clatter somewhere far down the alley.

"They aren't supposed to *fly*, either, but that one did a pretty fair job."

"Rock on!" A hungry light lit AJ's eyes and he launched into a frenzy of kicking that sent rats flying like furry black footballs into the gray mist. He was joined immediately by his friend. In the face of this unexpected onslaught, the rat army retreated, slinking under dumpsters or perching out of reach on ledges or piles of stinking detritus.

The boys stopped, panting.

"Nice solution..." AJ muttered. "Very direct... I like it." He took a quick step toward a rodent creeping out from under a broken recliner, but it scurried back to safety with a belligerent squeak. "Anyway, that's a start. Now what?"

Kelly eyed the fog warily and shook his head. "I'm fresh out of ideas and well and truly freaked. You?"

"Same." AJ's brow creased. "Okay..." He drew a deep breath. "This is gonna sound strange, but... if this was in-game, what would you do?"

"Grab another Dew and turn on some lights."

"That's not helping."

"Sorry. I don't know if it's the scary living mist or the attack of the possessed ratlings from Hell, but I'm not thinking too clearly right now."

"Yeah," AJ swallowed. "All I can think of is that Kit's out there. *Somewhere.*"

"Right. Right..." There was fear in Kelly's eyes, but a steely resolve had dawned there as well. "And I say we get him back."

"Get him *back*...? You mean... go out *there?!*"

Kelly gave a curt nod. "That's exactly what I mean. You with me?"

"Dude... I've spent my entire life in my mom's basement playing make-believe games and fantasizing about imaginary supernatural creatures - of course I'm ready. I'm not goin' unarmed, though..." AJ cast about a moment, then selected a short length of rusty pipe from a nearby pile of garbage. He gave it a few trial swings, feeling his courage build.

"Now you're talking!" Kelly dove for his own pile and came up with a length of broken two-by-four. "This one's even got *nails* in it! Okay, let's do this."

When he turned back, AJ was gone.

"NOOOO!!!!"

Kelly lunged to the section of wall where his friend had been standing mere seconds ago. A noise snapped his head upward, where he thought he could just make out the soles of AJ's black tennis shoes as they disappeared into the swirl of murky gray above him. A faint, sickening gurgle and the mad clatter of feet against bricks told him the journey was no pleasure trip.

Swearing loudly, Kelly stepped back, desperately sweeping the alley, probing shadows, trying in vain to pierce the impenetrable mist. The rats were back in force, crowding in, intent, eager, fearless now and seeming to bristle with hungry anticipation. Kelly started as a cold wet nose touched his ankle; he lashed out and stepped back quickly into the center of the alley. He was turning constantly, eyes probing, heart racing, mind numb.

There was no one left. He was next.

And he knew it.

"Just one swing..." he muttered to himself, clutching his makeshift weapon so tightly that the wooden edges bit into his palms. A bead of cold sweat trickled down his cheek. "That's all I want... just one swing..."

As it turned out, when the end came seconds later, that's precisely what he got.

Chapter Two

Hard Times in the 'Hood

"...missing for several days. The three teens were last seen in the Belfry district, which has been the site of several other unexplained disappearances in recent weeks..."

The radio was sandwiched into a shelf behind the counter, stashed between a few boxes of Pokemon cards and several stacks of jumbo-sized, limited edition Freezie cups emblazoned with propaganda for Hollywood's latest blockbuster. The battered device blared its message with blind importance, competing for the attention of an empty room, unaware that its only audience was a sleeping figure kicked back precariously on the counter stool, a rumpled newspaper draped over his face. The paper rose and fell gently with the rhythm of slow, steady breathing.

"...for any information leading to the recovery of the missing boys, as police have announced they have few leads. Sad story, eh Phil?"

"Indeed it is, Chuck. Indeed it is. And now, for the weather! It's

 16

another bea-u-tiful spring day here in Las Calamas, and you know what that means... that's right, get those bathing suits ready, folks, cuz the beach is callin'! In spite of the recent unseasonable showers and cloudy weather, meteorologists are predicting sun, sun and more sun right around the corner! We're looking for highs in the..."

The radio droned on, imparting its crackling wisdom to the silent magazines, snacks and household products that packed the tidy shelves of the mini-mart. Under his newspaper blanket the clerk twitched and shifted, the old stool creaking ever so slightly closer to a rude awakening. Oblivious, the clerk muttered something unintelligible, blissfully unaware of his impending engagement with the well polished floor.

Breathe in.

The paper fell.

Breathe out.

The paper rose.

A moment later the tranquil nighttime symphony of the mini-mart was joined by the electronic chime on the front door. Unlike the rest of the store, which was in good repair, the chime was not at its best and seemed in need of a tune-up, its tone sounding sick and warbly, like a record played at the wrong speed. As sad as it sounded, it brought a smile to the face of the young lady who stepped from the darkness outside into the washed-out fluorescent lighting. She was pretty, but looked like she either didn't know it or didn't want to be reminded of it - her long blond hair was stuffed under a red stocking cap and her fine, pale features undisguised by cosmetics. Her clothes were functional but equally unflattering - baggy khaki cargo pants tucked into well-worn work boots, with a white tanktop and brown canvas jacket thrown over her trim shoulders. She stopped at the counter, a smile playing over her thin lips. Clear, intelligent blue eyes swept the sleeping clerk, the empty store, back again. She studied him closely, listening to the steady, reassuring sound of his breathing.

After a moment she broke quietly away, made a few selections from the well-stocked shelves and returned to the counter, placing her items carefully on the cool glass.

The clerk made no move.

"Ahem..."

The paper rose and fell, its rhythm undisturbed.

"Ahem!"

The sleeper twitched and gave a soft snort, but did not awaken.

 17

"Sorry, Carson..." she murmured. "It's either use the bell or starve to death..."

Reaching out a slender but calloused hand, the young lady rapped smartly on the counter bell, disturbing both its *"Use Only In Case of Snack-Related Emergency"* sign and the dozing clerk. Both wobbled precariously, but by some miracle of gravity failed to topple.

Fighting his way out from under the newspaper, the clerk righted his stool with an effort and blinked quickly to clear the sleep from his eyes. "Wha...? Who's a...?! Fifteen...? Batman!!" Slowly his eyes focused on the pretty face before him, now graced with a wide grin that made it even more pleasant to wake up to. "Oh... hey, Kiki."

"Good evening sunshine. Or should I say 'good morning.'"

"Hmm?! Oh... uh... yeah... morning. Right. Good one." Carson gave a weak smile, stretched and yawned.

"You've uh... er... you've got a little..."

"Oh, sorry..." Carson wiped at the thin sheen of drool that decorated his cheek. "Darned Z slugs. Thanks."

He stifled another yawn, rubbed his face vigorously and addressed the small pile of sundries on the counter. "Alright! Groceries! I'm awake! Let's see what we got here..." He began ringing up Kiki's purchases, squinting at the packages as he struggled to focus his eyes.

"Ring me up a corndog too, wouldja?"

"Yeah... no prob..." Carson finished beeping the last of the items and turned to the warmer. Kiki watched him idly as he hunted for the largest and freshest of the batch.

Carson was in his early twenties, with casual brown hair that constantly schemed to creep onto his face, partly due to its style and partly because it was usually in need of a trim. The face it framed was clean-cut and ordinary, almost handsome but not quite, with the stub of a beard clinging to its chin and warm green eyes. He seemed tall, but Kiki was sure that was mostly due to her vantage point, which was much closer to the ground. When he moved, it was with the springy step and quick reflexes of youth, and he was lean and fit if not powerful. He wore a long-sleeved gray t-shirt under a short-sleeved green one that proudly bore the faded logo of last year's hottest first-person shooter, with a brown button-down, currently unbuttoned, over it all. A pair of loose fitting jeans with a hole in the knee completed the ensemble, along with a pair of comfortably worn sneakers that seemed more like old friends.

Carson passed her the deli bag, crisp, fresh and invitingly warmed by its contents. She noticed that he'd slipped an extra corndog inside and smiled ruefully, knowing that it wouldn't show up on the bill and wouldn't do any good to mention it. He would neither accept its return nor take money for it. Same old Carson.

He turned to bag the groceries, moving casually. Kiki's eyes followed him as she became momentarily absorbed with her friend, analyzing what made him *him*. Finding out what made things tick was a hobby of hers, had been since childhood, and it didn't matter whether it was machines or people. Carson was an especially interesting case. He *was* casual. Everything about him. She thought of other words to describe him, absently flicking through her mental dictionary, categorizing as she usually did: laid-back., friendly, open. Almost everything about him seemed non-threatening and amicable, from his disarming lopsided smile to the way he handled corn dogs. Even his trademark posture was invitingly average, hands in his pockets or slouching comfortably against the counter, the Freezie machine or anything else that happened to be nearby and nailed down. In fact, Kiki couldn't remember the last time she saw him standing fully upright under his own power. Even now, bagging the groceries, he had one foot propped on the rung of the stool and an elbow on the counter. He was the only person she'd ever known who could actually bag groceries with an elbow on the counter.

Still, he wasn't lazy, as one could easily see from the condition of the store - the floor was always clean and shiny and there were always paper towels and soap in the bathroom. The slouching was more casual than slothful... just another *normal* feature of a very *normal* person.

Normal. The word clicked in her brain and she smiled, satisfied with it. It was a good word for him, as good as "casual" and perhaps even better. Everything about him screamed Regular Joe, and Kiki liked that just fine. She liked it because it made her feel at ease, and because she had had quite enough that was *not* normal in her life already. Carson wasn't the kind of guy you'd put in charge of anything, but he was definitely someone you'd ask if you needed to use the bathroom or where to find the ketchup and know that he would give you a straight answer and some pleasant conversation to boot. After all she'd been through, those kinds of someone's were a welcome change.

"Here ya go, kiddo." Carson handed over the groceries and punched the subtotal, stifling another yawn.

Kiki traded money for goods. "What's up with you? You're not usually the kind to sleep on the job."

"I dunno. Sorry. I guess... heck, it's just there's nothin' to do! It's been so slow lately, like the whole 'hood is empty or something. This place is usually hopping - you know how it is - but the last couple of weeks business has been taking a long, slow slide into the toilet. Graveyard shift isn't what it used to be. It's... well, just like it sounds - it feels like I'm *working* in one." Carson rang open the cash register, revealing a till that was empty except for Kiki's few lonely bills. "A few more weeks of this and I'll be killing time down at unemployment - if Jack doesn't toss me first for sleeping on the job. Man... this stinks." Carson slouched dolefully against the Freezie machine and adopted a passionate frown.

"No customers, eh?" Kiki took a bite of her corn dog and chewed thoughtfully. "Maybe people are finally reading the ingredients on this junk." She picked up a nearby snack cake and eyed its wrapper. "Most of these labels read like a page from my chemistry textbook."

Carson snorted. "Hardly. If it doesn't have at least three kinds of sugar, yellow dye #5 and something ending in '-polysucraphosphate', most of my customers won't touch it. You're not down on the boardwalk, sweetheart - this is the Belfry District."

"Fair enough. Maybe it's competition, then. Didn't I read there was a new mini-mart chain opening in town? S'posed to be run by some big Asian corporation or something."

"Yeah, but they're not open yet. They had a little wrinkle with their marketing campaign."

"Oh?"

"Translation issues. Apparently America isn't quite ready to shop at the 'Super Maxi-Pad.'"

Kiki smiled around another bite of corn dog. "Ouch."

"Yeah. Their slogan is 'Here Comes the Flow of the Month.' Catchy, hunh?"

Kiki's silvery laugh broke the mood and, at last, brought a grin to Carson's face. "Well, that's a hundred grand they'll never see again." She dabbed a spot of mustard from her lips with a paper napkin. "Okay, then, I give up. If it's not a health kick or competition, where'd all your happy little junk food addicts go?"

Carson shrugged helplessly. "Beats me!" He threw up his hands. "Maybe it's just a slump. Or maybe you're right, maybe there's someplace new where everyone's gettin' their grub on. You know the neighborhood... lots of little side streets, cul-de-sacs, nooks and crannies. Could be something opened up that I don't know about - new shops are always popping up these days, seems like. Like that little place across the street... " Carson jerked a thumb toward the window, indicating a nondescript storefront hunkering in the shadows across the street. "That curio shop... what's it called?"

"The Curio Shop?"

"Yeah, that's it. One day it's not there, the next *bang!* there it is."

"Hmm," Kiki squinted at the little building, barely visible under the shroud of night. "Now that you mention it, it did sort of just... appear. How long has it been there?"

"Around three weeks. I remember, cuz it was about then business started drying up."

A dutiful electronic *ding* announced the arrival of a customer at the gas pumps outside.

Carson perked up. "Ah, another victim of fossil fuel arrives... we have our *second* paying customer of the night. Perhaps all is not lost." He casually stabbed a button on the gas console and watched as dollars and gallons flickered past.

"There you go, sport - cheer up. At least there's one customer who hasn't fallen prey to the Phantom Curio Shop... until it starts peddling regular unleaded along with monkey paws and shrunken heads."

"Good point - I'll talk to Jack about bringing those items in. But just between you and me, I don't think that shop is giving us any competition."

"No?"

"No. Seems to me you have to *do* business in order to *steal* business... and I don't think the Curio Shop is doing *any* business at all. In the last three weeks I haven't seen *anyone* come or go - not a single soul. And don't think they don't have any merchandise. That place is loaded." He wandered absently to the window, eyes fixed on the shop. "Got bored last night and wandered over for a look-see. There's stuff inside, and lots of it. Shelves are full of all sorts of junk. Didn't see any shrunken heads, but definitely some odd bits." He shrugged and turned back to the counter. "Oh well. Didn't think anyone could be doing worse than we are, but there you have it. I don't envy 'em. More mustard?"

Kiki nodded and Carson passed her a handful of yellow packets. He glanced at her hands, which looked pink from a fresh scrubbing but still sported grease under the nails. "Moonlighting again, eh?"

"Yup... changing out a transmission." Mustard squished out onto the second corndog in a thick yellow coil.

"When are you gonna stop working on cars and buy one?"

"When they cost as much as your corndogs." Kiki waved her meal wistfully and took another bite.

"Lucky Earl's Electronics Boutique ain't exactly paying the bills, eh?"

Kiki rolled her eyes. "Not exactly. Between school and rent there's hardly enough left for books. Might have to give up my weekly facial and massage."

"That's a shame. What's up with that college, anyway? Don't they have scholarships for smart people like you?"

Kiki's face hardened, pulling itself tight like cellophane stretched across a package of Snow Balls. "I pay my own way."

"Er... uh... right. Sure." Carson was acutely aware that he'd touched a nerve and was quite eager to untouch it.

"Uhhh... so, how is Lucky Earl?" He busied himself straightening the Freezie cups and straws. There was an awkward silence, and for a moment he wasn't sure she would answer.

When she did, her voice still had an edge but the cellophane had relaxed a bit. "Not so lucky. He cut off the tip of his thumb again. Wire snips."

Carson winced. "Ouch. Isn't that hard to do?"

"For most of us, yes. You don't know Lucky Earl."

"I guess we should just be happy he owns an electronic shop and not a gun store."

The sickly door chime warbled again and a pretty brunette entered, waving a hello and beaming a smile at Carson as she headed for the cooler. Carson was still in mid-wave when the chime sounded again and, following so closely on the heels of the brunette that she seemed like a panther stalking prey, another young lady entered. The newcomer was tall, whiplike and ghostly pale, clad from head to toe in skimpy full length black leather. She tossed her head impatiently, sending long, raven-black hair cascading over her shoulders. Pausing, she licked her lush ruby lips, casting quick, hungry eyes about the store.

"Hey, Vanessa." Carson called a greeting and the gaunt figure swiveled her head in a sharp motion, eyes narrowing. Lips twitching into the faintest of smiles, she gave a cursory flick of her head to acknowledge him and then stalked off between two aisles with a barely audible creak of leather.

"Well, anyway," Carson went on. "Expensive or not, I bet you're tearing things up at good ol' Las Calamas Community College. A tech whiz like you is probably flying through the... the... well, whatever it is you're flying through."

"Entry level Information Technology courses, mostly: a little hardware, a little software, some basic programming. Flying is hardly the word for it, though. Pre-req's are a pain and they don't offer much weekends or evenings." She shrugged. "But that's the way it is. You want the paper, you've got to jump through the hoops. I'll get through it. All it takes is time."

Carson relaxed a fraction. Whatever ill wind had blown through Kiki's evening seemed to have passed now, and she was back to her old chipper and resilient self. "That's the spirit. You'll be making the big bucks in no time, doing... doing... well, doing whatever Information Technology people do. Maybe you can even fix that tweaked-out door chime for us. Heck, I bet I could get Jack to hire you to do it right now... Find everything okay?" Carson turned to face the pretty brunette, who set a bottle of flavored tea on the counter and began digging through her purse.

"Yes, thanks. And I've got pump 3."

Carson took her credit card and punched up the total. "You got it. Anything else this evening? Snack? Magazine? Struggling mini-mart franchise?"

She laughed. "Business that bad?"

"If it was any worse... well, it couldn't be any worse."

She laughed again, smiling as her green eyes scanned the 24/7's generous offerings. "Too bad you don't have espresso... if you did, you'd have a sale for sure."

"Nope, no coffee indulgence... but behold!" Carson swept a Hershey bar from the candy rack and presented it with a flourish. "Chocolate - the next best thing!"

"Now you're talking. Ring me up. And throw in some Tic-Tacs."

"Yes, ma'am!" Carson swiped her credit card. "Just need some ID... thanks, Ms. Herron. That'll do." He bagged the goodies and handed them across the counter. "You made my night. Stay safe!"

The girl waved and left. Vanessa appeared suddenly at the counter, as if she had been there the whole time.

"Whoa... er... hey again, Vanessa. Just the breath mints? That'll be $1.80."

Without a word Vanessa dropped a pair of crisp bills on the counter, eyes fixed hungrily on the front door.

Carson rang up the sale. "Super-spearmint... big date, hunh? Well, here's your..." he looked up. Vanessa was gone. "...change." He shrugged and dropped the coins into the take-a-penny-leave-a-penny cup.

Kiki was staring at the door. "I didn't know the *Rocky Horror Picture Show* was in town."

"What... Vanessa?" Carson chuckled. "Yeah, we get all kinds in here. But I'll settle for getting anyone at all... and she's one of the only steady customers I have left." He let out a gusty sigh and sat down, resuming his precarious perch on the stool.

"So what am I, chopped liver?"

Carson glanced idly at her. She stood straight, one hand on her hip, the other resting on the counter beside her modest bag of groceries. Kiki was smiling, but Carson noticed suddenly that it didn't go very deep. Underneath it was weariness and stress. He had been so preoccupied with his own troubles that he hadn't really been paying attention to how she looked - which was not particularly good. Kiki was smart, independent, tough and knew how to take a joke, which made her a good friend in his book, and he suddenly felt guilty. As he thought back to the contents of her grocery bag and the infrequency of her purchases, he realized she would probably be living out of its contents for the next week or so.

"Far from it... in fact, right now, lady, you're the only thing keeping us afloat. Which entitles you to a complimentary Freezie, on the house." He slid off the stool and reached for a cup.

At the mention of "on the house" she frowned, the tight lines from moments ago threatening to return. Then, with an effort, she softened. "Freezie. Okay. Like the night we met." Kiki watched the icy mixture pile into the cup, the slurping, slithering hiss of it somehow comforting. "You must think I'm a cheap date."

Carson was about to answer when the sickly chime on the front door announced the arrival of another customer. "Wow, it's a regular rush... five people in one hour. Hey Pete! What's the word on the street?"

The newcomer flinched, looking startled, then squinted about under the brightly buzzing fluorescent lights, his hands raised in an awkward defensive posture reminiscent of the Saturday night chop saki specials. After a moment his rheumy eyes focused on Carson and he relaxed, adjusting the battered ballcap that restrained his tangle of greasy gray locks. The logo emblazoned on it was as faded, unreadable and stained as the old man's face.

"S'quiet, soldier. Real quiet. Y'might say... *too* quiet." He cast warily about the store, then sniffed the air. Apparently satisfied that the mini-mart was not under imminent danger of attack, he sauntered up to the counter, preceded by a wily scowl.

"Red Freezie and a cup o' hot water... and make sure it's to the top, boy." His fingers toyed with the soiled red bandanna looped about his neck, eyes playing about the store like an old badger watching for hawks.

"Sure thing." Carson reached for a cup. "You a paying customer tonight?" He asked idly.

The old-timer's eyes narrowed, pulling his crow's feet into forked lightning and his scowl a grim leather mask. Then the clouds broke and a grin shone through his scratchy gray stubble. From his pocket came the hearty jingle of coins.

"Whaddaya take me fer, some kinda freeloadin' carpet bagger?! 'S can day, soldier. I'm a rich man!"

"Can day. Nice. You're walkin' the talk, my friend." Carson busied himself with the drinks.

Pete's grin spread, a jackal in hobo's clothing. "Damn Yuppies throwin' away a fortune in 'luminum. I'm only too happy to cash in. Too lazy to haul their crap to the re-cycle thing-a-ma-bob. But not me... no siree... I ain't too proud, not ol' Pete..."

"Sweet. Think green. You're really living in the now, my friend. The Earth thanks you."

Pete's coins jingled again. "Roger that... green is good... veeeeeeery good..." The old gray head bobbed in satisfaction, as behind him Kiki discretely covered her nose and sidled away toward healthier environs. Carson, who seemed not to notice the general downturn in air quality, slid two brimming cups across the counter. He waited patiently as Pete first lifted their lids to verify that they met his expectation of "full", then carefully counted out quarters, dimes and pennies.

"Good haul this week, eh?" Carson asked as he watched the meticulous procedure unfold.

"Negative. Lots of recon, not much payoff. Resources were scarce."

Carson grunted. "I hear you there... people were scarce too."

Pete paused over a grimy dime, snapping his bloodshot eyes to Carson's face. Something flickered in their hazy, unfocused depths. It hung there a moment, barely discernible yet unmistakable. Then it was gone and he was back to his work.

"Y'don't say."

"Yup. Business has taken a porcelain detour, I don't mind saying. And I also don't mind saying," he added on sudden impulse, "That it's starting to feel just a little weird."

Pete looked up again, this time holding Carson's gaze for just a moment longer before returning to his decision between the more appropriate of two pennies. "Roger that. Y'got a good ken, boy. There's somethin' in the air indeed... somethin' not right."

"You can say *that* again," Kiki muttered from her vantage point a few aisles away.

If Pete heard her, he made no sign, but leaned in close to Carson, threatening to jostle his neatly stacked skyline of coins. The old hobo's eyes had a light in them now, and they loomed in Carson's face like a pair of grimy, red rimmed headlights shining out of a thick fog. The spark was back. "Look, kid... I'm gonna let you in on a little secret. I've seen... *things* lately. Bad things. There's an ill wind blowin' here in LC, I can tell ya that fer sure. Certain sure. There's more shadows here than there should be, an fewer people. Ain't felt this kinda bad hoodoo since back in 'Nam."

Carson's own eyes narrowed. In spite of the nearly overwhelming odor of his unwashed confidant, he couldn't tear himself away. There was something earnest about Pete's statement, something so matter-of-fact and dead-on confident that it froze his hands to the counter.

He shivered involuntarily as the slightest thrill went up his spine. "You know something you're not telling me, Pete?"

Pete shifted slightly, sliding his eyes side to side under bushy gray brows. The badger was on full alert now. His breath blew across Carson's face, startling in the compost pungence of its scent, but seeming somehow only to underscore the intensity of his words. "All's I can tell ya fer now is... watch yer back. And keep yer eyes open."

Then he was gone. The only sound in the mini-mart was the fading echo of the mortally wounded door chime. Seconds later, it was followed by a hacking, phlegmy cough from the parking area and a tremendous wet spit, muffled through the glass but still disturbingly audible.

After a moment, and still covering her nose, Kiki cautiously ventured from hiding. "What's 'hoodoo?'"

"Beats me." Carson's eyes bored holes through the darkened front window, where the night had already swallowed the lean, shabby form of Stinky Pete. His pulse was beating fast, and a strange sensation was tickling across his skin, symptoms no doubt caused in part by exposure to Pete's aroma, but not entirely. He was feeling strangely charged by this encounter, as if he had, for the first time in his life, had a moment so real, so undeniably *on*, that it refused to pass. It was as if he had brushed up against a truth that others only guessed at or dismissed as a dream. He let his breath out slowly, not even realizing that he had been holding it.

"Whaddaya think?"

"I think he's nuts. Mixed, salted, shelled and served up on a taxicab floor. I don't trust him. *And* I don't like him. Don't trust him, don't like him. Not a bit. He's not right, Carson. Not right at all. 'Bad hoodoo.' What the heck is that?!" She shook her head. "People like that will do you dirty every time. Trust me. I know his kind."

"Maybe..." Carson murmured, so caught up in this new sensation that he neither registered the heat of her diatribe nor paused to consider what lay behind it. "But maybe not. Maybe... just maybe... the old geezer is onto something. Maybe there *is* weirdness going on around here - bad hoodoo, bad mojo, bad karma, whatever you wanna call it."

The hands on the clock started ticking again.

"And if there is..." Carson added on impulse. "I'm gonna get to the bottom of it."

Chapter Three

When Vampires Attack

"Actually, it was Han who fired first."

"No kidding! I always thought Greedo got off the first shot."

"Well, sure, that's the way it is *now*... or at least that's how it's been from the *second* revision on. Really, it all depends on which version you're watching. You see, in the original, Lucas had Solo getting the drop on Greedo and blowing him away. *Vap!* Just like that. It was awesome. Total Solo - the guy's a smuggler after all, a criminal, and here's this bounty hunter trying to collect on his life. What else is he gonna do? But anyway, some fans complained because they thought it made Han look too... sinister... too much like a bad guy. Go figure. So, Lucas flip-flopped. In the re-release he doctored the scene so that it *looked* like Greedo shot first."

"Man." Carson whistled softly. "Total sell out."

"Yeah. Tell me about it. Solo was on the top of his game - no *way* he'd let one of Jabba's low level goons get the drop on him. Oh well... so much for integrity in filmmaking. Of course, that's not the end of the story. As it turns out, enough people complained about the revision so that he revised it *again*... in the latest release Greedo and Han basically shoot at the same time."

"*Double* sell out?!"

"Yup. Sort of turns your stomach, doesn't it?"

Carson shook his head, looking somewhat awed, slightly jaded and a good deal wiser. "Wow. *Star Wars* lied to me. I don't know if I'll ever be the same."

"Hey, it's no biggie. I've got the originals - and I mean *the* originals - on DVD. Feel free to borrow them any time and undo the damage."

"Hey, thanks, Mr. Carey!" Carson brightened. "That would rock!"

"Don't mention it." Carson's lone customer took a pull on the straw of his bucket of soda. "I'll drop them off next week."

"Sweet. Anything else to watch for?" Carson leaned in, the gleam of impending geeky sci-fi rapture making his green eyes shine like fire.

Mr. Carey scratched his goatee thoughtfully, pursing his lips. The fluorescent lighting gleamed off his bald head, stoking his powers of concentration. "A lot less CG, thank goodness. For some reason Lucas tried to wedge in some gosh-awful extra bits here and there; I guess he was trying to flesh the film out, but mostly it just looks like a bantha threw up on it. If you ask me, *Star Wars* needed those extra scenes about as much as it needed Ewoks."

"Yeah. Stormtrooper armor – not so good against blasters, even worse against rocks."

Carey chuckled.

"Well, thanks for the inside scoop, Mr. C. Can't wait for those vids so I can commence my re-education."

"My pleasure. Always happy to help the younger generation find the truth. Well, I'd better be getting home. It's comics day and I've got some catching up to do."

"Gotcha. My chores are calling, anyway. Stay safe!"

The sickly echo of the front door chime heralded Mr. Carey's exit. The store was empty once again. Carson shook his head, still in awe. "Han shot first... I *knew* it!" He pondered this fresh revelation for another few moments, then lurched up from the duct-taped comfort of the stool and busied himself with his nightly duties.

A few days had passed since his ominous conversation with Stinky Pete. In spite of the lingering sensation that all as he knew it was about to suddenly and irrevocably change, nothing had. Business was no better than before - in fact, it was worse. Mr. Carey had been only his third customer since he clocked in over three hours ago. It was midnight already, and there was little hope on the dark horizon. Carson stared out into the blackness of the warm spring evening, pausing as he rotated the cheese-filled Polish sausages bathing and sweating under the glory of the heat lamp.

Nothing.

He sighed. Not a single hungry kid, passing swing-shifter, insomniac, late night cruiser or vagrant in sight. Headlights appeared, and for a moment Carson's hopes lifted. Then the vehicle whooshed past, scattering loose papers and spinning an empty Freezie cup on its way to places more lively and less like a big empty mini-mart.

Carson sighed again. "This sucks."

With no further recourse, he settled into daydreaming, staring absent-mindedly out the window. Before long he realized that his gaze had settled once again on the dim outline of the Curio Shop, squatting mutely in the shadows across the street. He had taken to watching the shop more and more now, drawn to it by some nameless curiosity, catching himself staring at the unremarkable little building during idle moments when his mind would wander to thoughts of television or video games. Moments like this one. Lately it had become so familiar that at times, especially late at night, that it *almost* seemed the shop was watching him back.

Carson was hard pressed to explain his fascination with the place; for some strange reason he just felt himself drawn to it. The building was as empty and lifeless as when it had first appeared, giving no reason to have attracted his attention... or anyone else's for that matter. No one came. No one left. No lights. No life. No activity.

He snorted softly. "Just like over here," he muttered. "We probably look the same way from *their* front window... except for the shrunken heads."

With an effort, he tore himself away from the window and returned to his busywork, snagging a corn dog from the warmer to ease his pain. He made his way to the back of the store to put some distance between himself and his distraction, setting to work on the invigorating task of turning all the beverages in the cooler label-side out. Ten minutes later Carson was half-finished with both the top shelf and his corn dog when a noise caught his ear.

He paused, listening.

The noise came again, faint, muffled by the rear wall of the store, coming from somewhere outside. It had the complex, almost melodic ring of trash in motion, as if someone were moving garbage cans or climbing through a dumpster. Carson's brow furrowed, his hands full of bottles of strawberry milk and the corn dog clamped for safekeeping in his mouth. He cocked his head, straining to hear. The noise had stopped. Stowing the bottles, he stepped to the rear door of the mini-mart, letting the cooler door close behind him to shut out the generator hum.

For a moment, there was nothing. Then, through the thick industrial metal of the back door, the noise came again.

Tink. Clank. Rattle.

It ended with the sound of a rolling bottle and a tinny clatter. He concentrated - tin can, possibly aluminum. Still wearing a frown, Carson reached for the handle of the door. He paused with his hand on the cool metal.

Behind the 24/7, he knew, was an alley, the same basic kind you would find behind any self-respecting mini-mart in Las Calamas: stinky, dirty, cluttered with trash, garbage cans, cardboard boxes, food crates and a king-sized green dumpster. It wasn't unusual to hear noises out there, or to discover a stray cat or hobo browsing for dinner, and Carson was certain that one of the two was the cause of the disturbance. But for some reason, he hesitated. It might have been the haunting echo of Stinky Pete's foreboding reference to "bad hoodoo" that suddenly swam up from the inner recesses of his memory, or the mere fact that the neighborhood had been so ominously quiet lately; what it was, he couldn't say for sure. But whatever the cause, Carson felt, along with it, the slightest twinge of unease.

On a whim, he ducked back into the store, hurrying back to the front where he fetched an old friend from behind the counter. It was a baseball bat, well-used and well-loved but still sturdy; the faded "Louisville Slugger" emblem still visible in the tough hardwood, the hard won notches of countless homers and base hits proudly displayed in its battle worn exterior. Carson gripped the leather wrapped handle and felt an immediate surge of confidence. The bat had been with him since childhood, a family inheritance and a reminder of the carefree summers of his youth. The weight of it gave him reassurance, the familiarity of its grip a shot of courage. He noticed that his palms were slightly sweaty and he wiped them on his jeans, chastising himself for his nerves. The noise outside was probably nothing... but it never hurt to be prepared.

It was with a firmer step that Carson made his way back to the alley door, putting his ear close to the cool metal to reconnoiter.

Silence.

He was about to turn away when the noise came again. This time it was slightly louder and joined by what sounded like a soft moan. Carson threw the latch, hefted his bat and pulled open the door.

The air from the alley hit him, bearing the undesirable smells and odors of a thousand undesirable bits and blobs and underscoring the undesirable time and place that he now found himself in. The pale fluorescent light from the store spilled out into the alley, illuminating a narrow band of refuse, a bare patch of asphalt and a few mystery liquids gleaming on the pavement. Carson noted with displeasure that the store's alley lamp was burned out, leaving the rest of the narrow, cluttered space in deep shadow.

Undesirable shadow.

In the black, empty expanse, nothing moved. The noise had stopped. Again.

Carson drew a breath, intending to call out, but realized he was still clutching the half-eaten corn dog in his mouth. He pulled it out, glanced around for a place to stash it, considered stuffing it in his shirt pocket, discarded the idea and settled for holding the dog in one hand and the bat in the other.

He cleared his throat. "Hello?"

His voice sounded as empty and hollow as the darkened alley. Almost immediately there was a rustle and a clink from the depths of shadow directly across from him. He hadn't expected that. Bat and corn dog came up instinctively and he felt his heart jump, then settle into a loud pattern of drumming that he felt his feet should be making instead as they carried him back into the safety of the store. For some inexplicable reason, though, he held his ground. He stared hard into the murky shadows across the alley.

Something moved.

Carson jumped. His common sense hammered him to duck back into the safety of the store, but again he hesitated. Now that his eyes were growing more accustomed to the dark, he thought he could make out the faint outline of something... *someone...* on the far side of the alley... someone lying prone amongst the piles of trash and soggy cardboard boxes. Gripping his bat and corndog tighter, he edged into the alley. The shaft of pale light from the doorway threw his shadow in weird relief across the stained brickwork, illuminating faint wisps of gray fog which he hadn't noticed before. He flicked a glance at them, mildly curious, then locked his gaze back on the sprawled figure. There was no time to ponder atmospheric anomalies. Carson kept his attention focused on the shape wedged amongst the boxes and shuffled forward.

Had he spared a moment to look, he would doubtless have noticed the clinging patches of mist that now swirled and tugged at his sneakers, or seeped in ever-increasing billows from all sides of the narrow passage, surging up from the cracks and crannies with unnatural, almost supernatural, speed. He also would have noticed several pairs of tiny, beady red eyes boring into him from the empty depths of an industrial-sized nacho cheese can at the back of the alley, and deduced that they were rats. Big ones. But he saw none of it, his attention focused completely on the still form ahead.

"Hello...?" Carson called again. He was closer now, halfway across, and could clearly see the outline of a person. The figure - a man - was sprawled in an uncomfortable position, face down in the refuse and half piled over with cast-offs, as if he were an oversized rag doll that had been carelessly tossed out with the rest of the garbage.

There was no response. He edged closer. "Uh... hey, guy... you okay?"

Carson was close enough to touch the figure now. Although the mist was beginning to crawl over it and mask the supine form, he could see the awkward angle in which it was sprawled, noted the startling stillness of its limbs. While there was no comfortable position in which to lie face down in an alley, Carson couldn't help but note that this one looked *particularly* unpleasant. He paused, swallowing past the dry lump in his throat. It was too dark to make out any more details, but there was a nagging tug at the back of his mind. Something was familiar about this figure... about this man. Disturbingly familiar.

Carson steeled himself and reached out, fearing what he would find, heart hammering, palms sweating but unable to tear himself away. Around him the fog was thickening, swirling, pooling in great eddies and swells, but he was oblivious, every ounce of watchfulness locked by the motionless figure. Dozens of pairs of red eyes had joined the first few, looking on with fevered delight and breathless anticipation.

Gently, ever so gently, Carson shook the man by his shoulder. "Hey... uh... you want an aspirin or something?"

The body shifted and rolled, slipping from its perch atop a crumpled box and spilling fully into the narrow shaft of light. The pale fluorescent beam gleamed off a bald head, glassy staring eyes and a sticky red carpet of blood that soaked the figure's chest and ran in rivulets across the clutching cardboard. In that one horrifying instant, Carson new three things: the man was a customer, the man was a friend, and the man was definitely, definitely dead.

"Mr. Carey...!" His hoarse whisper echoed through the sudden, deadly stillness of the alley.

An instant later, that stillness was shattered by a sudden sound, an angry and purposeful crash from the rear of the alley as several loose garbage cans were hurled aside. Carson whirled, dropping the corndog and taking the bat in both hands, his body snapping into stance as if facing the heat of a star pitcher with two strikes and the bases loaded. There was a great deal of mist now, and although he hadn't noticed its stealthy approach, its presence was now a force to be reckoned with. It filled the entire alley, obscuring details and edging out light and warmth, concealing everything from the street or any window or door nearby that might have chanced to give a glimpse into the space. The mist must have been playing tricks with his eyes as well, Carson thought fleetingly, as for a split second he thought he detected a crouched human form, perched low and dangerous atop the dumpster from which the crashing sound had come. Crouched as if to spring.

Then, there was a low, beastly growl which built for a moment, then erupted suddenly into a savage, terrifying, ear-tearing roar that ripped the air like a curtain and drove him back on weak knees. The noise was followed an instant later by a huge hairy shape that hurtled at him through the fog, and he was swinging out of instinct and fear and with all of his strength.

The bat hit something, hard, and he heard a ferocious grunt. Then his foot slipped on something soft and round and he went down, the great hairy form sailing over him, jaws snapping closed where his throat had been. Carson landed hard and rolled, fighting his way through trash and panic to regain his feet. From across the alley, far too close for comfort, the sound of terrible claws scrabbling for footing on slick bricks added hustle to his efforts and pushed him to his feet in record time. In the second it took for Carson to be up and ready, back against cold bricks and graffiti, bat cocked and waiting, the thing was ready too. Carson could just make out its fearsome shape, crouched low and dangerous just inside the swirling curtain of mist, a feral, rumbling growl idling ominously in the back of its throat. The beast took a step forward, long heavy claws rasping on stone, almost as if it was dragging them on purpose. The Louisville Slugger's leather wraps were slick with sweat as Carson choked up his grip, tensing, judging distance, trying to ignore the hammering of blood in his ears.

Then it happened.

Through the murky gray shreds of mist, a light appeared - faint, luminous, red. For a moment, Carson's fevered, terror-wracked brain locked.

"Uh..."

Something was glowing. He fought to make sense of it. It was no flashlight, no glow stick, no lighter, not electric or natural in any way. The glow was unearthly and unreal, unlike anything he had ever seen. Mesmerizing. His whirling thoughts flashed unbidden to children's tales of Christmas fantasy, where magical reindeer saved the day with glowing noses, bringing goodwill and cheer to all.

But there was no cheer in this red glow - only malice, terror and a heaping helping of the supernatural. It was then he realized what the glow was.

Eyes.

The glow came from a pair of luminous red eyes, there was no mistaking it. Hot, hungry and blazing with an infernal lust that held him frozen in place and sent a chill of terror through the center of his being. And the worst part was, they weren't animal.

They were human.

And then they were gone.

Carson stood alone in the alley, unable to move, sweating and shaking as 110% of his daily supply of adrenaline slowly worked its way through his system, watching the swirling mist slowly fade away, and wishing fervently that he could simply fade away with it.

Chapter Four

Bad Hoodoo

As it turned out, Carson's wish hadn't changed much by the next day. To his great dissatisfaction, neither had his physical location. It was late the next day and he stood in the doorway to the alley, slumped against the steel doorframe which should have been comforting in its strength but which was actually rather disconcerting due to its other qualities, namely that it was hard, chilly and unsympathetic. In that respect, it was exactly like the reality in which he currently found himself. He watched moodily, hands jammed in his jeans pockets, as the police photographer snapped a few more pictures. The scene in the alley hadn't changed much ether, except for the addition of fading spring sunlight, an impressive labyrinth of bright yellow police tape and the awkward chalk outline of a body crawling over some crumpled boxes. It was a crude parody of a human form and looked as if a child had drawn it. This was especially true after the boxes shifted during the removal of the body, further distorting the image. The head was now greatly enlarged and the limbs bent in ridiculous angles, making it look less like a vicious slaying and more like a hydrocephalic had collapsed during a pilates routine. The crime scene investigators had joked about it, ribbing the frustrated chalking officer with the good natured, down-to-earth humor that one expects to find at the scene of a brutal homicide. No matter how distorted its shape, however, Carson remembered vividly what had occupied the outline a few short hours ago. It had proven difficult to ignore, even when he closed his eyes.

Beside him stood a tall black man in a rumpled brown trenchcoat, reviewing hand scrawled notes in a small pad and occasionally jotting additions. In his tweed jacket and corduroy trousers, the man looked more like a college professor than a policeman, although the dull brass badge and sidearm on his belt marked him as something more. Lines of care etched in his long face showed that he took his job seriously, and the deep furrows in his brow showed that, on this particular day, things were more serious than usual. Looking up from his notes, he surveyed the alley for the hundredth time, scratched the close-shaved, graying sandpaper on his head and pursed his lips.

The camera flash went off again and Carson flinched. He found it particularly annoying, grating on his raw nerves almost as much as the cool detached efficiency of the photographer himself. To him, it was just a job. To Carson, it was like standing in the waiting room of a nightmare that refused to end.

He cleared his throat and shoved off from the doorframe, itching to put the scene behind him and ready to do something about it. "So, Detective... anything else I can do for you?"

The detective gazed into the alley a moment longer, glanced over at Carson, glanced down at his notes. He shifted his feet and tapped the pen on the cover of his notebook. The man had a steady, plodding, determined manner that, at other times, Carson would have found reassuring, but which, under the present circumstances, seemed irritating and contrived. He did a lot of tapping and a lot of thinking, both of which had begun to grate on Carson's nerves like a leaky faucet.

"Just one more question, Mr. Dudley." The detective's tone was soft, friendly, thoughtful, but there was a hint of something else that was reflected in the deep brown pools of his eyes. Under that gaze, Carson felt uncomfortable and exposed as if he were back in Mrs. Munson's third grade class and had been called on to answer some horrid History question for which he hadn't studied and didn't know the answer.

Suspicion. That's what it was.

Tap. Tap. Tap.

"Was it a *person* or was it a *dog*?"

Carson struggled to remain calm, feeling his frustration boiling to the top. He brushed tousled brown hair back from a bandage on his forehead and drew a deep breath.

"Look, I already told you... I *know* it sounds crazy, but I'm *not* making this up. I've said it before, I'll say it again - it *looked* like a person at first, but *then* it was a wolf... a dog... *something.*"

The camera flashed again. The detective watched idly as his mind worked, re-cataloging the alley, scanning every detail once more, mentally reviewing it for what must have been the umpteenth time, and yet proceeding as methodically as if it had been the first. Carson drummed his legs with impatience, rolling his eyes. Inadvertently, they happened across the chalk outline with its grisly red necktie. He yanked them away again, fighting the urge to bang his head against the back door.

"Well, we did find evidence of an animal presence... scratches on the pavement, a few bits of hair that *could* belong to a canine... but the wounds on the body are just not consistent with animal attack." The pen tapped.

Carson sighed, forcing his hands to unclench. "Look, detective, I don't know what else to say. I saw what I saw... maybe I didn't see what was really there, maybe it was just my mind playing tricks, but there you have it. That's all I know. Real or not, that's all I've got."

The detective looked at him again, dragging his attention from the scene and registering Carson, as if for the first time, as a human being. He smiled, slowly, with warmth and compassion. And still a little suspicion. "Sure, Mr. Dudley. Sure thing. I appreciate your honesty and the terrible ordeal you've been through. Seeing something like this... it's never easy." He gestured vaguely at the outline of the body. "But neither is catching the person who did it. And I need to ask the questions I do, the way that I do, in order to make that happen."

Carson forced himself to look at the outline again. "Do you think there's any chance you will?"

"Well, I'm not going to put out an APB on Lassie," a brown eye winked to show that he meant no harm by the joke. "But there's always hope. Besides, we think all this might be tied to another series of attacks in the Belfry District. You're the closest we've come to an eye witness. You never know when a perp will slip up and tip his hand."

Carson frowned. Another series of attacks? Something inside squirmed uncomfortably and he perked up. "You mean... someone else... in *this* neighborhood?"

The detective gave a fractional nod, his eyes roving over the alley again.

"Were they similar? Did other people see an animal? How many have their been?"

"I'm afraid I'm not at liberty to say, young man. The details of the case are confidential. However, let's just say that both of them have similarly... unusual... circumstances." The detective paused and a shadow crossed his brow, making him look old and tired. Then his smile returned and chased it away. Almost. "Well, if you think of anything else, please give me a call." He held out a plain white business card that bore the words, "Patch Parsons – Homicide Division" along with the official emblem of the Las Calamas Police Department. "You'll do that; won't you Mr. Dudley?"

"Of course... yeah, sure." Carson stuffed the card in his pocket and turned gratefully to follow the detective into the store, finally putting the scene of last night's carnage behind him. "So... are we done here? Is it okay if we open up?"

"Don't see any harm to it. Just keep clear of the alley. We'll let you know when forensics is finished. Shouldn't be long now."

They reached the front door and Carson busied himself unlocking it and flipping the "Open" sign. Behind him Detective Parsons was staring back into the store, eyes haunted, transfixed by the alley door as if he were dying to get one last look at the crime scene. Carson noticed that the pen tapping had stopped.

"Remember, Mr. Dudley, if you think of anything - anything at all."

"You bet, Detective. You'll be the first."

Carson swung the door wide and without further comment the detective disappeared into the gathering gloom. Kiki appeared almost immediately in his place, eyes wide and lips tight.

"It's about time!" She exploded. "What's going on?! Are you alright?! What happened?! I've been standing out here for an hour...! Why are the cops here?!"

Carson ushered her inside to the dying strains of the dying door chime. He shook his head, feeling tired. Everything around him seemed to be dying. In spite of the hollow, aching feeling in his gut, he managed to summon enough energy to relate, once more, last night's encounter. Kiki listened intently, not saying a word or asking a single question. When he was finished, she stared silently out the front window, watching the setting sun as it spilled red and orange across the black oil stains in the parking lot.

"Wow," she breathed. "I mean... *wow!*" She shook her head slowly, her features more pale and tired than usual. They stood out in stark contrast to the red of her stocking cap, making her look faded and wan, like an old photograph. "Right here at the 24/7. *Right here* in our neighborhood."

"Yeah. That's pretty much how Jack took it." Carson was seated on his stool behind the counter, twirling a naked corn dog stick absently.

"He was here already? He knows?"

Carson nodded curtly. "Yup. Poor guy. News hounds were mobbing him, cops were mobbing him, shop owners from next door were mobbing him... and you know how he hates the limelight. Boy, there's nothing like one of your customers getting torn apart by a wolf in the middle of the city to bring in the gawkers."

"That'll pretty much ruin your day."

"To top it all off, one of the day guys quit - got spooked and just didn't show. Guess he figured he might be next."

Tap. Tap. Tap.

Carson tapped the corn dog stick moodily on the glass counter top, his eyes drifting to the alley door.

Kiki eyed him closely. "Are you... okay?" Her voice was cautious, quiet.

It took Carson a moment to answer. "I've never seen a dead guy before."

Kiki reached out, still cautious, and gently touched his hand.

They stood that way for a moment. The corn dog stick had stopped tapping.

"I can't even imagine what it was like."

"It was different."

Again, silence. As the moments crawled past, the sounds of the mini-mart began to slowly register themselves on Carson's awareness - the soft hum of the Freezie machine, the clunk of hot dogs shifting in the warmer, the faint bubbling of the chili-cheese goop simmering in its sturdy, sanitary, stainless steel box.

Carson took a deep breath and squared his shoulders. "I am. Okay, that is. To answer your question." He patted her hand and looked her square in the eyes, green locked with blue, like a magician showing his audience there was nothing up his sleeve. "It was weird at first... I was about as far into freaked as you can get and still come back. Took me five minutes to figure out how to call 9-1-1. But now... well, it's not as bad as I thought it would be, actually." In a funny way, Carson realized, it wasn't. "Not that seeing a dude you know with his throat torn out is any picnic. I feel just plain sick for the guy. Mr. Carey... man! He was cool. I'm gonna miss him. And scared?! Hoo boy! You can still follow the yellow brick road if you know what I mean. But y'know... it just makes me more *angry* now than anything else. I mean, he's *gone*... and we don't even know who did it. Or why..." The corn dog stick was tapping again, faster.

"So is that... is that how he died? His throat...?" Kiki sounded hesitant, cautious.

"Well, he didn't die of exposure. I'm no doctor, but I'd guess that having a hole in your neck the size of Wisconsin is bound to have a profound effect on your health."

"What do you think did it? That... um... animal you mentioned?"

Carson grunted. "Now we're headed for some weird places, that's for sure. Buckle up." He squared his jaw. "It's like I told you... I would swear... I mean I would absolutely *swear* that the thing that jumped me out there – the thing that did this to Mr. Carey - was a *wolf.* A big, bad, drooling, shaggy, toothy, Little Red Riding Hood style wolf. I mean, it's not like I've got a lot of experience with wild animals, but I've seen enough Discovery channel to know one when I see one. But where it came from or what it was doing there, I have *no* idea. And then there's this mystery person - one minute he was there, hunkered down in the fog on top of the dumpster, and then BAM! it was fido. It was like some sort of Satanic Shaggy DA. I tell you, there was something weird about the whole thing." Carson's thoughts drifted back to last night's terrifying series of events and fixated on the weirdest feature of the entire thing, the one detail that he had as yet not related to *anyone* - the eyes. The hungry, glowing red eyes that loomed larger than anything else every time he ran the instant replay. For a moment, Carson considered telling Kiki. Up to this point, he figured that the mention of luminous monster eyes wouldn't help much to strengthen his case. In fact, by now he wasn't even sure if he had seen them or simply imagined them. He hesitated, almost blurted it out, then at the last moment decided against it.

"Weird?!" Kiki was saying. "Yeah, I'd go with 'weird'. I'd even go with 'freakin' weird,' or maybe even 'Ow, I think my brain is melting' weird. Frankly, it's the strangest thing I've ever heard. Even when I was... well, I've heard a lot."

"It pretty much tops the charts, don't it? You wanna hear

something else crazy?" Carson plunged ahead despite the vehement shaking of her head. "That detective... Parsons... he shouldn't have believed me... I don't even know if I believe me... and he didn't act like he *did*, but at the same time he didn't act like he *dis-believed* me either. Like he didn't really *want* to believe me, but maybe he kind of sort of *did* anyway... a little bit. Y'know... like he should have tried a little harder to *not* believe me. Does that make sense?"

Kiki blinked. "Maybe you should go home... take a little time..."

"No way. No, thanks! No ma'am. If I was home it'd just be me and the houseplants, and that'd go nowhere real fast. Jack offered me time off, but I don't know... I can't do it. I need... I need... I need this." He waved the corn dog stick to indicate the familiar surroundings of the 24/7. "This is home. It makes me feel safe, somehow." And indeed it did, Carson suddenly realized. Despite the fact that the traumatizing events of the previous night had taken place not more than 30 feet from where he now sat, he couldn't imagine being anywhere else.

Kiki frowned. An undisguised look of worry decorated her face like a Mr. Yuck sticker slapped on an otherwise attractive bottle of drain cleaner. "Alright." She said the word with some effort. It was apparent she was dropping the subject in spite of her reservations about Carson's mental well being, and that she was none too happy about it. "But would you at least put that thing down? You're making me nervous."

Carson stopped tapping and cradled the gnawed corn dog stick protectively. "Hey - this corn dog saved my life. I am *never* letting this out of my sight, woman." Carson had discovered the stick along with the remains of his half-eaten dog shortly after his heart had started beating the night before. It was the corn dog that had caused him to slip when the wolf - dog, beast, thing or whatever it was - had attacked, sparing him from the opportunity of knowing what its teeth felt like in his throat. It had been a lucky break, pure and simple, and the impact of it had not been lost on him. In the aftermath of the encounter, the stick somehow served to ground him to a reality that was a lot less stable than it had been a few hours earlier. "This is my good luck charm now. It's goin' *nowhere.*"

Kiki sighed and rolled her eyes. "Okay, then... fine. However, even though it sounds like you've got things well in hand with a crusty snack stick and the cryptic comments of an overworked homicide detective, there might be something little old Kiki can do to help, too. If you're interested."

"Oh?"

"Yeah."

The stick stopped in mid tap. Carson sat up a little straighter. "Er... like what?"

"I take it you're interested?" She held his gaze, her blue eyes cool but loaded with mysterious intent.

"Interested in finding out what the heck unleashed all this crazy on the Belfair District? Yeah, I"m interested. Way interested."

"Alright then. I'll see what I can find out."

"But what..."

"Uh uh!" Kiki cut him off. "*I'm* not making promises, and *you* shouldn't ask any questions. We'll see what we see."

"Okay, I just..."

She held up a finger. "Don't make me use this."

Carson didn't. He let it drop, tipping back on his stool to signal defeat. "Whatever you say."

Kiki pushed back from the counter, straightened her stocking cap. "Good. If I find anything, you owe me a Freezie."

"Deal. I'll even throw in the limited edition color-changing straw." Carson tapped a display of novelty straws suggestively. Kiki's grin was her only reply. She turned on her heel to go, then paused.

"You sure you're gonna be okay?"

"I'll be fine."

"And this place... you still think it's safe?"

"Safe as sandwiches. Besides, Jack took steps. He hired some security service." Carson rummaged in a stack of papers behind the counter, producing a crisp, professional business card that glinted gold. "Gold Shield Security. Dude starts first thing tomorrow."

The news seemed to appease some of her worries. "Good. Hang in there. I'll see you soon."

Leaving behind a brief wave and the ghost of a smile, she was gone. Carson watched as the night swallowed her trim figure, feeling a mixture of curiosity and concern. He wasn't sure exactly what was happening, but that feeling was becoming more and more common. He found he was almost getting used to it.

After Kiki's departure, the night dragged slowly on. Traffic was light, but not as abysmal as it had been, though Carson suspected most of his customers merely showed up to try and get a glimpse of the bloody alley or perhaps even a fresh corpse. Local news had run a story on the incident, and although the occasional dead body was no real shocker in Las Calamas, the allure of the macabre always proved strong enough to attract lookie-loos. By midnight, however, even the thin stream of thrill-seekers had dried up.

Finding solace in his duties, Carson busied himself with the myriad of tasks that kept the mini-mart humming. He found himself relaxing a little as time passed, although he still jumped at the door chime and discovered a newfound affinity for his baseball bat, which seemed to accompany him on most of his chores. Slowly, Carson slipped into the comfortable, numbing routine of numbing routine. It wasn't until hours later, in fact, with his hands full of bulging garbage bags and his feet taking him on the familiar path to the back alley dumpster, that he remembered it was still off limits. He was only too happy to redirect his steps and haul the bags out the front.

On his way out, he passed the smiling, cheerful photo of a teenage boy, whose face was plastered on a "MISSING" poster that someone had hung in the front window earlier that day. Carson recognized him as one of the gaming group boys, and he found it haunting. The flat, smiling, empty eyes stared through him like a ghost. He hurried past.

Outside, the night was cool and refreshing. Carson dragged the bags to the curbside cans and hefted them in. As the clinks and clatterings subsided, his gaze strayed across the darkened street, past the pale, flickering glow of streetlamps and over the shadowed shapes of parked cars. They lit on the Curio Shop, and Carson found himself once again drawn by the vacant windows and faded sign. Faded, he noted suddenly, even though the shop had only recently opened. Odd. Other than that it was, as usual, quiet. Quiet, dark and still. Nothing had changed. Nothing ever changed. He shook his head. He wished he could say the same about his own little shop.

Behind him, there was a noise.

Instantly a chill shot up his neck. It had been a stealthy sound, the kind that a person knew right away he hadn't been intended to hear and the fact that he did scared the bejabbers out of him. Carson's mind flashed to the Louisville Slugger and his empty hand clenched involuntarily, itching to feel the reassuring grip of the leather wraps but knowing it was stashed out of reach behind the counter. His hands had been too occupied with garbage to bring it. The small, detached part of his brain that wasn't busy weighing fight-or-flight options advised him to stick the thing down his jeans leg next time, no matter what statement that made. Forcing himself to calm down, he tried to isolate the direction of the noise, pick it out of the mix of nighttime sounds, sense its direction.

Then the smell hit him.

Carson relaxed. "Hey, Pete! Come on out, dude - I know it's you."

A lone shadow separated from the dark mass of them huddled at the corner of the store and stepped into the light. The ragged army coat and battered ballcap identified the figure as that of Stinky Pete, although it was the *eau de hobo* that truly gave him away. He sidled up to Carson, glancing warily about the lot.

"You're a marked man, Dudley." Pete's voice was rough, ominous and foreboding, grating like a handful of gravel tossed across the parking lot. There was a pause. "Got anythin' ta eat?"

Carson patted himself absently as his mind grappled with Pete's words. He located a Snickers bar in his breast pocket and handed it over.

Stinky Pete carefully peeled back the wrapper, his roving, bloodshot eyes keeping watch from under the relative seclusion of his ballcap. The usual squadron of black flies that accompanied the old vagrant buzzed in annoyance as he swatted at them, then zoomed back in to eagerly join the feast. After his first swipe, Pete seemed neither to notice nor care about their involvement, and tucked into the candybar with the air of a soldier addressing his rations. He chewed and swallowed with a detached, professional air, hardly seeming to taste the chocolate and continuing his surveillance the whole while, jaw working, eyes roving.

Carson didn't care what he smelled like or how he looked. He was glad to see the old man. These days, he was glad to see practically anybody. He smiled as he capped the garbage cans. "A marked man? You know something I don't, Pete?"

"Roger tha'." Pete's voice was thick with chocolate and caramel. "You got eyes onya, soljer. Hostile eyes. But don' worry. Ol' Pete's got yer back. Ain't nothin' gonna get past me, bucko... don' you worry."

Pete's roving gaze was sweeping the parking lot in a methodical pattern as if he expected something dark and terrifying to leap from the shadows at any moment. While the word "alert" hardly applied to Pete under any condition, Carson couldn't help but note that something was definitely different in the old man's demeanor. He also couldn't help giving the lot a going over of his own, and as he did so, he picked out what looked like the corner of a large cardboard box peeking out from the shadows from which Pete had emerged.

"Pete... are you sleeping here?"

"Affirmative."

"Er..."

"Don't mention it. S'no problem. Been here a couple days now. Off an' on. Didn' set up th' bivouac 'til I heard th' news, though... tough break, kid. But don' worry. Ol' Pete's got yer back, yessir... the Sarge is in charge..." Bloodshot eyes were roving again, probing every shadow. Pete's behavior was starting to make Carson nervous.

"Uh... yeah... and boy, what a relief *that* is. Say... don't you think we'd be... umm... safer... inside?"

"Hmm? Whazzat?" Pete tore away from his dogged reconnaissance long enough to eyeball the clerk. The change in perspective seemed to disorient him and he tilted precariously before he could refocus. "Affirmative. Roger that. Inside, good recon from there. But only fer a sec, pal. I'm on duty. Ol' Pete don't let his friends down, that's fer sure. Yesiree... gotta stay frosty..." His voice trailed off into unintelligible muttering.

Carson led the way into the store, bewildered. He had known Pete for over a year, and had never seen his eccentricities hover quite so close to just plain nutty. He frowned. Something was wrong.

"Can I get you something to drink, Pete? Freezie, maybe? It's on the house."

"Don't mind if I do, shooter. Freezie. Help me stay frosty. Freezie... frosty... cold as ice. That's her..."

More mumbling.

Carson watched the old man carefully as he filled the cup, hoping that the promise of refreshment and a change of scenery might relax him. There was, however, no immediate change. Pete was scouring the interior of the 24/7 as aggressively as he had the outside, probing every nook and cranny, squinting under the fluorescents. He listed slightly to one side, and for a moment, Carson thought he was going to tip over again. He was about to lunge for the old man when he suddenly righted himself and Carson realized he had been leaning for a better view around the chip display.

"Er... so... what's up, Pete? Clue me in here. Don't keep me in suspense. Can you let the Marked Man know who's got him marked?"

"You want the sit-rep, do ya?" Pete swung close to the counter, accepting the tall, frosty Freezie from his friend. He took a long pull on the straw, which squeaked quietly against the lid like a neon-blue bow pulled across a plastic violin. To Pete, it was a symphony. He closed his eyes and permitted a satisfied smile to slide across his cracked lips.

"S'good. 'S real good. Thanks, soljer." Pete wiped his red lips with the back of his hand, adding to the multicolored decorations on his fingerless glove. Suddenly weary, he relaxed his vigil of the mini-mart, loosening the red bandanna about his throat like a salesman would his tie. He tipped back his ballcap and scratched his thinning, greasy hair. "I'll tell ya what I can, Dudley, but it ain't much. 'S need to know right now, and right now it wouldn't do you to know too much." Bleary eyes focused momentarily on the alley door. "S'that where it happened?"

Carson nodded. "Yeah. That's it."

The gray head shook, sadness pulling Pete's tired, worn features down into a frown. "Poor Joe. Prob'ly never knew what hit 'im. They never do."

"Uh... yeah. Yeah, it sucked, that's for sure. Especially for Mr. Carey." The by now all-too-familiar feeling that he didn't have a clue about what was going on was settling in once more like a cozy old bathrobe. Only this time, it felt like the bathrobe was being wrapped around his head and cinched into a tight knot, making it not so comfortable and in fact making it hard for him to breathe. "Uh..." Carson shook his head to clear the feeling. "Uh... so... so you heard about the attack, I guess. About the... *wolf* and all..."

Bloodshot eyes snapped to him like a gopher trap, pinning him to his stool and the moment. "That's what yer tellin' yerself, then? This 'wolf' yarn?" The raspy old voice had a clip to it, a sudden edge that hearkened back to a different time, a different man.

"Uh... well..." The bathrobe was back. "I mean... I saw... I saw what I saw..."

"Was there glowin'?"

Carson's heart stopped. His mouth was suddenly dry and the room seemed to be spinning slightly. He licked his lips. The vision of luminous, rage-filled eyes swam vividly through his recollection, chasing the mini-mart into slightly faster revolutions. "I don't..."

"Was... there... glowin'?" Each word was deliberate, flinty. The edge was still there, and Carson felt himself caught on it.

"Well..." He stammered, thoughts racing, mind struggling to sort and accept the things his eyes had reported but that his brain had as yet refused to entirely accept. He still wanted to believe that things could go back to the way they had been. He wanted it desperately. Then he looked into Pete's eyes. They were cool, strong, steady. The second hand ticked on the clock and he felt something inside him *give*, just a little. Suddenly he found that maybe, just maybe, he didn't wish that quite as much as he thought he did.

"Yeah... maybe... I guess. There might have been a *little* glowing..." Carson wondered in passing how Pete might know this, but his thoughts were racing too fast to stop and consider it, zooming on to things of greater interest and less sense.

"You didn't tell the cops 'bout it - how come?"

"Well... it's just plain crazy, Pete. Look, it already sounds crazy enough... I don't even know if I believe it myself."

"That's a lie. A durn lie. You know what you saw, kid - you may not *like* it, but you *know* it. Tellin' yerself anythin' different is jes yer brain tryin' to make the best o' things. When life starts tuh get crazy... I mean *really* crazy... you've got to remember jus' one thing - *the eye don't lie*. Pictures'll fool ya, stories'll fool ya, other folks'll take ya fer a ride just as sure as look at ya. But this here's the real deal, soljer. One o' the best weapons them ghoulies have is the human noodle. We're skeptics at birth, you'n me... s'way the Good Lord cooked us up. We don't wanna believe, most of us, even if we see stuff firsthand, and we want to *tell* people even *less*, cuz they'll jus' think we're *nutjobs*. But the plain fact is, boyo, mos' of the time, these'll tell ya the truth..." Pete jammed a pair of forked fingers toward his own eyes, deeply set in a scowling mask of grizzle and whiskers. "...that is, if you're willin' ta listen."

Carson stared, trying to pierce the red film that veiled the old vagrant's eyes, wanting desperately to see what shred of lucidity, if any, lay behind them. He was willing to concede that Pete was an authoritative expert on crazy, but felt he was not yet entirely grasping the man's point. There was something in the urgency and intensity of his voice. Something compelling. Something genuine.

Something real.

Then it hit him, sudden and startling in its simplicity. This wasn't Pete's first time. He'd been here before.

"Pete..." Carson asked breathlessly. "What have you seen... exactly?"

There was a flicker, the faintest stirring of recollection, and the battered red curtains that obscured the windows to the hobo's soul parted just a fraction, revealing the barest hint of something invaluable and incalculable:

Clarity.

The room was starting to spin again and Carson gripped the counter to keep from tipping in his stool. He forced his lungs to work.

Pete blinked slowly, deliberately, scowled up at the lights and gave the room another once over, brows furrowed in concentration. Memories danced and capered behind his watery red eyes, dark shapes gliding under dark waters, just out of sight but full of suggestion and a haunting, ominous intensity.

Carson knew the look. He'd seen the same one in the mirror ever since last night.

"I was three years in the bush." Pete's voice was barely a whisper. "Seen a lot o' killin', thet's fer sure. But I never seen anyone... anythin'... better at killin' than *it*. Nuthin' even come close. Thet's a fact. Take a man right outta his bunk. Right outta his boots. Suck 'im out, suck 'im dry, leave the shell is all. They tol' me it was jus' imaginings... superstitions... jungle fever. But I seen it. Yessir, I seen it alright. And these don't lie, boy." He stabbed forked fingers at his eyes again. "They don't lie. Like a ghost it was... nuthin' ta stop it, nuthin' ta show it, nuthin'... nuthin' at all. 'Cept those eyes. Those gol-durned, red, glowin' eyes..."

Carson simply stared. He had no words.

Pete's rheumy gaze snapped back from the jungle and locked onto Carson's face, merciless and fierce in their honesty. "And now it's here, kid. *Right* here. I feel it. Been usin' yer store... huntin'... plenty o' warm bodies, plenty o' cover. It's a real keen one, too, this here one is. Smart. Careful. But it never reckoned on Ol' Pete. That's fer certain sure. I know its little game, yessir... yesiree... dirty bloodsucker... its time is a-comin'..."

Pete seemed suddenly to rediscover the Freezie that chilled his gnarled hand. He shook himself from his musings, took another long pull. The straw squeaked and sang its mournful song. Pete wiped his mouth and set the empty cup rattling on the counter. With a purposeful hand he cinched his red neckerchief snugly about his neck, jerked the brim of his cap down to its familiar position. Long shadows returned to his weathered features and crow's feet.

From their hunkering depths, his bloodshot eyes once more took up their roaming vigil. "Talked long enough. Better get back to the bivouac, kid. Jus' don't forget... *the eye don't lie*." Pete took a few shuffling steps, then paused at the door. He stared out into the dark, oily shadows in the dark, oily lot. "Bad hoodoo," he muttered softly and to no one in particular. "That's fer certain sure."

Then he was gone.

This time, not even the door gave its chime.

Chapter Five

Bringing In the Guns

From the moment Kiki entered the store, it was clear that things had changed, and not for the better. It had been several days since her conversation with Carson and she was bursting to tell him of her discoveries, but it was instantly apparent that he had other things on his mind. He was behind the counter polishing the Freezie machine, and it was obvious from his scowling countenance and vigorous motions that he was angry. Furious, rather, she decided – fuming, seething and ready to blow. She could see it in his rigid posture, read it etched into the taught lines of his face reflecting from the already spotless surface of the machine which he seemed intent on wearing a hole through with his fierce rubbing.

A pleasant greeting died in Kiki's throat, just as quickly as the door chime behind her. She was bursting with news and dying to tell it, but something about her friend's demeanor told her she needed to approach the situation carefully. She checked herself from triumphantly brandishing the white paper envelope as she had rehearsed a dozen times, thrusting it instead into a back pocket.

"Hey." Instead of her ebullient greeting, she settled on a half-smile and what she hoped was a non-threatening wave, giving the store a cursory glance in an attempt to identify the source of his animosity.

"Oh... hey." Carson flashed an unconvincing mini-smile of his own, not pausing an iota in his work. Kiki eyed the worn rag in his hand, imagining that if he carried on polishing with his current vehemence it would quite likely burst into flame. There was smoldering of a different kind that she could read easily in his eyes.

"Glad you're okay..." he muttered. "I was beginning to worry." He paused a moment and looked her up and down. "You are okay, aren't you?"

"Uh, yeah... yeah, sure, okay. Very okay."

Carson returned to his rubbing. Silence.

"Er... how about you? Everything... okay?"

Carson grunted. The noise was unintelligible and non-committal, but spoke volumes.

Kiki continued to cast about for possible irritants, but found nothing. She was reluctant to share her news until Carson was in a more receptive state of mind. "I see they took the cop tape down from the alley. Must be good to be able to use the dumpster again."

Another grunt.

"That Freezie machine sure looks... clean. Lookin' very good. Very... hygienic."

This time, there wasn't even a grunt. She changed tactics. "I uh... I saw the Gold Shield car parked out front. New security must be here."

Pay dirt.

At the mention of the security guard, she could see Carson's shoulders tighten and his hand clenched on the rag. His green eyes stabbed out through the windows into the darkness of the parking lot. Now she was getting somewhere.

"How's that workin' out?" She asked, in what she hoped was a casual, I'm-really-not-digging-into-your-personal-business kind of tone.

"Super," Carson spat the word. "Business is *way* up."

Kiki arched a brow. "It is? All because of this security guy?"

"Oh yeah, it's all because of him alright - but not the way you think. Oh, super... here he comes again... the Great Appetite himself!"

A shadow loomed for a moment outside the glass of the front door - a very *big* shadow. Then the chime was warbling and an imposing figure swung through into the light. The man was large, larger than most, in fact, but more in the sense of a gorilla than a star athlete, the buttons of his crisp blue shirt straining dangerously against the girth of his stout belly and his thick arms showing little definition but plenty of power. Pinned to his barrel chest was a cheap-looking gold badge declaring the sovereignty of the Gold Shield Security company. Below the badge was pinned a nametag that read "Officer Dexter Jackson," but it looked like the pin had come loose from the strain and that it might spring off at any moment, fly across the room and strike someone in the eye. The guard was dark-skinned, with a heavy face, large brown eyes and a mop of shaggy dreadlocks atop his head that seemed jarringly out of place with the rest of his ensemble. A thick black belt encircled his waist, straining desperately along with his uniform to keep their contents where they should be. Although this was enough of a challenge by itself, the belt was almost cruelly loaded with tools of the trade, including two sets of handcuffs, pepper spray, taser, multi-tool, flashlight, several spare clips, radio, steel baton and a handgun that looked like the firearm counterpart of its owner - bigger than it needed to be, fully loaded and looking to prove something. Officer Jackson had a swagger when he walked, a purposeful, almost rhythmic stride, his thick boots planting firmly with each step but still hinting at a grace that belied his impressive size. He was middle-aged, and in spite of the extra pounds he carried, the faint lines and creases on his face showed that his life had not always been an easy one.

Carson bristled visibly and the tension in the air ratcheted up several notches. "Good evening, sir," he grated, voice dripping with sarcasm. "May I help you? No, let me guess... the Hostess aisle, I believe..." Carson swept his arm in an exaggerated gesture, draping his dirty rag over it like the maitre d' of a swanky four star restaurant. "Yes sir, it's right over there, can't miss it - the glaringly empty shelves right in front of the giant boot-shaped impressions that look like they were made by an overpaid security guard."

Officer Jackson scowled. "Very funny. I'm on break." The timbre of his voice was as thick and powerful as his arms, and it was also not very happy. Kiki could sense immediately that the hostility in the room was completely mutual, and that it had had several days in which to ripen and mature. By now it was bordering on open warfare.

"Oh, 'break.' Right... that's what you said *last* time. Y'know, when your office said you worked 5-on, 5-off, I thought they meant *days*."

Officer Jackson made his way to the snack shelf, ignoring the comment. He rifled through the collection of Ho-Ho's and cupcakes, making multiple selections. His scowl, however, had collected some new grooves and an impressive depth of expression when he turned back, making it look downright mean. It made Kiki feel uncomfortable.

"Listen, &@!$#... you do *your* job, I'll do *mine*."

"Oh, profanity again, that's great," Carson rolled his eyes and waved his rag in the air with an exasperated snort. "That's *very* professional. Very cutting edge. They teach you those delicate social skills in the rent-a-cop academy, or is it more of an instinct thing?"

The big man stomped up to the counter, dropping his snack cakes onto the glass with an ominous thud and directing the gathering stormclouds of his countenance toward Carson. He leaned across the counter and looked down - a loooong way down, Kiki noted - to stare him directly in the face.

"I'm - on - break," Officer Jackson gritted in a voice like distant thunder. "I been standin' out in your *&%$!@ parking lot all &^*(@! night and there ain't been so much as a *&*$#@! jaywalker cross the lot. I didn't *ask* for this &%$#@! assignment, and I didn't *want* it! And I don't want anymore of your 'tude, either. It's *quiet*. I'm *hungry*. I'm on *break*. So ring me up... or don't. Either way, I'm gettin' fed."

Carson swept the treats one by one across the scanner, tossing them into a plastic bag with a flagrant disregard for their spongelike softness and creamy centers. Officer Jackson winced with each abuse.

"Your genuine concern for the financial well being of the 24/7 is duly noted," Carson growled. "But you're supposed to *protect* my customers, not *become* one!"

"I don't *see* any customers, smart guy."

"Oh duh! Thanks! *Now* you're finally starting to catch on! Look, here's the deal, and I'll keep this simple because it looks like that collar might be cutting off the blood flow to your brain: you take *a lot* of breaks. You take *too many* breaks. When you take *breaks*, you don't do your *job*. If you don't do your *job*, *I won't have one*! And that, genius, means *you won't have one either*!"

Officer Jackson's next words came out through clenched teeth, careful and precise. "*I - am - doing - my job!* My *job* is to solve *problems*, which I can't do if there *ain't* any problems. Look around you... you see any problems?! Hell no! Why not? Cuz there *ain't* any! That's *none*. Zero. Zilch. Nada. If there's a problem, yo... I'll solve it."

"Thank you, Vanilla Ice."

"Hey!" A finger the size of a hot dog stabbed at Carson's face.

"Watch it! Those are fightin' words."

"You?! Fight?! Yeah, that'll happen... when both of us are going for the last package of Ding Dongs! And here's a newsflash, gigantor - in order to fight you'll have to move those boots, which, based on your job performance up to this point, I'm not sure is possible!"

"If you ain't careful they'll be movin' alright... someplace you don't want 'em!"

Officer Jackson scooped up his treats in one ham-sized fist, scowling in a way that made Kiki want to duck behind something large. "You don't like my work, counter monkey, you pick up that phone and call your boss. I got better places to babysit than some whacked out loony bin where giant scary wolves eat up all the customers." Carson stiffened and Officer Jackson knew he'd hit a nerve. He grinned evilly. "That's right - I do my homework. I've heard the bull you been shovelin'. I might just bug out at that... let ol' wolfy make a meal outta you and take away this pain in my *&$!@."

Carson snorted, struggling to recover his composure. "You? Leave? I don't think so. First of all, my luck has been way too crappy lately for that to happen, and second of all, we still have some chocolate cupcakes left."

It was the guard's turn to stiffen. "So I got a sweet tooth... so I like my cakes..."

"*Like* 'em?! If you visit that shelf one more time, it'll constitute common law marriage!"

"There's that mouth again! Listen, cracka... you don't watch it, some day that &%$@! pie hole is gonna get you in trouble - deep!"

"Oh, great, more swearing. Super. Apparently the only four-letter word you *don't* know is 'work.'"

"Yeah... and I got plenty more I'm dyin' to share with you."

"I'll keep a pencil handy, *Dex.*"

"Keep a first aid kit handy, *Dud...*" Officer Jackson paused suddenly, baring his white teeth in a malicious grin. "Yeah... *Dud.* I like that. Like a wimpy little firecracker that's all fizzle and no pop."

"Are you sure you don't mean &*^#! Dud? That's a little more colorful."

"We'll just try plain ol' 'Dud' for starters. I can always add color later if I need to dress it up. Oops, lookie there," Officer Jackson glanced exaggeratedly at the watch he wasn't wearing. "Break's over. Gotta get back out there and scare off the Big Bad Wolf!" With a smug grin, the big man turned on his heel.

"Ha! The only way he'd be afraid of you is if he was dressed like a Twinkie!!"

And then he was gone.

Carson gave vent to a wordless noise of pure frustration and punched the air violently. Then his shoulders slumped and he buried his face in his hands with an exasperated groan. "A dozen rent-a-cop shops in town and Jack had to pick *this* one..."

Kiki stepped out from behind cover, clearing her throat hesitantly. "Whoa. Intense."

"Hmm...?" Carson started, suddenly remembering he wasn't alone. "Oh... sorry. Yeah, just... guy stuff..." His face flushed and he smiled sheepishly. "Too much testosterone in one place, I guess."

"Yeah, I get it. Kinda like male bonding except without all the bonding and a lot more offering to kill each other."

"Pretty rough, hunh?"

"I feared for your life. And mine."

"Sorry, kid. Sorry you had to see that. I just... I mean... *man!*" He punched the air again. *"*That dude *seriously* gets under my skin! He's like a giant walking attitude in blue polyester pants! Came in here the first day, grumpy as a grandpa and spoiling for a fight... a *total* sourpuss. Always moping around, stuffing his face with sweets - which is good for the bottom line, mind you; I can see the value in it, but that's totally beside the point - and in general trying to make everyone as completely miserable as he is. I don't know who took a tinkle in his Corn Flakes, but they spent some time at it, that's for sure. Maybe it's a chemical imbalance, I don't know... but the dude has *serious* issues."

Carson slumped and his forehead hit the counter with a thud. Kiki gave him a moment, then gently touched his shoulder.

"You okay?"

She had never seen him this way. Carson always had good rapport with the customers, most of whom he was on a first name basis with. She had even seen him waving goodbye and trading gaming tips with a shoplifter once as the young man was hauled off by police.

"Yeah... yeah, I guess..." His voice was muffled. He took a deep breath and let it out, lifting his head.

"I dunno... maybe there's more to it than good ol' Officer Sunshine. Probably just all the stress catching up, I suppose. First no customers, then a dead customer, and now the Security Guard From Hell who's my *only* customer. Cripes! I tell you, that dude knows how to push my buttons. You know, yesterday he stopped the Hostess guy in the parking lot - he tried to buy a case of Twinkies right off the truck!"

"No kidding."

"Scout's honor. That guy, I tell you, he's a regular..." Carson bit off his words and threw up his hands, giving up in exasperation. "Never mind. Don't get me started."

"You did more than get started already. You sure it's a good idea to ride him that way? You were making with the wisecracks like it was your job."

"I know, I know... but I can't help it. You know me - I get nervous, I joke. I get mad, I joke. It's just how I deal with stuff, I guess."

"That may be true, but I'd watch it with this guy. He's got 'loose cannon' written all over him."

"You're right, I know... I'll watch it. It's probably not worth the effort, anyway - you can bet nothing's getting through. It's like shooting paintballs at a tank. A really *big,* annoying tank that eats all your Ho-Ho's and has a mouth like a sailor..." Carson stopped himself again, sighed and dropped back onto his stool. "I know, I know, there I go again. Alright, I'm done. I'm not letting it get to me anymore." He smiled and Kiki thought he looked a little more relaxed. Now might be the time.

"Good." She smiled back, slipped the envelope out of her back pocket and tapped it nonchalantly on the counter. "That's a healthy attitude, in more ways than one." Carson's eyes caught the plain, unassuming slip of white paper, watching it like a cat might a string.

"So... whatcha got there?"

Bullseye.

"Well... remember I said I was going to do some poking around?"

"Yeah?"

"I poked."

The envelope stopped tapping. It lay flat on the counter, now not so plain, not so unassuming. Now it was suggestive, compelling and packed with the promise of dangerous knowledge.

Carson blinked. A second passed. Then he reached for it eagerly, as if it were parked under the Christmas tree. "You rock..."

Kiki grinned. "A girl tries."

A moment later Carson had the envelope open and was leafing through its contents. "Whoa... these are police reports. That's Patch Parkinson's signature, I recognize it from my statement... and for that matter, there's my statement! Where'd you get these?!"

 56

"Let's just say I've got friends. And let's say these friends are some very tech savvy people with very little supervision and a real distaste for paying parking tickets and leave it at that."

"Fair enough. What happens in Las Calamas stays in Las Calamas." Carson was only too happy to drop his questions and for the next several minutes he poured over the official-looking documents, flipping back and forth between their official-looking pages. Occasionally, a soft whistle or muttered "Dude!" was heard, but otherwise all was silence as he hungrily devoured their contents. Finally, he slumped back in his stool, drumming his fingers on the thin stack of papers and studying the ceiling with a furrowed brow.

"Well?" Kiki's keen mind was itching for dialog.

Carson looked at her. "You read 'em?"

She rolled her eyes. "Whaddaya think, I'm waiting for the movie?! Heck yeah, I read 'em! So?! What... do... you... think?!"

Carson rose from his seat and started pacing. He seemed restless, anxious, like the counter was a cage. "I think..."

"Yes?!"

"I think things are starting to get..."

"*Yes?!*"

"...interesting."

"You got that right!" Kiki exploded. She snatched the packet, spun it to face her and pored over its grainy, faxed-once-too-often pages, sharp blue eyes flicking over details and skimming text like a master Scrabble player working the board for a triple word score. "Multiple disappearances, mysterious circumstances, inconclusive evidence, no suspects or motives... look at this: 'mutilations and ritualistic tendencies!' It's all right here in the reports... all right here in the Belfry District! I mean, 'mysterious circumstances...' c'mon, how often have you heard the cops use a term like that in an *official* document? They're stumped!"

"And trying to keep it quiet, too, by the look of it..." Carson plucked the by now omnipresent corn dog stick from his shirt pocket and started twirling it, his face a mask of concentration. "But who can blame 'em. What a mess. I had no idea this was going on for so long. Judging by that report, the victims who have made the news are just a handful... which explains a lot about the dive our foot traffic has taken. I mean, just look at *that*..." He paused and stabbed his lucky corndog stick toward the front window, which by now was mostly obscured by "*MISSING!*" flyers and "*Have You Seen This Person?*" posters in various colors and levels of urgency. "They've been cropping up here and there over the past week, one or two a day... now they nearly block the view. It's like some crazy neighborhood family album." Carson tapped one of the newest, a cute young brunette with a round face and laughing green eyes. "I just sold tic-tacs to this lady. Tic-tacs! And now... she's a blurry photocopy on my window and a line in a police report."

Kiki was still absorbed in the reports, skimming pages, reviewing data, analyzing and categorizing as always, struggling to put the pieces together. "Well, if they're stumped," she mused absently. "That makes two of us. Nothing in here makes any sense... there's no common thread, no links, just a series of random attacks. Even the condition of the victims... look, this one has bite marks on the throat, this one on the wrist and ankle... here's one that 'suggests animal attack...' Some took place on the street, some in private residences... this one says the victim was found on a *roof* of all places."

"Yeah, well, I'll tell ya what *is* starting to make sense..." Carson's voice was soft.

"What's that?"

"Pete."

Kiki flipped a page, still absorbed. "Pete?"

"Yeah Pete... Stinky Pete. Y'know..." Carson gave a few sniffs and made an exaggerated fainting motion.

"Oh, right." Kiki made a face. "Bad hoodoo guy." She was obviously displeased with the direction the conversation had taken. "What makes you say that?"

"Well..." Carson faltered. Kiki's eyes were burrowing into him from the shelter of her red stocking cap, pulled low over her brow. It made her look angry, which Carson found fitting since she clearly was, although he was at a loss to explain why.

"'Yes?" She clipped. "Well what? Tell me he's got something besides 'bad hoodoo' this time. Something besides booze delusions or... or... post-traumatic Vietnam flashbacks about his 'time in the bush' or something."

"Er..."

Kiki's eyes were like blue spotlights. He could tell this wasn't going to go well.

"What have you got against Pete?" He asked nonchalantly, in what he knew immediately was a vain attempt to hedge. "Besides the obvious, I mean."

"Nothing... much. Like I said, I know his type. Just tell me what's up."

Carson could tell by the look on her face that it was definitely not "nothing" and more like a very big "something," but he could also tell that he wasn't likely to get out of her what that something was. He let it lie.

Still, regardless of the baggage she was carrying she had him pinned. Quickly he considered, then discarded, the total brush off. It was no use. He had stuck his neck out now and there was no clean exit. Besides, the strangeness of it all had been building maddeningly inside of him and if he didn't tell someone, *anyone*, no matter how hostile, he could see gaskets bursting.

Carson took a breath. The corn dog stick tapped faster. "Well... it's like this. Pete's got this theory..."

"*Theory*? Why do I have the feeling I'm not going to like this?"

Carson's palms were sweaty and his mind started spinning again as the details of his midnight conversation with Stinky Pete swam through his recollection. "He said he's seen things like this before. Weird stuff. Bad stuff. In the... well, in the bush, actually, funny you should mention that... people in bunks... something about boots... and eyes... definitely something about eyes... I didn't understand that part so well, but it was *really* intense and I'm sure it was important. In fact, it was *all* important. And it was *crazy*, too! But not... you know... like *him* crazy, more just *general* crazy, like... y'know, psycho, spooky, out there crazy. Too crazy to be just plain crazy. Just crazy enough to be... I don't know..." he paused. "...true."

"Carson... what are you talking about?"

The stick stopped. He gave up and dove headfirst into the pool. "He thinks it's a vampire."

Carson braced himself for her rebuttal. Nothing came.

Kiki was silent.

A moment passed.

"You're not saying I'm nuts."

"I'm thinking it."

"Well, that's a start. Look, I don't even know if I believe it myself."

"Now *that's* a start..."

Carson wagged his head, vexed and anxious, tugging at his short beard as if he could pull hard enough to yank something down out of his brain that made sense. "He just sounded so... sincere. And all the pieces fit... what I saw in the alley, Pete's story, and now that report from the cops..." For the millionth time, the haunting red eyes resurfaced, glaring hungrily at him from the foggy recesses of his memory, hateful and fierce and full of hellfire.

Kiki was watching him strangely. It was as if the kid sitting beside her on the bus had just picked his nose and eaten it and she wasn't sure whether she should change seats or just sit it out. "Look... you've been through a lot, I know, and there's more than the standard amount of what-the-hell operating here... but a *vampire*?"

"Bloodsucker, actually," Carson muttered. The corn dog stick was twirling again.

"Excuse me?"

"He didn't actually say 'vampire,' he said 'bloodsucker'. That's my paraphrase."

Kiki rolled her eyes. "Whatever. He might as well have said 'Boogie Man'. Carson, let me spell it out for you... he's nuts! This guy has too much wine and not enough sense; he's off the deep end! And what's worse, he's taking you with him! The only *bloodsuckers* Stinky Pete has ever seen are the one's who poke the needle in his arm when he's donating his pint down at the clinic. It's sad, yes, tragic even, but that's the way it is!"

"Look, I know it sounds whack..." Carson paused momentarily, realizing that, even though this was the first time he had spoken his theories out loud, they didn't sound as "whack" as he thought they would. "...but the least you can do is *talk* to Pete! Just hear him out! Listen to what..."

The front door chimed and Officer Jackson lumbered through, forced to turn his broad shoulders slightly to avoid scraping the frame. Carson's urgent plea faltered and he switched gears instantly from begging to brooding. Already frustrated by Kiki's lack of enthusiasm, the reappearance of Officer Jackson was like fresh salt in a fresh wound. He could feel his insides bubbling.

Kiki noted the transition with awe. Carson reminded her of a small cocker spaniel she had once owned that had been quite friendly to her but had developed an intense animosity for the mailman and had finally bitten him severely on the thigh. He had exactly the same look in his eye.

"Has it been five minutes already?" Carson wasn't wasting any time. His voice was dripping with sarcasm. "My, how time flies."

"I'm hungry... *Dud*." Officer Jackson was once more showing off

 60

every one of his strong white teeth in a smug and self-inflating smile. "I believe I'm in the mood for donuts. You got any donuts?"

Carson turned to Kiki with flaring nostrils, gesturing mutely and emphatically at the guard as if he were a prosecuting attorney resting his case and there was no greater evidence he could present.

"Donuts, *Dud.*" Jackson's grin was threatening to do permanent damage to his face.

Carson glared at the guard, then gestured violently toward the far side of the room. Judging by his expression, Kiki figured words would have been ill-advised. Officer Jackson lumbered off casually in the direction of the sweets, humming tunelessly.

"What's *he* so happy about?" Carson muttered angrily, his eyes boring holes in the big man's back. Without waiting for an answer, he seized his rag and resumed his therapeutic polishing of the Freezie machine, its mirror surface reflecting back his darkened brow and angry eyes. Kiki let the threads of their broken conversation dangle, sensing that rational discussion would have to wait for cooler heads.

A moment later, Officer Jackson swaggered back to the counter, keys, cuffs and radio jingling merrily on his belt, providing accompaniment to his humming. He dropped a package of jelly-filled donettes onto the counter along with a five dollar bill. Carson ignored him, pretending to work at an imaginary stain on the Freezie machine.

Jackson shrugged, caught up the donettes and tore into the package. He sank his grin into the yellow dough with a puff of powder and a gush of thick jelly that squirted down his chin. "Whoops..." He smiled cheerfully around the mouthful of goo, snatching a handful of napkins out of the dispenser. "Better be careful! All that red mess runnin' down my face... wouldn't want you to think I'm a *bloodsucker...* or I guess you prefer the term 'vampire'."

All polishing stopped. Carson stared hard at the security guard. "So that's it. You were listening in... *spying!*"

Officer Jackson stared at his donut, his face blissful, relishing both the pastry and the moment. "Hey, no thanks necessary. That's what I'm here for, me and my big ol' immovable boots. Plant ourselves where we can be useful, keep an eye on things, watch what's goin' on... and yeah, listen in from time to time. That's what you wanted, ain't it? What's your beef, bro? First I'm *lazy* cuz I wasn't doin' my job, now I'm *nosy* cuz I am? Make up your mind."

"This is different! This is... this is... well, I don't know exactly *what* it is, but it's not polite, thank you very much! And just for the record," he added defensively. "I didn't say it *was* a vampire - I was just sharing a theory."

Jackson snorted. A thin line of powder from the donette decorated his upper lip, robbing him of some of his dignity but still leaving him plenty in control. "That's some theory. Now allow me share *mine*. First of all, I don't believe in all that supernatural crap... you want to talk vampires or the Boogie Man, get yourself a comic book or go to the movies. *Someone's* out there killin' people... not some-*thing,* some-*one.* He's a whack-job, I'll give you that, but he's as human as you or me. Well... maybe me." The guard popped a pair of donettes into his mouth, chewing slowly and with great delight.   The squelching, squishing sound of jelly was so loud that Carson felt like he was in there with it. He watched the spectacle with disgust. "Well, if the Gold Shield's finest says it's just a man, then who am I to argue? Your finely tuned rent-a-cop sense probably had this whole thing figured from the beginning, right? Of course, it's easier to just take a flying guess than to do any *real* work, isn't it?! Say what you want, believe what you want, laugh at me all you want... but I know what I saw. The eye don't lie."

"You saw saw a *corpse*, man... woop-de-doo!" Officer Jackson's retort rumbled around the pulpy mass of donette. "Some poor slob got his throat torn out, that ruined his day, you got an eyeful and it ruined yours. He's takin' the big sleep, you got one less customer and that's that, tough break for everyone. But it's over, and *that's that!* Move on, man... you're pathetic!"

"Hey... show a little respect!" Carson dropped his rag and stepped to the counter, drawing himself up to his full height and staring Officer Jackson squarely in his badge. "A dude is *dead* here... a dude who happened to be a friend of mine!"

"So some guy got ganked, big deal. It ain't the first time someone died in this city..." A shadow passed over Jackson's face, briefly but leaving an obvious ripple. Carson paused, momentarily caught off guard. As quick as it came, however, the shadow fled and Officer Jackson was bullying on, his volume on the rise and his nostrils starting to flare. "It's just like they say - *&$@ happens. Then you die. But it's *people* doin' the killin', not zombies or mutants or Bigfoot or even *vampires!* There ain't no such thing as monsters, and anyone who says different is just smokin' the crank!" Officer Jackson yanked another donette from the package, which was by now quite distressed from the unconscious working of his enormous hands, and jammed it into his mouth. A puff of white added emphasis to his words.

"Well for your information, I'm not the *only* one who's smokin' the crank... this particular theory *also* happens to be shared by Stinky Pete!" The red was starting to crawl up Carson's neck and his volume was on the rise as well.

"Well, *excuse me*!!" Officer Jackson jerked his tree-trunk arms into the sky, as if enlightened by sudden revelation. "Why didn't you tell me?! If *Stinky Pete* says it's a vampire, then it's *gotta* be true!!"

"Say what you want, jumbo, but I happen to believe him! Sure, he stinks like low tide, and that's unfortunate, but he's been around a *long* time! He *knows* stuff... he's *seen* stuff... a heckuva lot more stuff than *you*!"

"Yeah, he's seen things alright... pink bunnies, space aliens and the damn Tooth Fairy..."

"Oh, right, good, that's rational - and what have *you* seen... besides the bottom of too many donut boxes?!"

They were both bellowing by this time, locked nose to nose across the glass counter. The package of donettes lay between them, now a sad, shapeless wreck. Despite his obvious rage and the intensity of the exchange, Officer Jackson was still fishing them out and popping them into his mouth. "There you go again about my eatin' habits! I'm *warnin'* you, cracka...!"

"Well, warn away! The only thing that has a reason to be scared of you around here are those donettes!"

Jackson stopped, mouth open, another morsel just inches from going down the hatch. He hesitated, but his appetite got the better of him and he jammed the defenseless pastry ruthlessly into his mouth. When he spoke, his voice was thick with jelly and rage and bits of yellow cake flew into Carson's hair. He didn't flinch.

"I am *sick* of this place!! I am sick of this *job,* sick of this *life,* and most of all, brother, I am sick of *you*! It's *you* that's been keepin' me stuck at this dead-end op guardin' your sorry *&*% in the middle of the night, and the whole *&*!#% time all you been doin' is ridin' me, sayin' I'm doin' nuthin', sayin' I'm lazy, sayin' there's *somethin' goin' on out there*... but all you got is some crap story about '*bloodsuckers*' and whatever, all cuz some guy called Stinky Pete had some bad hobo trip. You got more crazy in you than my ex! Did somethin' happen to you as a kid to make you this way?!"

"Yeah... it's called 'school,' you should try it!"

At the front of the store, almost completely drowned out by the intensity of the argument, the front door made its weak, sickly chime. Kiki was the only one who heard it.

"Uh, guys..." She coughed softly. The shouting continued unabated.

"There's that mouth again!" Jackson thundered.

"Correct! It *is* my mouth! Well done, big fella, that's progress! Now... what are these?" Carson stabbed fingers at his ears. "Once you can identify them, maybe you'll start *using* them!"

Jackson's fists clenched into great ham-sized balls of flesh and knuckle, the unmistakable glint of murder shining brightly in his eyes. The lone survivor of his onslaught against the donettes lay still in the box, forgotten at last as his rage finally overpowered his appetite. "I *told* you someday I'd bring the thunder, counter monkey!! Know that I ain't lyin' when I say that day is *fast* approachin'...!" Jackson banged the counter with enough force to topple several stacks of Freezie cups.

"Oooh, scary!" Carson threw up his hands in mock terror. "Careful... if you kill me, you may never find out what aisle the ice cream sandwiches are on!"

Kiki cleared her throat and tried again, louder. "Uh... guys?! There's a...." Again her words were hopelessly trampled.

"I wouldn't buy more sweets from you if my life depended on it, *Dud*!"

"I've seen the way you eat... your life *does* depend on it, *Dexter*!!"

The guard fumed, at a loss for any more clever insults. "Punk!" He bellowed.

"Jerk!"

"Loser!"

"Rent-a-cop!"

"Pantywaist!"

"Potty mouth!"

"*&%@$!"

"*HEY*!!!" Kiki had finally had enough. Her shout cut the air like a knife, and just for good measure she banged the counter bell so hard that the clap broke off the ringer.

Both men stopped as if slapped, yanked at last from their private war, breathing hard, fists and teeth clenched, bridling with anger. They stared at Kiki, then followed her finger to the figure standing in the doorway.

"Oh... hey Vanessa..." Carson's furious expression melted,

reddening even more as he realized she'd been listening. "Uh... sorry... just... uh... a little labor dispute..."

Officer Jackson, however, had a much different take as his eyes registered black form-fitting leather, curvaceous lines and porcelain beauty. The argument, as heated as it was, was instantly forgotten. One second he was puffed up like a pit bull, bristling and ready for action, the next he was leaning on the counter in a suave, come-hither stance.

"Damn... maybe there's some perks to this gig after all." Still oblivious of his powdered-donut mustache, he hiked up his belt and lifted his chin in greeting. "'Sup, mama?"

Carson rolled his eyes, flabbergasted and slightly nauseous. "Don't mind him, Vanessa... he was *just leaving*. We'll finish this little chat later, Officer Jackson." Carson speared the guard with his eyes and nodded emphatically toward the door. Jackson, however, was oblivious. His eyes were fixed on Vanessa, who was striking a decidedly feminine pose near the impulse buy racks. It was apparent that she was creating all manner of impulses already.

"He's on duty, after all, plenty of work to do..." Carson flashed a plastic smile and jabbed the big man in the arm. Officer Jackson didn't budge. On his face was the same look as when he had opened the box of donettes.

A look of amusement danced across Vanessa's cold, delicate features. "Really?"

This single word was like a lightning rod. Carson blinked. He realized, dimly, that it was the first time he had ever heard Vanessa talk. Her voice was soft, sultry and packed with feminine allure, penetrating the mini-mart and snatching everyone's attention as if they had been slapped in the face by a velvet glove with a brick stuffed inside of it.

"Zat is unfortunate..." she continued. "I vas hoping he vould stay for a moment. I vas very much interested in your... discussion." Adding to its innately hypnotic qualities, her voice was thickly flavored with some obscure Eastern European dialect, making her sound like an escapee from an old Bela Lugosi film. Carson was momentarily torn between fascination at the sound and frustration at the suggestion that Officer Jackson's presence could be anything more than wholly unpleasant.

"Damn... I *love* an accent." Jackson's toothy grin was back, spreading slowly across his face.

"You, uh... you were?" Carson struggled to adapt to the sudden change in atmosphere, eager to find a way to dislodge his sparring partner from the store but intrigued by Vanessa's appearance. There was something about her that Carson couldn't put his finger on, something engaging, almost entrancing. Maybe it was her voice. Or maybe it was the tight leather peek-a-boo lap-dancer outfit. Carson couldn't be sure, but he *did* know that whatever it was, when she talked, he wanted to listen.

"I vas," she was saying, the words dripping like melted chocolate from her lips. "I vas *indeed*." To the ambrosia of her tone, Vanessa introduced a broad, scintillating smile, showcasing perfect, dazzlingly white teeth and luscious, ruby red lips. The lips were sensuous and agile, quirking in subtle punctuation to her moods and words and startlingly vivid in hue, an inviting splash of color in the delicate doll-like beauty of her face. She took a single, languorous step into the room, one stiletto heel clicking softly on the tile floor, the shift of her hips subtle but as unmistakably feminine as a lingerie commercial. "I apologize for... how do you say... 'eavesdropping' But it vas difficult not to overhear. Your vords vere quite heated."

Both men began speaking at once, clamoring to explain their behavior.

"He started it..."

"It wasn't as bad as..."

"Please, you misunderstand..." Vanessa lifted a slim, supple hand and instantly all talking stopped. "I found it quite intriguing, especially your comments concerning the supernatural elements. I must say, my dear, sweet Carson-boy, that you make some very interesting observations."

"It was? I mean, I do? Er... I mean..."

"Indeed. And, unlike your large friend suggests, I do not find you unbalanced. In fact, quite the opposite. I think you might be... how do you say... 'on to something.'" She took another couple of steps, hips swaying like a runway model. The soft creak of leather was an invitation to look.

Carson blinked. "You... you think... I'm sorry, what now?"

"I think you may be correct."

"You do?!"

"I do."

"Yes! See?!" Carson shifted his attention pointedly to Officer Jackson.

"Great." The guard rolled his eyes. "Why do the sexy mama's always gotta be crazy?!" he muttered.

Carson ignored him. "Well, thank you, Vanessa! Thank you very much." He folded his arms defiantly across his chest. "I appreciate your open mindedness. I must say, it's a breath of fresh air around here. Very welcome change. Please, do continue."

"Certainly, my delicious, virile young friend. Vould it surprise you if I said I know a little something about such things? Vhere I come from, tales of such happenings are not so strange, not so foreign." She was halfway to the counter, her words, lithe, swaying figure and pouting lips an anchor for attention. In spite of his rebuff, even Officer Jackson found himself riveted.

"Ha!" Carson crowed. "Not so strange after all!"

"In fact, you might say that 'bloodsuckers,' as you call zem, are a part of the local culture vhere I come from. A prominent part at that."

"Ha! Local culture! Prominent!"

"In fact, many from my country believe zey are not merely creatures of folklore... but that zey are *real*."

"Ha! Real!"

"I believe zem."

"Ha! She *believes* zem! Er... *them*."

"And as it turns out, my succulent young friend, you are indeed correct - zere *is* a vampire in your town."

"Ha! There *is* a vampire in my town!"

"I know this because... it is *me*."

"Ha...! What...?"

Vanessa stood before them now, close enough to touch. Her arms hung loosely at her sides, head cast back, night black tresses spilling across the firm, supple muscles of her shoulders and upper back. At this range the cool, alabaster landscape of her features was knifelike in its beauty - clean, sharp and wounding. She stood like a goddess in black leather, hips cocked, lips curved in a half-smile like a scythe, long dark lashes lowered over half-lidded eyes that were lit with a haunting mixture of towering superiority and amusement.

Carson blinked. "Uh... you... okay, now that's not helping anyone..." Carson shot a sidelong glance at Officer Jackson, checking his reaction. There was none - his face was a mask.

"Shall I tell you vhat has happened to your missing ones?" Vanessa gave the slightest toss of her head to indicate the wall of "*Have-You-Seen-This-Person?*" flyers. "Zey are not, as these parchments say, missing."

"Not missin'?" Officer Jackson found his voice. It sounded

slightly husky, as if he had just woken up. "Then where the hell are they at?"

"Zey are dead."

The comment fell as if she had dropped the bodies right on the floor in front of them. There was something in her voice that brooked no argument and they knew, suddenly and undeniably, that she had spoken the truth. The store was quiet. Deathly quiet. Even the hum from the Freezie machine seemed to be gone.

Kiki's voice broke the silence, a whisper from somewhere near Officer Jackson's elbow. "How do you know?"

"Zat is simple, my fragile little kitten-girl. I killed zem."

It was here, Carson realized, that he should do something - shout, weep, swing, fall down, run around in circles screaming, anything - but none of his limbs seemed to be interested in joining the effort. He was experiencing a strange sense of detachment, as if the carpet of reality had suddenly been yanked out from under his feet, and he was stalled, suspended in mid air, waiting for his body to hit the ground before deciding whether or not it was worth it to get up again. He noted, absently, that he could smell Vanessa now. She had a rich, earthy scent with a hint of Wintergreen breath mints and the faintest waft of something almost unidentifiable but too close to the smell of undercooked hamburger to be comforting.

"I drank zeir blood." Vanessa leaned casually, languidly across the counter, well within his bubble and looking like she was planning on getting *a lot* closer. Carson, able to make out every perfect pore in her stark, porcelain features, stared into the bottomless depths of her black soulless eyes. "And now... I vill do the same to you."

A heartbeat passed.

No one breathed.

Then, every life in the 24/7 suddenly changed forever.

Vanessa's face burst into a nightmare mask of horror, fangs and darkness. Black hair billowed in a wild tangle as her head snapped back and her arms flew wide. Three inch claws sprouted from her fingertips and a hideous, animal scream tore through silence and soul alike, shredding both like a tornado through a mobile home park. Carson gave a great, unintelligible shout and promptly fell over backward, tripping on his stool and crashing to the floor. Kiki stood rooted in the shadow of Officer Jackson, her face a frozen mask that mirrored perfectly the shock and mind-numbing horror that locked brain and body in place, holding her immobile and helpless against the

 68

threat of imminent vampiric destruction.

Only the security guard managed to produce a meaningful action, yanking his heavy pistol clear and jerking the trigger three times in rapid succession. Unfortunately, the reaction was more out of reflex than intent. His face wore the look of a man whose brain had suddenly turned to cabbage, and it was immediately apparent that the cabbage had not informed any of the other body parts that the weapon's safety was still engaged. His finger worked in obedient futility against the properly secured and completely unresponsive trigger, as some small, still-functional part of his brain screamed at the rest of his body that something was terribly, terribly wrong and struggled to comprehend exactly what that might be and rectify it.

Vanessa's hot eyes ate up the scene for a split second, relishing the mental devastation. Then, almost casually, she slapped the weapon away with a force that broke a finger and sent the pistol flying across the room, where it embedded itself in the side of the nacho cheese warmer. In the same movement, almost faster than the eye could follow, she seized the big man by collar and belt and heaved him across the room like a massive, cabbage-brained rag doll. Jackson's heavy frame crashed down on the business end of ten feet away, completely demolishing a large section of metal shelving that, ironically, would have done much more to cushion his fall had it not been recently emptied of snack cakes. He hadn't even had a chance to curse before Vanessa was on him.

Launching herself into the air with a frighteningly effortless leap, she rebounded from another shelf and lit by his side with a hiss and a vicious kick that caught him square in the chest. It was the second time her shapely leg had caught his attention this day, and this time it made an even bigger impression, lifting him three feet off the floor and cracking several ribs. Jackson came down on his side with a hearty *woof!*, slid to a stop against the hard, cool metal of the standalone freezer chest and was promptly kicked in the back of the head. His large skull rebounded first from the boot-tip and then from the side of the chest with a distinctive *ping* that rang through the mini-mart like a bone dinner gong. Stricken, disarmed and now enjoying the fruits of a moderately severe concussion, the guard was, at least for the moment, finished. Vanessa, however, was just getting started.

Hoisting his body from the floor like one might hoist a bag of dog chow, the vampiress dumped him effortlessly across the cool glass lid of the freezer lid, slamming his face into the glass. She held it pinned, sliding up onto his back, hissing and gnashing like a bobcat, demon light dancing in her red eyes, tongue lashing across the bared tips of her uncomfortably prominent canines. She postured for a moment, exulting in unbridled power and fearsome magnificence. In triumph, she cut loose with another straight-from-the-bowels-of-Hell-hear-this-and-never-sleep-again banshee shriek that set off car alarms several blocks away. Then, quite unnecessarily and in a way so wrong it seemed cruel, she licked him. Her tongue - too long, too red and too much - drew a languorous slimy trail through the quivering beads of sweat on the guard's exposed throat. Officer Jackson kicked feebly and gurgled, helpless as a kitten, cheek and lips mashed almost comically against the thick glass.

Then it started all over.

With an effortless grace that would have been charming if it wasn't currently being used to destroy a human being, Vanessa dismounted and dropped to the floor, yanking her victim to his feet and whipping him about. Fearsome claws lashed out, slashing the front of Jackson's blue polyester shirt to shreds and carving deep, jagged furrows through his chest. Jackson fell back, barely able to stand but at last able to curse. Though most of it was unintelligible and clearly not his best work, he made up for it with volume. Vanessa leapt and slashed again, carving another set of furrows, then followed up with a casual backhand that snapped the guard's head back like a rubber band and split his lower lip clean through. Staggering with the force of the blow, he lurched past Kiki who still stood frozen, slack-jawed and wide-eyed, and came up hard when the front counter rammed into the small of his back.

Like a panicked Jack-in-the-box, Carson popped up from behind the counter an instant after he hit, baseball bat in hand, eyes wild, looking for a target and a reason to swing but not looking like he was going to wait for either before cutting loose.

Jackson met his wild eyes, shielding himself instinctively as Carson barely managed to check a frantic swing. "A *baseball bat*?!" Jackson bellowed, sucking air and at last managing to find his voice. One arm was clamped across his cracked ribs, the other clutching at the counter to keep him from collapsing. "What're you gonna do, hit a home run?! Get my gun, whitey... *we got a situation here*!!"

Before Carson could force his traumatized brain to produce a reply, they were rudely interrupted by a giant, burly mass of wiry gray hair and gnashing fangs that lit on the counter amidst a defining thunderstorm of ear-splitting roars and savage barks. Vanessa had changed. Claws scrabbled and tore at the counter, sending Carson ducking away under a shower of hot saliva. Officer Jackson leapt back as if he'd already been bitten, a fresh chorus of profanity painting the air behind him where powerful jaws now snapped and clicked, a split-second and a fraction of an inch from tasting flesh.

Letting him go, the Vanessa-wolf whipped about, glowing eyes hungrily searching for Carson. They lit instead on the heels of his tennis-shoes as they disappeared around the far end of the counter, where he was well on his way to safer environs and a world's record for speed crawling. Frustrated, she bunched her powerful hindlegs, found a tenuous purchase on the slick countertop and launched herself after the stumbling, staggering figure of Officer Jackson instead. Her body morphing back to human form in mid-air, she turned a neat somersault and landed with both feet on his heaving chest.

In spite of the vehemence of the blow, Officer Jackson kept his feet, although this was largely due to the fact that he had slammed with full force into the door of the walk-in freezer. Inside, several items could be heard to leap from their shelves and burst upon the floor, mimicking the sickening feeling of Officer Jackson's own insides.

As the big man stood slumped, stunned and shaking against the door, Vanessa suddenly slowed, trading her crouching panther's charge for a sauntering, sultry, almost idle pace, letting her hips do the talking. She paused every few steps to run her long red tongue over her inch-long incisors in a meaningful suggestion of things to come. Officer Jackson got the message. Despite the general discomfort in every square inch of his body and the powerful desire to lay down and pass out, Jackson moved - not far and not fast, but an impressive effort in its own right. A few shaky steps bought him just enough time to fumble for the handle of his steel baton and yank it from his belt.

"You want some more o' this, honey?!" He bellowed, though his words were badly slurred due to his head injuries and came out sounding more like "*You want your oatmeal runny?!*"

On Vanessa's next step, somehow, he swung.

The blow, which would have neatly split a two-by-four and should have done the same to Vanessa's skull, stopped cold with a meaty *smack!* as she reached out lazily and caught it with her bare hand. Vanessa yanked the weapon away as if taking a rattle from a disgruntled 400 pound baby, bent it into a "U" and cast it aside.

Officer Jackson stumbled back and groped in his belt for another weapon, groping as well for some suitably crushing battlefield rhetoric but falling short. "Oooooh! Mutha...! You a *bad...!* Less go! ...in yo face, baby!!"

A frantic moment later he was armed and firing. This time it was pepper spray. Vanessa walked through the burning mist as if it were a summer breeze. She snatched the can, crushed it with her teeth and continued the advance.

Keenly aware that he was running out of options, Jackson's face showed it as he backed against a wall and stopped - hard. Clawing one last weapon - a taser - from its holster, he jammed it desperately against Vanessa's chest and squeezed the trigger. Overwhelmed by physical abuse and terror, his brain fired away simultaneously with a single, roaring epithet:

"STINKER!!!"

A mad, frenetic clicking filled the air as thousands of volts of electricity coursed through Vanessa's body. Her back arched, blue arcs lacing the reds of her eyes, dancing off bared teeth, raising her hair in a sparking, staticky cloud as the charge built up in her body... and then fading slowly, as the light and the charge died away, leaving the weapon as cold and dead as she was. Her body relaxed.

She smiled.

A second later Officer Jackson hit the ground, sent there by a powerful backhand. His head bounced smartly off what seemed to be developing into a neverending sequence of hard surfaces, and this time he blacked out.

He was not out for long, however. Desperately the guard fought against numbing waves of darkness that had washed the mini-mart away. Somewhere deep inside he was aware that his life depended on the simple act of waking up, and it was this single thought that he clung to as he dragged himself back toward consciousness a few seconds later. When he came to, it was not to good news.

The first thing Officer Jackson could feel was Vanessa - he was flat on his back on the floor and she was pressed tightly against him, slick and hard like a leather-clad cinderblock, pinning him down and trapping his arms at his sides. She grasped a handful of dreadlocks in one clawed hand and yanked his head sideways, exposing the pulsing artery in the side of his neck and sending fresh fireworks through his brain. He could hear the blood hammering in his ears and saw Vanessa's eyes fixed upon the vessel, mesmerized, tongue lashing in rhythm with the coursing blood. He tried to wriggle, twist, anything, but could not. Claws dug into his flesh and the earthy, meaty smell of her washed over him in full force, her eyes blazing feverishly above a cruel, twisted smile as she dipped her head. A hiss spilled from the back of her throat, unconscious and sinister, like a serpent's warning before the strike.

"You have shown me yours..." she whispered in a tone that in any other setting would have been seductive, but at this particular moment only made Officer Jackson want to wet his paints. "Now I vill show you *mine*!" Her head flew back and her jaws flew wide - impossibly wide - baring needlepointed fangs which glistened like pearl stilettos in the fluorescent light.

Then she struck.

At that precise moment, the unmistakable *smack!* of hardwood on skull snapped the vampiress' head to her shoulder, lifted her bodily and sent her flying into the beverage cooler, where the dramatic introduction of her head created a neat starburst in the glass. In the space she had just vacated stood Carson Dudley, eyes wild and bat in hand.

"You don't have to be playin' baseball to hit a home run..." he muttered savagely, and to no one in particular.

Officer Jackson did a quick double-take, blinking furiously in an attempt to re-engage his brain. He seized Carson's outstretched arm, blinked some more and struggled to get his legs working as the clerk hauled him upward. "Yeah... yeah... nice hit! Baseball bat. Yeah... gotta get me one of them..."

"You okay?!" Carson stared into the vacant brown depths of Jackson's eyes as the guard lurched unsteadily to his feet, searching for some indication that the big man was in charge of his faculties and not seeing much to convince him.

"Yeah... yeah... jus' a sec... gimme a... there's a... ...rung my bell... What? Yeah... jus' a sec..." Jackson shook his head weakly, sending his dreadlocks dancing and scattering bits of plaster and glass this way and that. His eyes were badly unfocused and dilated and he seemed about to fall. "'S jus' my head... ribs... back... arm... these two fingers... I'm jus' gonna get my legs... rung my bell... then I'm gonna find me that bloodsucka... open up a can of..."

"Forget it! We're grabbing Kiki and gettin' outta here!" Carson whirled to go. Another slurred, vacant comment by Officer Jackson brought him up short.

"'S funny... we break a pipe?"

"What?!"

"We got... steam..."

Sure enough, a thick cloud of mist was rising from the floor all about them, swirling over packages of goodies and spilling up from under shelves and overturned displays.

"Uh-oh."

"Whazzat...? Why you... what's *uh-oh*?!"

"Oh, man... that's not good. Not good at all..." Carson licked his lips and choked up on the bat, staring into the rapidly thickening mist that was now hedging in on all sides. "It's not steam, dude... it's mist. *Her* mist. 'Uh-oh' means it's one of her little tricks, and it means we're in big trouble. Stay frosty!"

"Got it... got your back, bro... stinker!" Officer Jackson shifted, putting his back to Carson's and his clenched fists toward the roiling fog. The move caused him to wobble threateningly, but he caught himself on a magazine rack and steadied his balance. "The witch... still got some game, hunh?"

Carson nodded tersely.

"So much... for your home run, man." Jackson's voice sounded a little steadier.

"Let's call it a base hit - practice swing. I'm ready for her this time!" He hefted his bat. "C'mon, you dirty bloodsucker..." he shouted into the mist. "*Batter up!*"

"You said it, bro! Bring it *on*! I know her... I know her moves now... I know her style. I got her *down!* And this time, freaky mama... this time papa is gonna *mess you up!* You hear that?! I'm gonna *mess you up!* I'm gonna... wait a sec..." His voice dropped. "Wait a sec... I think I see somethin'..."

"What is it?! Is it her?!"

Silence.

"Talk to me, dude! What's..." Carson's question died as he chanced a quick glance over his shoulder.

Officer Jackson was gone. He was alone.

"Oh, snap..."

For the second time that week, Carson stood in the middle of a thick cloud of swirling gray that chilled like ice but felt more like a large frying pan. As he struggled against both an overwhelming sense of deja vu and a rising panic, he came to a single, powerful revelation - he didn't like it. Not at all.

"Vell... here ve are again, my savory little flesh biscuit."

Carson started, snapped his head about.

Vanessa's voice floated out of the impenetrable expanse of mist, as vaporous and intangible as the thick tendrils of gray that swirled and eddied about him. It seemed to come from everywhere, echoing throughout the once-familiar but now terrifyingly surreal landscape of his beloved 24/7. Ears straining, he desperately tried to pinpoint the direction of the haunting, dusky tones, which he was finding increasingly less seductive as the evening progressed.

"It has not been so long since our last encounter... and yet so much has changed."

Carson thought he detected a faint shadowy movement from the corner of his eye and shifted quickly, bat at the ready. The mist swirled, contorting into imaginary faces, curling around shelves and fixtures until everything looked alive and moving.

His eyes shifted, shoulders dropping as he forced himself to relax.

Nothing.

Or something?

Carson licked his lips, suddenly dry.

"How different your little vorld must seem now, my sweet, scrumptious, pudding drop... my tender, pink, beloved dumpling... how strange, how frightening, how... *perilous!*" The last word was a whisper in his right ear, so close that the hairs on his neck jumped up and prickled like a startled porcupine. Carson whirled reflexively and lashed out with all his might. Fueled by the rivers of adrenaline coursing through his system, the bat whiffed through the air and crashed solidly into a nearby display, neatly obliterating several cans of hairspray and an assortment of toothpaste.

"Ooooh..." the disembodied voice purred. It had moved again, this time off to his left, but still close. "Such hostility... such aggression. You are a fine hunt, my plump, tantalizing meat snack. Exciting! Vigorous! I have so much enjoyed our time together."

"Great - why not just call it even, then? I had fun, you had fun, we both have some fun stories to tell... how about we just go our separate ways?" Carson tried to force some bravado into his voice but it came out sounding as weak and fearful as his insides felt.

She *tsk'ed* him from the fog. The words that followed were pouty. "Now, Carson... zat vould *never* do! *You* know and *I* know zat ve cannot leave our business unfinished. Ve are joined, you and I, inexorably connected, predator and prey, hunter and hunted. The table is set, the invitations delivered... the meal *must* be served. You vould not vant to deny my... *hunger!"*

Again her seductive whisper tickled his ear, this time from the left, and again he jerked a swing. Several packages of tampons and a quart of motor oil went flying into the mist as this blow, too, missed its mark.

The fading echoes of the crash mingled with a sinister, musical laugh. "Ahhh, Carson, my dear, delicious, succulent morsel... zat is vat I vill miss the most about you. Your *zeal*! Your *spice!* Your *energy!* Even vhen all is hopeless, all is lost... you still vill not give up, like so many of your patrons have done before you. Veak, they vere, pathetic and miserable, groveling for their vorthless lives. Not so you! Not my Carson... but alas, your efforts are doomed. Do you think you are the first to face me? I have done zis before, for hundreds of years, in dozens of cities. Men have tried to hunt me - hunt *me, the huntress!* - but alvays it has availed zem not. Sadly, you vill end up just like zem... cold, lifeless and dead, food for the vorms. After, of course you are food for me. Zat is the vay of things, darling. You must not blame me and you cannot stop me. No one can stop me."

He felt the slightest caress on the back of his neck, like a trace of fire, and whether it was ruby lips or scarlet fingertips, Carson didn't know for he was already whirling and swinging, his nerves taught and explosive. A dim shape loomed out of the shadows and mist, and he connected violently, sending a very threatening loaf of white bread and most of a rack of hot dug buns flying off across the store where they would never bother anyone again.

Maddeningly, agonizingly, the sinister, throaty laugh floated from somewhere out of the mist, grating on the taught, frayed wiring of his nerves. This time, it came also with a warning. "Tut tut, my savory, mewling chop of lamb... you had best be careful vith your svings. Otherwise, you might hit something... breakable."

There was a whimper.

"Kiki!" Carson took an impulsive step, even though he realized as he did so that he had no idea what direction the noise had came from.

"Aha..." Vanessa purred. "At last our delicate little flesh kitten has contributed something useful to this altercation."

"Let her go, Vanessa! Let her go, or... or...!" Carson's voice faltered. Given his present situation, he couldn't think of anything terrible to visit on the vampiress that would be meaningful, much less convincing. He knew only anger, frustration and helplessness. More importantly, he knew Vanessa had him right where she wanted him.

"Mmmmm..." Vanessa's tone had shifted now, taking on a hungry note. Carson could tell she was savoring the moment, anticipating it, toying with it, like the first bite of a sausage hot pocket fresh out of the warmer. He didn't know if vampires drooled, but he imagined it thick in her mouth, pooling around the base of needle-pointed incisors. The image didn't help. Unbidden, his imagination rushed to fill in additional details, adding the hot, blood-red glow of her eyes, as he fought back against a fresh tide of fear. Kiki whimpered again.

"At last," Vanessa gloated. "You realize the futility of your situation. You poor, poor, sveet, delicious, succulent man-morsel. So alone... so afraid... so vulnerable... so soft... so *tender*..." There was a faint click of stiletto heels, and he knew without a doubt that Vanessa was close. His nerves jangled and his muscles itched to swing, but this time, he held himself in check. A laugh of sheer delight, at once triumphant and bloodcurdling, bubbled up from the black depths of Vanessa's throat and rippled across the room like a funeral shroud dancing in the wind. "I do not vish this moment to end so soon. *Beg* me, my darling, precocious, sveet meat... *beg* me for your life and those of your friends! It vill not, I confess, alter the outcome of the evening, but it vill at least delay it and provide dear Vanessa some entertainment. And I do so enjoy the *music* of it! Come... *beg* me!"

It sounded good to Carson. "Umm... okay. Try this: 'Please, please, O great and beautiful Queen of the Night... let us go and spare our lives.' There. How was that? A little rough, I know, but if you give me a minute I can work up to something a little more genuine. I mean, I'm *really* motivated here, but you're totally freaking me out and it's making it hard to concentrate. Hey - you like tears?! I mean, heck, I'm pretty close right now, I bet I can even whip some up for you...!"

He paused, listening.

The laughter had stopped.

"Vanessa?"

"You mock me." Vanessa's voice had taken on the cold, hard edge of a granite coffin lid.

"What?! No way! You said 'beg', I begged!"

"I have changed my mind."

"Hey, it was *your* idea!"

"*Enough!!* I tire of you now, you foolish, ripe, inviting boy-bite. The end has come for you, save for a final act: now zat friends and pride are gone, there is but one thing left to take from you." With a faint rush and a swirl of mist, a black shape ghosted before him, snatched the bat from his hands and vanished before he could so much as blink. The weapon was gone. His one source of hope in the entire sickening decline of the evening - *gone*. Carson's mouth worked, but no sound came out.

"And now," Vanessa's haunting tones surrounded him, penetrating his brain, paralyzing him, deceptively smooth yet decidedly deadly. "I have stripped you of all I can, save that vich I desire the most. Let the end begin..."

The black blur ghosted in again and Carson caught an iron bar to the mouth, rocking his head back and throwing him through the air. He hit tile, sliding a few feet, and came to a stop, ears ringing, face numb. He had seen the same happen to Officer Jackson, but now it was his turn. It hurt *a lot* more, Carson decided, in first person.

He shook his head and scrambled awkwardly to his feet, putting a hand to his mouth. It came away bloody. He swallowed hard, brain racing but foggy with pain and panic. Begging hadn't worked. He switched tactics, turning frantically as he tried to pick Vanessa's shape out of the crowding gray fog. "You're taking a big chance here! Someone could come in... they could see you!"

Again her triumphant, bloodcurdling laughter pealed, but by now it was mostly bloodcurdling and just a little bit triumphant. It sent Carson's stomach into his sneakers.

"*Who?!*" She crowed. "*Who* vill come, foolish, dancing blood-filled dumpling? Your patrons have become my victims! All who have come *seeking* sustenance have instead *become* sustenance! There are *none* left to help!"

"Ha! So it *was* you!"

Vanessa spluttered. "Vhat?! Of *course* it was me... I have confessed that already to you!" Again, the black shape lashed out of the mist, this time with a little more anger and a little less flair. Carson took a shuddering impact on his chest and felt himself flying backward, collided with a wire-frame display rack and added himself to the debris littering the floor. It hurt.

"Foolish pink man! You are ready to believe so much, yet are unable to see it even vhen it is right... under... your... nose!"

"Yeah?" Carson coughed weakly, struggling to draw breath into his throbbing chest and willing himself to roll to his knees. "One... more day... I'd have figured... it out. Breath mints... that was the key..."

"Unlikely, little mouthful. I have been using your establishment as a hunting ground for veeks now, and you vere oblivious the entire time! Although, I must say, you have been an excellent host and it has been the perfect environ: plentiful victims, late hours, no questions, a suitable lair nearby... the perfect habitat for a hungry - how do you say - 'bloodsucker?' Your district vas ideal... and, may I say, *delicious*."

"Uh-huh... thanks..." Carson staggered to his feet and stood reeling. "Delicious. Terrific. Something we agree on! That's a starting point - maybe we can still talk this through." He cast about for an exit, a weapon, anything that might help. Before he could take a step a hand lashed out of the darkness and seized the short hairs of his chin.

He yelped. "Ow! Not the beard!"

Callously, cruelly, the vampiress jerked his head side to side and his body followed frantically, propelled first into one display rack, then another. Finally, she cast him free and he slipped and fell again...hard...taking his wind.

"Talk... alas, no," she purred. "For the time of talking has passed. It is time for the hunter to find a new hunting ground, and to put to rest the last of her prey. Pity. I so much vanted this to last." She giggled suddenly, wickedly, like a guilty school girl. "But then, who else is left?"

Carson struggled to his knees and, for the first time since the mist appeared, his blurry eyes focused fully on Vanessa. She appeared impetuously, imperially before him in a parting of the fog, which clung to her shoulders like some ghostly majestic raiment. One hand rested seductively on a fulsome hip, while with the other she clutched Kiki by a clawful of hair. Kiki's stocking cap was gone, blond hair disheveled, face deathly pale. She was half-slumped in a faint. Casually, Vanessa cast her aside. She fell to the floor, face first, with a sickening, defenseless thud that made Carson want to throw up, then lay motionless. Vanessa stepped over the body without a second glance, closing on him and giving him, at last, the answer to whether vampires drooled.

In his head, the small part of Carson's brain that hadn't turned to pudding was screaming at him in deafening stereophonic sound: *"Run! Move! Crawl! Fight! Do something... anything!"* But it was too small a part to have an effect on the rest of his mind, which had just tipped off the end of ,"this is too much, thanks, I'll be checking out now", and had apparently taken the rest of his body with it. His numb, aching limbs refused to cooperate, and he felt himself stop moving. He opened his mouth to scream, but not even that worked. All that came out was a sluggish unintelligible groan.

"Guuuuwwuuuuhhhhrrrrr..."

Vanessa's grin split her face nearly ear to ear in a blood-red gash of lush lips and peekaboo fangs. "It vas a vampire you vanted, succulent man-meal..." she drawled. "And a vampire you shall have. Now let me show you vhy they call us 'bloodsuckers'..."

Vanessa gathered herself to leap, legs bent like a pair of coiled steel springs, breath hissing softly from the back of her throat, claws grasping reflexively. Her jaws gaped wide... then wider... then impossibly, inhumanely wide, making a soft, sick *pop* as they unhinged, pulling the clean, white porcelain of her face into monstrous lines, bulging her blood-pooled eyes and thrusting her fangs into a shark-like grimace. It seemed to Carson, from his excellent vantage point, helpless on the floor at her feet, like he could see all the way down into the dark, inky, irrevocably lost depths of her soul. He watched with sick fascination, as part of his temporarily unhinged brain reached the conclusion that it would be nice to have one more corn dog before he died.

And then a strange thing happened.

The savage hissing in Vanessa's throat faltered, faded and died. The feverish red glow in her eyes dimmed, flickered, then went out, as if the hellfires that cast it had suddenly been doused by a bucket of ice water. Her body seemed to soften, draining of tension and color, becoming even more ashen and pale than before. Carson stared, watching with wonder and detached interest but still unable to move or think. Then, just below the plunging v-neck of her top, slightly to the left of the milky crease of ample cleavage, his dumb gaze detected a slight bulge in the tough leather, an insistent presence that pressured the suit from within, like a child trying to force its arm through a shirtsleeve but missing the hole. Carson's eyes fixed on it, mesmerized, watching as it stubbornly worked against the stiff leather.

Something was inside her, trying to get out.

Then a face, grizzled, lined and badly in need of a wash and a shave, leaned around hers from behind. "And let *me* show *you* why they call these 'stakes'!"

It was Stinky Pete.

"Sorry, sister... nobody here wants what you're sellin'!" He twisted his wrist sharply and the tip of what was now properly identified as a wooden stake gave a wiggle under the tough leather covering her breast. Vanessa's body writhed and a faint, almost inaudible groan forced itself from her throat.

"How d'ya like *that,* eh?" The old hobo cackled, his red bandanna bobbing with the up-and-down motion of his Adam's Apple. "Howzat taste?! Y'know what that is, dontcha, ya dirty l'il minx... that there's good ol' fashioned *American pine*, sharped up and stuck where it counts. But then you *know* that by now, I reckon! No? Lemme jog yer thinkin'..." Pete twisted the stake again, grinning at the moan it elicited. "Yeh, thet's right... I'll show ya how we dealt with yer kind in the bush..." His rheumy eyes, now lit with a fierce self-satisfaction, lifted to focus - although with some difficulty - on Carson. "Sorry, soldier. Had to wait 'til her guard was down to make muh move. Heh heh... knew she'd start yakkin'. Durn bloodsuckers *love* to yak it up. 'I'm so bad, I'm so evil, I'm gonna tear *this* out, I'm gonna tear *that* out, I'm gonna bite off yer...'"

But that was as far as he got. A hand of porcelain steel shot up to seize his throat, cutting off his words in mid-gloat. Carson caught the faintest flicker of red light in the depths of Vanessa's eyes, previously unnoticed in the wake of Pete's dramatic arrival but definitely there. And definitely furious. Her movement was stiff and forced, but it was *movement,* and that in itself was not a good sign. Especially for Pete.

Vanessa's other hand darted back and clamped over the gnarled fist that gripped the stake. Pete staggered, gasping for air, eyes bulging and body struggling feebly against the fearsome strength of the vampiress. With a sudden yank and a horrible, wet, sloppy rasp, Vanessa jerked the stake free.

There followed a fierce blur of movement, and an instant later Vanessa clutched Pete from behind, one arm pinned painfully behind him, bent almost to breaking, her other hooked around his neck.

"Hunh," he gasped, and his face wore a bemused look under its rapidly purpling hue. "Guess I missed..."

"Vell, vell, my scrumptious blood sausage... it seems I vas wrong. There *is* someone else left to kill..." In her eyes, there was nothing but the cold, dead, angry rage of death. The ghost of a smile twitched at the corners of her ruby lips.

Then she struck, her fangs punching straight through the soiled red bandanna and burying themselves deep in the leathery old neck. A shower of blood sprayed the room and Pete's body jerked in stiff, awkward spasms as Vanessa set to work.

Carson felt like he had been pierced as well.

"*NOOOOOOO!*" His ragged cry echoed through the room, but his body, still numb and broken, refused to function. He could only watch as Vanessa drank her fill, her back arching with the fury and passion of her efforts, sucking at the wound with all the wild abandon and animal instinct of a baby tigress at the teat.

It took less than a minute.

Vanessa let the ashen body drop with a sick thud. She stepped back, swayed a little, eyes close in ecstasy, tongue tracing a line of sticky red that had strayed across her cheek.

When she opened her eyes a moment later, they were bright and hot, full once more of devilish malice and inhuman hunger.

They lit on Carson.

"Not bad... considering." Her voice was thick and slurred with the intoxicating effects of her meal. "Now, beautiful, delicious, virile, nutritive rich boy... I shall see vat *you* taste like..." She took an unsteady step forward, wavering a bit, though from her injuries or the feeding Carson couldn't tell. Whatever the case, he knew, it wasn't enough to stop her.

Nothing was.

"*Stop!*" A shrill shout tore through the tension and jerked the eyes of both hunter and hunted. Kiki, pale and shaking, had appeared at the edge of the mist. She looked every bit as unsteady as the vampiress, but her blue eyes were lit with a similar intensity. In her hand, she held something, but from his position, sprawled and helpless on the cold tile, Carson couldn't see what it was.

"Vell..." Vanessa slurred. "This night is full of surprises. Or should I say *delights*?"

"Say whatever you want - just leave him alone!"

Vanessa shifted into stalking mode, dropping again into her dangerous half crouch and starting to circle the new development. Kiki angled her body to match, keeping the vampiress in front of her. As they closed, Kiki seemed to remember the item she held in her hand. With a quick jerk she thrust it out before her, clutching it desperately like a loaded gun.

Only it wasn't a gun.

It was a bag of chips.

Carson's heart sank, and once again, he wanted very much to throw up. Vanessa, however, merely laughed in her cold, wicked way. "I admit I do not eat a balanced diet... but even such delicacies as this could hardly dissuade me from supping on the precious life flow inside of you, succulent juiceful girl." She gave a flick of her hair and a disdainful sniff. Kiki was visibly shaking, face tight with fear and lips pale and quivering. But she held her ground.

Vanessa took another gliding step forward, dropped a fraction lower. Carson could see the muscles in her legs and back bunching, straining against her tight black leather like coiled snakes. He knew the signs by now. She was ready to spring.

"Kiki..." he croaked. "Watch her...!"

"So, as kind as you are to offer, I am afraid I must decline, for I fear I vould find your tribute not to my liking." Vanessa's commentary ended abruptly and her jaw stretched, gory fangs exposed and strike imminent.

"Actually, I'm counting on that."

Kiki stepped directly to Vanessa and slammed her hands together on the bag, exploding its contents directly into her face. A handful of chips went straight into her gaping mouth and down the windpipe, the rest painting her face with greasy crumbs. Vanessa stood in shock for a split second, stunned. Then her eyes flew wide and she burst into sudden spasms and wracking, choking gasps. Kiki stood stock still, breathing hard and clutching at the empty bag like it was the last life preserver on the Titanic. Carson could now see the label clearly:

Uncle Arthur's Frontier-Style Potato Chips

And in smaller print beneath that:

NEW! Garlic Flavor!

Vanessa staggered about, clawing at her throat and smashing over shelves. A river of reddish tears streamed over her once pristine features, which had erupted into a swollen mass of angry red blotches. She hissed and spit with pain and rage, more animal than ever, her body wracked by frightening, ragged, wheezing coughs.

Above the hideous noise Kiki called out, her voice pitched high and trembling but full of grim intent. "Now *get out*! I don't know what rock you're hiding under, but you'd better get back to it... quick! Or you'll add a pretty nasty little sunburn to your list of hurts, and I'm guessing that'll be worse!" Kiki gestured toward the front of the store with a jerk of her head, where a warm, orange glow lit the mist-shrouded glass. Vanessa whipped into a crouch, hissing and wiping savagely at her blood-smeared eyes, her face a mask of rage. The quick motion was too much for her and she tilted sideways and crashed into a rack of candy.

"Very vell..." she wheezed, and through the horrifying mess of her face Carson detected the faint gleam of a hungry smile returning, although she was staring off in the opposite direction. "But our game is not yet finished!" She shrilled at no one in particular, waving threateningly at the nacho cheese tub. "You have novhere to run and novhere to hide. I vill return to you this evening, my darling fleshy blood kebobs, and you shall know vhat it is to stoke my wrath. And *you* my dear..." Vanessa jabbed a blood-red nail at the soda dispenser. "Shall be last!"

With a parting hiss she turned on her heel and leapt for the door, the mist sweeping after her in a rush and collecting about her body like a great billowing gray cloak, shielding her from view and jerking the interior of the mini-mart back into view as if a curtain had suddenly been snatched away. Missing the door by a wide mark she instead flew headfirst through the side window, taking a nasty fall and cutting short a final sinister laugh of wild abandon. To the accompaniment of tinkling glass and a fit of violent hacking coughs, she disappeared into the night.

Kiki collapsed in a heap right were she stood, shuddering and shaking and gasping for breath. It took Carson a moment longer to realize he was still alive, and not about to be permanently destroyed. And when he did, his mind focused on a single thought: Pete. A crushing sense of helplessness and loss washed over him and he was crawling madly forward, catching up Stinky Pete's limp and broken form in his arms. Remarkably, the rheumy old eyes flickered open, gazing up into Carson's twisted, grief-stricken face. Pete drew a shuddering, gurgling breath.

"He's alive!" Carson shouted hoarsely. "He's still alive... call...!!" The cry faded as he gently peeled back a corner of the blood-soaked bandanna, exposing the ghastly wound beneath. It didn't take a 911 call to know that the old hobo was dying.

Pete read the look on his face. He twisted his pale, blood-spattered lips into a faint smile. "Boy... sure could use a Freezie 'bout now. Don' worry, I'm good fer it... found a buck on the sidewalk this mornin'..." He gave a weak laugh, which faded into a wet cough.

"Don't talk, Pete. Just lie still... look, we'll call an ambulance... 911... we'll... we'll..."

Pete shook his head, the gesture feeble and barely discernible. His eyes fluttered closed. When he spoke, his voice was soft, faint, almost peaceful. "Naw... don' bother. I'm a goner, that's fer certain sure. She got me. Got me good. Ain't as quick as I useta be..." His eyes flickered open again and he stared at Carson, reading the pain and guilt. "Ahhh... don' sweat it kid... it weren't yer fault. Ya did good. An' this ain't over yet... jes remember what I taught ya... the eye don't lie. Ol' Pete told ya that, didn't he?" He paused, another wet cough shaking his body, but weaker this time. "Remember that, boy," he managed when the spasm had passed. "An' I'm sorry I let ya down. Told ya it was bad hoodoo, didn' I? Jes promise me one thing, kid... promise me you'll give her the stick fer me, alrighty? Lotta good folk gonna depend on you now soljer. Promise Ol' Pete that you'll see this through... promise me, now..." The rheumy old eyes locked with Carson's.

"I promise." Carson's voice was thick with emotion, but his answer came fast. Underneath, there was a hint of iron.

Pete smiled again, although it was just a ghost by this time. His eyes slid closed. Weakly he patted Carson's arm, gnarled fingers poking through fingerless gloves like the curled talons of an aged buzzard, clutching, then relaxing, then clutching as his breathing faltered. Carson could hear someone crying softly nearby. Kiki.

The old hobo coughed once more, and his grip relaxed. He gave a deep sigh, shuddered, and lay still.

He was gone.

Carson bowed his head and wept.

A short time later the sound of heavy, uncertain footsteps announced the arrival of Officer Jackson, who staggered into view wielding an empty magazine rack and looking like he meant to use it. He was clearly dazed and still bleeding freely from several deep gashes in his head. "Wha'd I miss?! Where is the *&%$!? She gone?!" Bleary eyes swept the scene, took in the limp, lifeless figure of Stinky Pete, still cradled in Carson's arms. Kiki had crawled over to join him and sat with a hand on his shoulder, head bowed. "Oh..."

The rack fell with a clatter and the guard followed it, slumping heavily to the floor in a heap beside the rest of the human wreckage.

They stayed that way for a long time, the three of them, silent and still in the midst of the destruction. Emotions washed over them in overwhelming waves, and they let them, too weak and sick and hurt and tired to do anything else.

It was Officer Jackson who finally broke the silence. His voice was distant and rummy, and his eyes had a glassy look, blinking through dried blood and matted dreadlocks. "I'm guessin'... we lost."

Carson lifted his head, sniffed and wiped his eyes with the back of his hand. "Worse. We got powned."

Beside him Kiki shifted, staring about helplessly at the carnage. "Carson..." Her words were almost too soft to hear. "What are we going to do?"

Carson looked down at the still, gray mask of Pete's face. He sniffed again. "Whatever it is, we're gonna need help. Pete's dead, he's the only one who had a clue. Vanessa is coming back tonight..." Officer Jackson swore, indicating he was at least alert enough to figure out what that implied. "You can bet on it. And this time it won't be to play games. So what are we gonna do?" He paused. "I don't have the *faintest* idea."

Officer Jackson swore again, louder and with more feeling. "I *hate* accents," he mumbled. "*Hate* 'em. Never again. Not as long as I live. Not *ever*... I don't care if she's got..." His rambling commentary faded into more swearing and grumbling, then stopped entirely.

Silence again enveloped them.

But only for a moment.

Carson's face suddenly lifted. There was purpose in it - grim and desperate, but purpose nonetheless. Gently, he lowered the body of his friend to the cold tile floor. Pete was at rest now; there was nothing else to be done. It was time to face the future, as grim as it may be. With some effort, Carson stood up and picked his way across the wreckage toward the phone, limping and wincing but determined.

"Carson... what is it? Where are you going." Kiki stared after him through puffy eyes.

"I know what to do. I know who to call."

"Who?"

Carson stopped and looked back, the phone in his hand and conviction in his voice. "My grandma."

Chapter Six

Bringing in the Nuns

"Garlic chips... that was just plain *awesome.*"

Carson peered out through the window blinds of the 24/7, squinting against the afternoon sun. Beside him, the doors were locked tight, a hastily scrawled "Closed" sign barring the way from outside. Constructed from the torn cardboard of a burrito box, the sign looked shabby and makeshift, but sparkled in comparison to the store and its occupants. They had cleared some debris and washed the blood from their faces, but in general everything and everyone inside the place gave the impression that they had recently been involved with a tornado.

Kiki smiled wanly. "Thanks. It was just dumb luck, really. I remembered seeing them on the shelf earlier and thinking how good they looked. Funny. When Vanessa dropped me, I landed right beside them. I didn't even know if it would work."

"Luck nothing - it was quick thinking, and it saved our lives. That and your little 'sunrise' trick. Man... using the heat lamp from the wiener warmer to make her think the sun was coming up... *that's* thinking outside the box, woman. Ol' Vanessa was probably halfway back to the coffin before she realized it was still the middle of the night."

Kiki's weak smile blossomed into a self-indulgent smirk. "Yeah. That's the part I *really* like. She might be a supernatural steamroller, but she can be just as dumb and gullible as the rest of us. Arrogant witch."

Carson grunted his agreement, fingering a fresh scar in the business end of his bat. It hadn't left his side since the altercation. "I hear you there. Next to giving her a smack on the noodle, my favorite part was watching her squirm after she huffed that garlic. It's good to know that, if your gonna be stalked by a bloodsucking temptress of the night, at least she's got a weakness. Man, did you see her face? I bet they don't make a cream for *that*." Carson grinned wickedly, but there was little pleasure in it.

"Yeah. I just..." her voice trailed off to silence. There followed a very large, very empty, very significant pause.

Carson glanced back from his vigil. "What's eating you?"

"Besides your choice of words?"

"Oh... er... sorry..."

"Don't sweat it. As for what's wrong, nothing. Or maybe... well, it's just that... I just wish I would have thought of it earlier. I wish I would have done *something*... anything. I was just so... I mean... I was just Jell-o, Carson... I couldn't..." she clenched her fists and frowned, her pretty face tight. "If I hadn't frozen, then maybe Pete..."

"Hey..." Carson scolded gently. "You stop that, girl. I think 'I just found out that vampires are real' falls under the list of acceptable excuses for freezing."

"Yeah. Maybe."

"You can't blame yourself for what happened to Pete. You didn't kill him." Carson turned back to his vigil, an ugly scowl scudding across his features. "She did."

There was another very large, very empty, very significant pause.

Kiki rose and started to pace. "So have you wondered what kept her from doing the same to us? Why didn't she come back to finish us off? After she figured out the sun wasn't really coming up, she still had plenty of time before dawn."

Carson shrugged. "Dunno. Maybe good ol' Uncle Arthur's chips were too much for her. Maybe she got too far before she realized she'd been punk'd. Or maybe she just wants us to squirm."

"If that's the case, it's working." Kiki stopped her nervous pacing,

 88

drawing up behind him and staring over his shoulder out the window. "Any sign of your friend?"

"Nope, nothing yet. But don't worry, she'll show. Granny said she'd call her just as soon as we hung up the phone."

"I hope she hurries. We're burning daylight." Kiki chewed her lower lip, watched the empty street for a few moments, then returned to her pacing. "What's her name again?"

"Bischoff. Becky Bischoff."

"That would be *Sister* Becky Bischoff, wouldn't it? She's what... a nun, right?"

Carson nodded, not taking his eyes off the parking lot. "Yup. According to Granny, she's the real deal, too. Card-carrying, habit-forming member of the local nun house."

"What... *exactly* did you tell your Granny about... about last night?"

"Not much. Just that I had some spiritual issues going on and needed some advice. ASAP."

"Well, there's a loose interpretation of current events. That's all it took, eh? She popped right up with this Sister Becky character?"

"Uh-huh. Said she'd call her and ask her to stop by. Apparently they go way back. Granny's known her for years, by the sound of it."

"From where?"

"Beats me. Granny's not Catholic - darn churchy, if you remember, just not that way. Said Becky's a good gal, though, and seemed real confident... though she did say she's a little... eccentric."

Kiki nodded. "Good. She'll need to be more than a *little* eccentric. Once she hears what we've got to say, she'll probably bolt for the door.... and I might join her. By the way, what *have* we got to say?"

"Heck if I know. This is all a little new to me." He tugged his beard, pondering. "Been thinking about it though. I figure I'll sound her out a little first... you know, get an idea of where she's coming from, sniff around about the supernatural stuff, find out if she's open to it. If things feel okay, I might hint around at what we've seen... careful like, of course, subtle. Then after that, just sort of... see what develops."

Kiki pursed her lips, cool blue eyes trying to read her friend's enigmatic expression. "Subtle or not... are you sure this a good idea?"

"Nope. Not at all. But what do we have to lose? What I know about vampires I learned from the movies, and if movies screwed up bloodsuckers as bad as *Pirates of the Carribean* did pirates, then we're in a world of hurt. I mean, I'm in the dark here, I'm grasping at straws.

The garlic worked, so that much of the lore is true - maybe the God thing is too, who knows? Anyway, the way I figure it, we're either suffering from collective insanity or we're about to get ganked by a she-vampire. Whichever way you slice it, it can't hurt to have some back up from Upstairs."

"Still don't see why we need her," Officer Jackson rumbled from across the room. "Waste of time, if you ask me." He was stationed at the front counter, the disassembled pieces of his sidearm spread out on a towel before him and undergoing a rigorous cleaning. He had pried his beefy automatic from the nacho cheese tub with the aid of a borrowed crowbar and a great deal of cursing. The weapon proved still serviceable but was in dire need of maintenance, a task which the guard had set to immediately. Jackson withdrew the cleaning rod from its barrel, yanked a cheese-smeared patch from the tip and reached for a fresh one. His progress was somewhat hampered by splinted fingers and an array of other hasty bandages, but he worked without complaint.

Carson shot him a pointed look. "Officer Jackson... did you fight a vampire last night?"

"Yeah, but..."

"Then we need her. We've gotta assume that guns aren't enough. We've been through this."

Jackson kept his eyes on his work, his expression surly and uninviting. He mumbled something unintelligible under his breath, which, although Carson was certain was neither flattering nor appropriate in mixed company, was still input and he considered that progress. The guard had not said more than a dozen words since the events of last night, and all of these had been the four letter variety. While the three of them had cleaned up, tended their wounds and rested, he had remained dangerously quiet, avoiding all attempts at conversation. He had accepted the offer to stay at the mini-mart until they could devise a plan, but that was about his only concession. Carson had hoped that a little time and space would help. It hadn't. He and Kiki had been walking on eggshells all day.

Perhaps, he realized grudgingly, it was time to try and lighten things up a little. After all, Officer Jackson had taken the brunt of Vanessa's fury last night, and he could imagine that being a considerable sting for an obviously self-styled tough guy. Maybe the pounding had softened up his attitude a bit - common enemies had a way of doing that. Carson didn't like the man, that much was certain, but like him or not they were all in this together. That and the fact that, if they were to live through the next day, anyone with a gun had to count for something.

"But then again, what do I know? Guns... guns are good. Guns can't hurt, that's for sure. I mean, they *can...* hurt, that is... which is why sometimes they're real handy. Like now. I can see how handy guns can be, for sure. And you're..." It pained him to say it, but he clamped down on his ill will and forced the words out. "You're a good guy to have in a fight."

Officer Jackson said nothing. The cleaning rod went in. The cleaning rod came out.

"And..." Carson cleared his throat awkwardly, not sure how to continue but knowing the olive branch needed to be extended further. "I just want to say that... I... uh... I don't know what we would've done without you. I mean, last night. It sucked alright, we got kicked right in the face... but it would've sucked even more if it hadn't been for the good ol' Gold Shield. For you."

Kiki suddenly caught on. "Yeah... I hear that. I don't know what they're paying you, but you earned your check last night, that's for sure. You took a heckuva beating - I've never seen anything like it. By the way, how are those bandages?" She strolled his way, eying the finger splint and the several yards of white gauze that bound up his various injuries.

"Okay," Jackson mumbled. He yanked another soiled swatch out of his cleaning rod, reached for another one, then paused. He shot Kiki a sidelong glance, hesitating as he weighed his words. He seemed to be considering the olive branch. "Thanks," he managed finally. "For patchin' me up. These field dressings... they ain't bad."

"My pleasure. It's amazing what you can pick up in a CPR/First Aid class. You may not play the piano again, but I think you'll make it. What do you think?" She tried a smile.

The guard dropped his cleaning rod on the counter and stretched treelike arms. For a moment, she didn't think he would answer. Then he shrugged. "I'll live. Just sore mostly." He massaged a spot on his shoulder, wincing slightly, then took up his pistol again. Kiki was about to turn away when he suddenly added, "You wanna know what hurts most? The fact that I got beat up by a girl." Jackson's dreadlocks, still matted with a residue of dried blood and plaster, tossed as he shook his head. "I'm still smartin' from that one. Only thing gonna take the sting outta that is a little payback." He thumbed the release, and the heavy slide of the automatic smacked home like a chrome-plated exclamation point.

Then Officer Jackson looked Carson directly in the face. "Thanks."

"Er... for what?"

"For savin' my life."

The words obviously brought the guard great pain, but he got them out. Carson thought back to the blurry, painful, chaotic events of last night, struggling to put them in an order that matched up with Officer Jackson's gratitude.

"Oh... er... you mean the..." he pantomimed a swing of the bat. "Yeah, well, no prob, dude. Glad I could help. You know, right place, right time, right piece of sporting equipment." He patted the Louisville Slugger affectionately.

Officer Jackson grunted again, but this time there seemed to be, if Carson wasn't imagining it, the faintest of smiles behind it. "Yeah... base hit, right? I'll give you that... or maybe even a double bagger. Not out of the park, that's for sure... but a real pinch hit. Not bad for a civilian."

"Frankly, I'm surprised I'm still alive."

"Me too." This time, there *was* a smile. "I was on my keister for most of it, but it looks like you took a few good shots."

"Yeah. I hurt. A lot." Carson gingerly probed the black and yellow landscape of his body. Jackson's grin stretched.

"You will, man. You will. That's the first rule of scrappin' - you get it through your skull beforehand that it's gonna hurt. Period. Then when it happens, you can keep your head in the game. Get on with business."

"That's either the voice of experience or a line from a Chuck Norris movie." Carson regretted his jibe as soon as he said it. "You sound like you know your way around a brawl," he added quickly.

If Jackson took offense, he gave no indication. "Been in a few scrapes. Don't let this fool ya." He patted his ample belly. "I did a turn or two in the trenches. U.S. Army. Got my schoolin' there, as far as hard knocks go. Folks'll tell ya it ain't what it used to be, but it'll still kick the weak outta ya, that's for sure."

"Dude, I'm sold on that. You're the poster boy for 'Go ahead - I can take it'." Jackson made a non-committal grunt, then fell silent. The silence stretched and Carson cast about for a new topic, wanting to capitalize on his inroads through the hostile territory of Jackson's demeanor. "So... Army, eh?"

"Yeah. Infantry."

"How far did you get?"

"Not far enough. Had a little... problem. My sweet tooth... somethin' about stress, comfort foods, some BS like that..." Jackson's voice dropped out. Carson sensed that a mood swing was imminent and quickly bailed on the topic. He had made enough progress for one day, he figured - the way his luck had been going, it didn't do to press it.

"Well, you won't find any temptations here for awhile." He waved about to indicate the wreckage. "I don't think I could find ten adjacent calories in this mess. What a train wreck, eh? I hate to think what Jack's gonna say."

Kiki pursed her lips, nudging a sad, flattened loaf of bread with her foot. "Jinkees. Jack. What are you going to tell him?"

"I have *no* idea." Carson shrugged helplessly. "Vandals, maybe, gang fight... something, I dunno. Frankly I'm a little too preoccupied with this whole notion of impending death to worry about it."

"Fair enough. Next question: how long do you think you can keep the store closed without someone catching on?"

"We made it a day so far. Worst case, I figure we can keep it up until tonight - after that it won't matter, one way or another. I hate to say it, but Vanessa was right. There's no one left. I mean, who's gonna pop into the ol' 24/7 now? All my customers are either victims or scared they will be." He shook his head dejectedly. "Can't say I blame them. It's almost like... hey, wait a sec... she's here!" Carson let the blinds go with a snap and hurried to the door.

Kiki stopped him, her hand catching his on the deadbolt. "Are you *sure* this is a good idea?"

"Look... if you can't trust the people your granny sends you, what people *can* you trust?"

"If you're expecting me to say 'nun', I won't do it."

Carson grinned. "That's my girl."

There was a firm rapping on the glass of the front door, just behind the makeshift "CLOSED" sign.

Carson glanced at it, then back at Kiki. "We're in this together. We can still call it off, if you've got butterflies."

Kiki sighed. She looked back at the destruction, then up at Carson. Their eyes met. "Oh, I've got butterflies, lots of them - but the biggest ones aren't from Sister Becky What's-Her-Name. And quite frankly, unless she turns out to be an axe-wielding homicidal maniac with a soft

spot for chopping up blonds, I don't see how things can get any worse."
Kiki shrugged and shivered at the same time – it was an odd sight but
somehow summed up the moment. "What the hey. Let's do it."

A moment later Carson opened the door.

He wasn't sure what he had been expecting, but the figure that
stood before him on the threshold of the mini-mart was, simply put, a
nun. But not just any nun - Sister Becky Bischoff was *the* nun. She
looked, in fact, as if she had been dropped off by the official nun
delivery service, hand selected for her nun-like appearance and
mannerisms. She was swathed entirely in tradition and black fabric,
from the hood of her habit to the soles of her stiff, flat shoes. A
seamed, care lined face beamed radiantly from the depths of the
garment as assurance that there was indeed a human soul somewhere
under it all.

She was short, although not stout as Carson had pictured her, but
slender and whiplike - at least that was the case if her narrow face were
any indication, since there wasn't an inch of skin otherwise visible
under the yards of fabric. That face gave other indications about the
woman too, as it was a veritable study in pious serenity, compassion
and sensibility. He wondered fleetingly at her age, which seemed at
first glance obvious, but after a little inspection, difficult to guess.
There was wisdom in her warm emerald eyes, a wisdom that indicated
long years of experience, contemplation and even suffering - but there
was also a dance of light and a youthful flicker that hinted at something
more. He couldn't be sure, but he'd be surprised if she were a day under
60. Or maybe 70. Or even 50. It was hard to say. But whatever her
age, and wherever things went from here, Carson was immediately
convinced that Granny had not let him down. He'd never seen a nun
before - a *real* nun - up close and personal. But now that he needed
one, he was satisfied that this one would do the trick.

"Good day, young man," the black hood inclined politely. "Am I
to assume that you are Mr. Carson Dudley?" Carson noted that her
voice had more than a hint of Irish brogue, warm and rich like a cup of
spiced cider on a cold winter day. He liked it instantly.

"Yes, ma'am."

"How nice. Such a polite young man, a rare commodity in this day
and age. Well then, Mr. Dudley, it is my distinct pleasure to make your
acquaintance." She extended her hand, which Carson took gently,
expecting a limp and bony fish. Instead, he winced. The nun had a
grip. "Your grandmother speaks well of you," she smiled serenely,

eyes flicking over his face, his clothes, his posture, taking the full measure of him at a glance. Carson felt himself straighten instinctively, as if he had arrived for his first day at a Catholic boarding school. The thought made him smile, and he relaxed.

"May I enter?" Sister Becky inquired politely.

"Yeah! Er... yes. Please. Come on in."

Carson ushered her into the mini-mart and made introductions. Pressed, proper, straitlaced and charming, Sister Becky shook hands all around and made small talk easily, about Carson's grandmother, the weather and her trip to the mini-mart, which had been by foot ("I can't see paying good money for a taxi car, what with the day so fine and the sky so fair - a brisk walk can put a spring in one's step, don't you agree?"). In conversation, she was softspoken, gentle and genteel, her manners formal and old-fashioned without being stiff. She had the unusual practice, for instance, of referring to them all by their surnames. This Carson found eccentric, but somehow comforting, as if he were being afforded a certain measure of respect that he wasn't sure how he had earned but that he found he quite appreciated. Somehow, it made him feel stronger and more confident.

After a few moments he became aware of something else, something profoundly important - for the first time in weeks, he was calm. *Calm.* Carson hadn't realized until now just how keyed up he had been. In fact - between the business slump, Mr. Carey's murder, tensions with Officer Jackson and last night's introduction to the world of vampirically endowed sociopathic Goth queens - he found it difficult to remember when the last time was that he had felt any semblance of peace. But he felt it now, and it *definitely* had something to do with this frail-looking Irishwoman who stood before him discussing the unfortunate state of public transportation in Las Calamas. There was more to her, he decided then and there, than met the eye. Much more. He wasn't sure whether he was just seizing hold of any random comfort in the storm of peril and terror in which he found himself, but he began to sense a certain undefinable strength about her, a sort of *power* lurking just beneath the surface. In a funny way, it made her seem stronger and more imposing than even Officer Jackson. Carson wasn't sure what to make of it, but it made him feel safe. It also gave him the faintest tickle of something he hadn't expected to feel ever again - hope.

A few moments later, almost as if she could sense his thoughts, Sister Becky fell silent. The others followed suit and the conversation trailed off and died. The nun turned her attention to the store, quietly surveying the ill-concealed wreckage, her sharp emerald eyes roving about the overturned shelves and decimated product. Carson could see wheels turning.

"This is a lovely chat, Mr. Dudley, and I could go about it all afternoon. But come come..." Her tone changed, indicated that the turning of those wheels had led her someplace interesting and caused her to shift gears. It was still pleasant, but had the clip of business. "As the saying goes, 'If a goat chews grass and not thistles, then a field will never flourish.' Perhaps, lad, you should tell me why you have summoned me here?"

Carson's stomach gave a squish as the reality of the previous night jarred its way back into his mind like a bus through a brick wall. He glanced nervously about, but was unable to avoid Sister Becky's cool, steady gaze.

"Uh... we've... uh... got a problem," he offered lamely, unsure of exactly how to proceed. He was suddenly more conscious than ever of the strength of her presence, and the voluminous black habit now made her seem more imposing than comforting. He squirmed, feeling not only her eyes but those of his friends on him as well.

"I can see that, young man. But this is not a maid's costume, is it? You certainly did not call me to tidy up." Her eyes, as gentle and green as the rolling hills of Ireland, danced with sparkles of good humor and her pious, angelic smile melted his anxiety. She reached out and patted his hand comfortingly. "If your problem were merely this unsightliness, you would have called on a chambermaid or a fix-it man. You did not. Instead, you called on me. There is a reason for that; I am quite certain. Why not just come out with it; that's a good lad."

Carson hesitated.

"We fought a monster."

Behind him, he heard Kiki gasp. Officer Jackson swore softly.

Sister Becky didn't bat an eye.

"Werewolves, demons, zombies... what are you up against?"

There was a pause.

"Vampires, I think... but I can't be sure. We've only had one brush so far, but all the signs seem to point in that direction."

Sister Becky leaned across the mini-mart counter, peering at the clerk through the shadows of her overhanging hood. "Signs, you say? Like what?"

Carson blinked, feeling disoriented and like he might need to sit. A wave of déjà vu washed over him and he struggled to put the train of his thoughts back on track. "The usual... uh... I think. Fangs, fog, blood drinking, turning into a big dog... uh... hey... are you... what just happened here?"

"I am sorry, Mr. Dudley, but I don't take your meaning."

"Did I just tell you we fought a vampire? And are you still *standing* here?! Aren't you gonna freak out, run away, or give me the 'There's a friend of mine I think you should talk to, here's his card' line?"

"Mr. Dudley, I am a servant of the Lord. Who should be more willing to accept the presence of Ultimate Evil than those who serve Ultimate Good?"

Carson blinked again. The room was still spinning. "You... you don't... you don't think I... we... you don't think we're... crazy?"

"On the contrary." Sister Becky flicked her emerald spotlights across the assembled faces, probing, measuring, weighing. "I find it quite refreshing to meet young persons who recognize the truth when they see it. This can be a difficult thing, young man, believing your eyes. The Devil's minions take many forms - that is their nature, and, I must say, one of their most effective tactics. If they make you doubt what your senses tell you, then you have no idea you are in harm's way until it is entirely too late to do anything about it. By the time you realize what's *really* happening you are most likely dead, or at the very least, doomed which is often just as bad a thing."

"But you... you..."

Sister Becky dismissed his doubts with another pat on the hand and another angelic smile. "My dear lad, your testimony is not the only evidence that something of dark intent has been roosting in our fair city. I have felt a sense of growing evil of late, an ill presence if you will. It is difficult to ignore - at least for those who are trained to notice such things. I am not at all astonished to hear that this lurking menace has at last taken shape. As the saying goes, 'One does not need to *see* the fox to know that it is in the coop.'"

"I just... durr..."

"Tut tut, dear boy, things will proceed much more efficiently if you dispense with all the stammering. Now then, let us have the truth. The full story, all of it, every detail. Leave nothing out." Sister Becky folded her hands in the cavernous sleeves of her habit and settled in to listen.

Carson needed no more prompting. The fact that he had even said the word "vampire" out loud to this stick of a nun and she hadn't immediately called the loony bin or taken after him with a ruler was argument enough. A moment later, he had found his voice and launched into an animated recap of the past week. For the most part, Sister Becky listened carefully, saying nothing but making appropriate listening noises and occasionally nodding her head in understanding. The only time she spoke was to curb a slightly overzealous Officer Jackson, who had become engrossed in the retelling in spite of himself and interjected enthusiastically at the point of Vanessa's initial transformation.

"Yeah!" he blurted out. "That's when the &*$#! went all *Lost Boys* on us... gave me this!" He indicated a particularly painful looking gash on his head.

Sister Becky's eyes shot to the big man and a polite smile blossomed on her thin lips. "Mr. Jackson... I am quite unaccustomed to such language and, although I hate to impose, I do find it offensive. If you would be so kind as to refrain from vulgarity, I would consider it a great kindness."

"Huh? Oh... uh... yeah... sure..." Jackson mumbled, looking like the world's biggest fifth grader who had just been put on the wall by the playground teacher.

Carson took up the tale again and finished with Vanessa's retreat. "Then she promised to come back tonight and, 'let us know what it was like to stoke her wrath,' which I'm assuming means kill us. There's a cultural thing there with the accent and all, so sometimes I missed her exact meaning - but I'm pretty sure that was the gist of it."

Sister Becky tilted her head, eyes pointed absently at the ceiling as behind them her mind, just as sharp and clear, sifted and sorted, carefully processing the details of all she had heard. "Tragic loss of life. I grieve for your friend, my children. His was a noble sacrifice, and it shall not go unheeded, I promise you. To lay down one's life for a friend... there is no greater act of courage or selflessness. May our Father in Heaven grant him the rest he has so dearly purchased." She crossed herself and her eyes flickered closed for a moment, then snapped open. "Now then, on to the matter at hand..." With a fluidity and suddenness that was breathtaking, the nun's entire manner changed, taking on a brusque, businesslike demeanor that was as crisp as the folds of her garment. "The first order of business is to establish as closely as possible the identity of the creature. Only by knowing its true nature can we be best equipped to combat it."

 98

Carson nodded quickly, eager to proceed. Part of his brain was still whirling, but he ignored it and pressed ahead. "Great! Er... how do we do that?"

"There are many shapes and forms that such creatures take, in order to confuse and distract those who hunt them. Although a vampire would be the most logical choice, we must also consider werewolf, based on your recollection of this monster's lupine transfiguration. In that case, a werewolf's *victims* offer the best evidence, since their wounds are often infected and transform them into lycanthropes themselves." Sister Becky's gaze flicked briefly at Officer Jackson.

Jackson blinked. Then realization dawned and his big features darkened. "What the...?! You think I'm a *werewolf*?!"

The nun flashed him a sweet smile that reminded Carson instantly of Granny. "No, Mr. Jackson. Of course not."

"Yeah, well... that's good..."

"When I shook your hand earlier, I brushed you with wolfsbane. If you were a werewolf, you would be screaming like the miller who met his saw, if you take my meaning."

Officer Jackson bristled. "You... you brushed my...? Why me?"

"Perhaps you should ask yourself that question, Mr. Jackson."

"What?! You sayin'...?!" At a loss for more conventional words, he cut loose with a seasoned oath.

Sister Becky's genial smile melted, the corners of her mouth tucking down into a slight frown. "Mr. Jackson... as I asked you once before, please kindly refrain from using profanity in my presence. I find it distasteful." This second rebuke was a little sharper than the first. "I tested you because you were obviously injured, and being injured by such a creature is how you become one. And, if I may be frank, you are also somewhat surly, which is a common trait amongst the werewolf-afflicted. There is no need to take offense; testing for lycanthropes is something I do to a great many of the people I meet - and if I must say, not a bad habit to be in." She did not wait for further reaction but pressed on, clipping into her next point with the precision, efficiency and subtlety of an antique typewriter.

"At any rate, that disproves the possibility of werewolves. Having ruled them out, I believe, based on the rest of your testimony and the clues provided, Mr. Dudley, that we can safely assume this beast is, indeed, vampiric in nature. Yes, a vampire. Quite definitely." She gave a firm nod in support of the conclusion. "Soundly reasoned, Mr. Dudley. Furthermore, this... 'Vanessa' creature sounds like an Old

World type. This does not bode well. We must take caution. Old Worlders take evil seriously, make no mistake. Thoroughly disreputable creatures, vile and unwholesome as the day is long... the blackest pudding in the darkest bowl, as the saying goes. Still, it is strange..." she mused. "Interesting. Old Worlders are seldom seen this far from home - if ever. They do not customarily arrive by chance. Usually, they are attracted to sources of great power and darkness. I wonder..." Sister Becky's voice faded and she became lost in thought. After a moment she clucked and shook her head. "I wish Father Nicholas were here."

"Who?" Kiki asked, and Carson was glad to see that she looked as bewildered and dizzy as he was. The old nun had set quite a pace and they were all struggling to keep up.

"An old acquaintance of mine. An expert in creatures of the Old Country. He would be a valuable asset in this matter. But, alas, there is no use in such talk; it's knitting on socks that'll never be worn, as the saying goes. Now then..." and she was off again..."since we have reasonably established the true nature of this monster, our next step is clear: the deceased. Please take me to the corpse. I must examine it." She rose purposefully, hands tucked firmly into sleeves.

"What... you mean Pete?"

"Indeed, Mr. Dudley. Where have you placed the body?"

"Uh... the freezer. We put him in the freezer."

Carson led the way to the stainless steel walk-in. He opened the door obediently and the biting cold greeted them, quickly chilling fingers and breath. It was not as chilling, however, as the room's most noteworthy occupant. Pete's lifeless body lay in a corner, covered respectfully in brown freezer paper and partially concealed by a stack of frozen peas. Sister Becky wasted no time but swept past him to the grisly form. She drew aside the wrap and flicked her eyes over Pete's remains, checking him carefully from head to toe. Pete gave off a considerable whiff of odor, even in death, but the old nun seemed unperturbed. In fact, she gave no outward sign of faintness or revulsion whatsoever, as if such grisly duties were part of her daily routine. It looked less like she was inspecting the mutilated corpse of a vampire's latest meal and more like she was deciding the best spot in the garden to plant azaleas. After a moment, her roving eyes came to rest on the gaping, blood-soaked wound at Pete's throat.

She frowned again. "Tragic. Heartbreaking, really. Such a waste of a noble life. You have my condolences once again, Mr. Dudley, in the loss of your friend."

"Thanks. That means a lot."

"We need to stake him."

Carson stared at her as if he had just been slapped. Behind him, Kiki squeaked and Officer Jackson muttered something unintelligible but undoubtedly colorful. "Uh... what...?"

"Stake him, Mr. Dudley. We must transfix his heart with a wooden stake, and the sooner the better." Sister Becky held him fixed with her emerald eyes, her withered face as implacable and unfluttered as if she had just suggested they have a spot of tea. If she felt for his uncertainty and discomfort, she gave no sign. Carson tried speech again, interested in getting his lips moving but not quite certain how to go about it.

"Uh... durr..." His words came out with a white puff and he felt numb and stiff, but not just from the cold of the freezer.

"Come, come, Mr. Dudley. You have accepted the fact that vampires exist, have you not...? Excellent. So you must take the next logical step in reasoning. The legends regarding such creatures are largely true, I can assure you: they feed on the blood of the living, garlic and holy symbols cause them pain, animal transformation and control over the elements are among their many powers... this much you have seen for yourself." She was speaking plainly, matter-of-factly, as if she were in an honors-level Sunday school class and not standing in a walk-in freezer beside the corpse of an old hobo that had just been killed by a vampire. "Once you have accepted those truths, you must also realize that these vile creatures are fully capable of inflicting their disease on other poor souls, a process which begins with a bite at the throat and the draining of blood. This unfortunate old gentleman, God rest his soul..." she crossed the corpse, then herself. "...*has indeed* been bitten, *and* drained, *and* we have no idea whether or not he has been turned. The safest course - the only course - is to make sure that he will *not* return as a servant of the Powers of Darkness. I cannot stress enough - *this must be prevented at all costs*! At this stage, the danger to his immortal soul is very real, not to mention the fact that *one* vampire is quite enough to manage, and facing two is like inviting a second elephant into the lifeboat, if you take my meaning. Driving a stake through his heart - God rest his poor hapless soul...," she crossed him again, "...is the only way to be certain that he will remain blissfully deceased and not join the ranks of the Enemy."

Carson made no response. He had none to give. The old nun watched him for a moment, then abruptly broke off and bustled past him into the mini-mart, squeezing by Officer Jackson who was planted in the freezer door, his jaw gaping.

"And I thought last night was weird," he rumbled.

Sister Becky cast about the wreckage. Her eyes lit on a broken piece of shelf, splintered to a sharp point on one end and reasonably flat on the other. Scooping it up, she gave it a brief, professional examination, testing the pointy end with her thumb. Satisfied, she gave a curt nod. "This should do. Now then... do you keep a hammer in your shop?"

"I... uhh..."

"Ah..." Sister Becky spotted a yellow toolbox in the nearby utility closet and made for it with a purposeful step. Her voice floated out from inside, muffled but still audible over the sound of her rummaging. "I know it sounds cruel, Mr. Dudley, but as the saying goes, 'If you are going to match wits with the Devil, it is best to blunt his horns'." Sister Becky emerged from the closet, holding the makeshift stake in one hand and wielding a worn rawhide hammer in the other. "I assume, as you were the departed's closest acquaintance, that you would prefer to deal the stroke." She marched straight to Carson and thrust the implements at him. "There. Not ideal, but they should do. The heart is your target, Mr. Dudley, left side, just between these ribs here. One good sharp smack should do it, and I should stand well to the side were I you - sometimes the work's a bit wet, if you take my meaning."

Carson stared down at her dumbly. His knees felt weak and his head light and floaty. "Uhhh..."

Sister Becky bored into him with her eyes. Then suddenly the tough, businesslike granite of her face fell, drawing aside like a curtain to expose the familiar, sweet, grandmotherly smile that had brought him such comfort earlier but now just made his head hurt. "Yes, dear, I know. This is grisly work, indeed, and not the course that any of us would choose. But it is the *best* course, I promise you. I think, lad, that you know that, do you not?" She proferred the tools again, gently, and this time Carson took them in numb hands. They felt heavy, almost too heavy to lift.

He licked his lips, staring mutely into the nun's kind, smiling face. "You want me to..."

"Yes, lad. It is an unseemly chore, no doubt - but I believe, from what you have told me of him, that your friend would have wanted it this way. And I do believe he would have chosen *you* to deliver the blow. Do you not agree?"

Carson looked down at Pete. "This is the... uh... the only... are you *sure?*"

Sister Becky nodded consolingly. "The only way, dear, yes. This body is merely a shell now, after all, and an empty one at that. And, unless you would like it to rise up and drain every ounce of your life's blood while you sleep, I suggest you follow my counsel."

"It's just..." Carson stared down at the body of his friend. "Isn't this... it just seems... wrong. I mean, y'know, desecration and all..."

"Mr. Dudley - either you desecrate him or he desecrates you. Those are the only two options."

Carson licked his dry cold lips again and glanced back at Kiki. Her mouth opened, then closed, then opened again. Finally, she gave a helpless shrug.

Carson knelt, placing the tip of the makeshift stake on Pete's still chest. The old face looked haunted and waxy under a thick layer of frost, surreal and distorted in death, yet there was enough of the old Pete left that it seemed he might open his eyes at any moment and ask for a Freezie. Carson felt the weight of the rawhide hammer in his hand. It weighed a ton.

With effort, he raised it.

The tool hovered in midair, just over his shoulder, immobile, wavering. He stared down into the old face, with its familiar scruff of stubble and dirty crow's feet. Pete seemed so peaceful. So serene. So still. The thought of the violence he was about to wreak on his old friend suddenly seemed deplorable, unnecessary and just plain wrong.

Carson's resolve weakened. He couldn't do it. The hammer dipped. "I... he just looks so... this seems so... do we *really* have to?!"

There was a gentle touch on his shoulder and he realized that Sister Becky had knelt beside him. When she spoke, her voice was warm with compassion and sympathy. "I must apologize, my dear lad. You have been through much in a short time, and I forget myself. Your loss is still fresh. I allowed my zeal to cloud my judgment, and for that I am truly sorry. I was wrong to suggest this. Wrong and insensitive. Please forgive me." Gently, she took the hammer and stake from him.

Carson let her. He slumped, relief flooding his body. "Thanks, Sister. Boy, that's a load off! It just didn't feel right, jamming a stake through the old dude. Sure, he *could* be a bloodsucker, but, I mean, we just don't *know,* y'know?"

In one fluid motion, Sister Becky set the stake to the old man's chest and drove it through with a single blow of the hammer and a loud, wet *smack*.

"There. Now we know." She laid the hammer reverently beside the corpse, crossed it and rose to her feet. "May I trouble you for a kerchief, dear?" She smiled politely at Kiki. Slowly, mechanically, Kiki drew a tissue from her pocket and handed it over, her jaw hanging slightly open.

Sister Becky dabbed at a few red droplets on her cheek. "We may never be certain whether he was turned or not.... but the simple fact is, it no longer matters. One way or another, this dear soul is at rest and we are now free to focus fully on the challenges that lie ahead. And that, lad, is peace of mind - do you not agree?" She returned the bloodsmeared tissue to Kiki with a warm smile and a pat on the hand. "Thank you, Ms. Masterson. A messy business, this."

Carson struggled unsteadily to his feet, leaning against a stack of frozen burritos and wishing the freezer would stop spinning. He couldn't tear his eyes from Pete's face. The old hobo was still pale and drawn, and the makeshift stake blossoming from his chest drove home even more the fact that his passing had been less than peaceful. But as he stared, Carson had to admit that, somehow, Pete's body looked... different. He wasn't sure if it was just his imagination, but it seemed that the lines of suffering and hardship etched into the old face had softened, and that his death-grimace had taken on the hint of what might almost be called peace. Maybe Sister Becky had been right after all.

Carson steadied his breathing, blew on his chilled hands and forced his thoughts to focus. "Whoa. Okay. Alright. So... uh... what do we do about the... the... what about Pete? We can't just leave him in the freezer. Should we... I mean do we..."

"We lay him to rest, Mr. Dudley," Sister Becky favored Carson with her gentlest smile. "With the utmost care and respect. And I would be honored to preside over the ceremony... if you would permit me."

"I'd say you've got the job." Carson was feeling better already, his brain beginning to function again. "But where do we plant him? I'm assuming we don't just call up the local funeral home and ask about their next opening."

Becky clucked disapprovingly. "Alas, no. I'm afraid the particulars become somewhat complicated in these cases. I have found over the years that informing the authorities can often lead to questions that are most difficult to answer."

"Well," Kiki stomped her frozen feet to restore feeling. "We can't

 104

just leave him wedged in there by the taquitos."

"Yes. Well, it certainly does pose a bit of a challenge, my dear."

Officer Jackson cleared his throat. "Construction."

Carson blinked at him.

"There's fresh construction up the street."

Carson blinked again. "I don't..."

"I drive by it on the way here every night. They're pourin' concrete - looks like a pretty deep slab, too. If a guy had a couple of garbage bags..."

Carson's eyes widened. "You don't mean..."

Kiki sat down on a tub of liquid cheese, looking pale.

"You ain't gonna get him into a family plot lookin' like that, bro. The old broad said it herself - you take him anywhere official and you're gonna get some questions you don't wanna answer. But hey, suit yourself." Jackson shrugged. "The way I see it, those questions are comin' whether you like it or not. Sooner or later you're gonna have to explain to the boss why you got a real sleepy old hobo with a busted shelf post jammed through his cavity stacked alongside the corn dogs. That could get a little awkward."

Officer Jackson was leaning against the doorframe, his great arms folded almost casually across his chest. He seemed least affected by recent events, and the fact that he could remain so cool at the prospect of dumping a body into a cement mixer was a source of both concern and strength to Carson.

The worst part was, it was starting to sound like a pretty good idea.

"Okay... okay, yeah..." Carson drew a steadying breath, trying to think things through but not too thoroughly. "We take care of him ourselves. He didn't have anyone anyway, so no one's going to come looking. He won't be missed."

"There now, Mr. Dudley, there is some peace in that after all, isn't there? Now, let's get you out of this drafty air before you catch your death." Sister Becky took his arm and led him gently out of the freezer into the warmth and light of the store.

Kiki was right on their heels. As Sister Becky bustled away to return the hammer, the blonde cast a final glance behind them into the freezer. She suppressed a shiver, then drew close to Carson. "Hey... you okay?"

"Yeah. Strangely enough, I think I am. I just watched a nun drive a stake through the heart of a deceased vagrant who last night saved my life from a vampire in leather underwear. I'm starting to think things can't get much weirder, so I've decided to roll with it."

"Fair enough."

Carson squeezed her hand and winked. "How about you, kiddo?"

"I'm deeply disturbed, but comforted by the fact that my autobiography won't be boring."

"Now *that's* making lemonade out of lemons." Carson rubbed his hands vigorously to warm them and addressed the others. "Alright. That takes care of Pete... or at least will. Now we just have to tackle the bloodsucking wench."

"That should be just a *little* more difficult."

"Well, at least now we have a plan."

"We do?"

"Er... yeah. Or at least, we have Sister Becky - and Sister Becky has a plan, right?"

"Quite correct, Mr. Dudley."

"Great! Umm... so... what *is* the plan?"

"The hunt." There was a queer light stirring in the placid green pools of Sister Becky's eyes. "You know *who* and *what* the creature is now, and have removed the threat of progeny. The hunt is all that remains. The vile beast will most definitely return as she threatened and continue her assault upon you and your friends - such creatures never threaten idly - and undoubtedly make good on her promise to exterminate you. That is, of course, unless you can find her first."

"The hunt... right. Okay... er... how exactly do we...?"

"The first step in a hunt is to locate the creature's lair. Old World types like this one *always* have a lair, the more traditional the better."

"Lair. Good. Find the lair. Then what?"

Lines of gentleness and compassion rearranged on the nun's face, drawing together in a pattern of fierce and relentless determination. "Destroy her."

The way she said it made Carson take a step back.

Officer Jackson, on the other hand, was just getting interested.

"Now you're talkin'!" His deep baritone rumbled through the room and he pushed away from the wall against which he had been leaning. "Only one problem - we don't know where this 'lair' is. How we gonna find it?"

"Indeed, Mr. Jackson. That is the question at hand." Sister Becky began to pace, hands folded in her sleeves, her wrinkled brow wrinkling even further as she mulled the problem. "She is clever, this one, of that I have no doubt. However, she is of the Old World, which means her

 106

twin weaknesses are *pride* and *tradition*. She sees herself as a Dark Queen, reigning over her trembling subjects with fear and intimidation." Sister Becky gave a disdainful sniff. "Pompous creatures... not a bone of humility in them. She will choose a lair central to her hunting grounds. It will be abandoned, as large as possible, several stories high, I suspect, with a commanding presence. To her it will resemble a keep or small castle from the days of her youth. Typically, owing to the clandestine nature of her affairs, it will be in an isolated, low traffic neighborhood, or possibly a derelict industrial quarter, if such a thing can be found."

Kiki slipped off Carson's stool where she'd taken up a perch. "I can track that."

"You think?" Carson quirked an eyebrow.

Kiki shrugged. "Old abandoned building, in or near the Belfry District, centrally located to the string of murders, rundown neighborhood or closed down factory... that's a pretty good start. I can think of at least three likely candidates already. I've got the info from the police reports, that'll help, too. With all this and a quick trip around the Internet... who knows? We may get lucky."

"Well don't just stand there, girl... the clock is ticking!" The seed of hope from earlier blossomed. "You got your rig with you?"

Kiki patted her worn canvas pack. "Never leave home without it. I know a hotspot just around the corner. Shouldn't take long." She was swinging for the door as she talked. "Leave a light on for me!"

Kiki left and the store fell quiet. Too quiet. After the terrors and intensity of the previous twelve hours, the stillness felt unusual and dreamlike. It made Carson uncomfortable. After pacing for several minutes, he threw himself back into the cleanup effort. It helped, but he was still restless. Working while waiting was still waiting.

"So... anyone want a Freezie or something?" He put his question to the room at large, hoping to spark a conversation. "Corn dog? Potato wedge? Jalapeño popper?"

Officer Jackson grunted in the negative, busy with his gun-cleaning kit.

"No thank you, Mr. Dudley," Sister Becky inclined her head graciously. "Growing up in the convent I never did acquire a taste for such foods. Although," she added in a tone that was almost bashful. "Being this close to a hunt again does stir the broth in the bottom of the pot, as the saying goes. I dare say a little nibble of something might be just the ticket after all, if it is not too much trouble."

"None at all, Sister. What's your poison?"

"Have you any beef jerky?"

"What self-respecting mini-mart doesn't?"

"That is the stuff then, Mr. Dudley. Beef jerky, if you please."

Carson rummaged diligently through nearby piles of clutter and came back with a dented plastic tub.

"Li'l Pepe's Fire-Blasted Pepper Jalapeño Jerky," he read off the label. *"Caution - may cause taste buds to explode!"* He flashed her a picture of an angry cartoon jalapeño pepper stuffing what appeared to be a flaming grenade down the throat of a hapless consumer. "Sorry, this is all I could find. Nasty stuff. It actually sent some dude to the hospital last month, poor guy. We had some other, I could look..."

"Nonsense, Mr. Dudley. This will be quite adequate, God bless your heart. You are a generous man - truly as fine a rug as your grandmother wove of you, as the saying goes." Sister Becky accepted some of the oily, dangerous looking meat and took a generous bite. Carson noted the strong, straight white teeth that she put to the task. He eyed her carefully, waiting for her taste buds to explode, but nothing seemed to happen. She just sat chewing happily around a pleasant smile.

Carson shook his head.

"You're amazing."

"Thank you, Mr. Dudley. But it is only a stick of jerky, hardly cause for amazement. Although it is quite delicious, I may add."

He studied her thoughtfully.

"I didn't know nuns liked beef jerky - or fire-blasted pepper jalapeño, for that matter."

Sister Becky smiled, working through another bite and swallowing politely before answering.

"A childhood spent in an Irish convent can have a strong effect on one's culinary tastes. I have had the opportunity to sample practically every edible presentation of root vegetables, and I can assure you that dried fire-blasted meat from a plastic tub is a welcomed change. I quite enjoy a bit of flavor from time to time."

Carson returned her smile, remembering the screams of the last of his patron's who had sampled L'il Pepe's "bit of flavor."

"Thanks - but I'm still keeping it off the bucket list." Returning to his labors he righted a shelving unit and began stuffing product back into place. Most of it was either crushed flat or leaking, but it felt good to have something to do. He worked for a moment, then paused again.

"You know, Sister, I have to say... you're not what I expected."

"I shall take that as a compliment, Mr. Dudley."

"As a matter of fact, you're about the furthest..."

They were interrupted by a loud bang and a hearty curse as Officer Jackson bruised his shin crossing the cluttered floor. Instantly, Sister Becky was on her feet.

"*Mr. Jackson!* I have asked you politely *twice* before and I shall now ask a third time: *please refrain from using profanity in my presence!* Your total disregard for my requests is simply unconscionable and marks you as a rude and disrespectful man, a notion which I was willing to dismiss early on in our acquaintance but which is becoming increasingly difficult to ignore. This language of yours is *simply unacceptable* and I will *not* tolerate any more of it! I am through asking, Mr. Jackson. If you persist in your profane speech, *there will be consequences!*"

Sister Becky's reprimand stopped abruptly on this ominous note. She did not specify what the "consequences" would be, but judging from her tone and bearing, three things were crystal clear: they would be dire, Officer Jackson would not like them at all and she was serious about carrying them out. Deadly serious.

Jackson stood with his mouth hanging open, speechless. After a moment, as no words seemed to be coming out of it, he snapped it shut, at which point it formed into a fierce, dangerous scowl. Without so much as a grunt, the big man turned on his big heel and stormed away, shaking the few shelves in the store that were still upright. The front door seemed to jump open before he even touched it, eager to be out of the path of his boiling anger.

"You were saying, Mr. Dudley?" Sister Becky's placid gaze was back on Carson. All traces of thunder and lightning were gone.

"Forget it - *that* was what I expected."

Sister Becky smiled benignly, smoothing her robes. "I apologize, Mr. Dudley. I do not mind telling you that I find that sort of discourtesy truly aggravating. I made three polite requests of the man - three! - and he showed no respect or consideration whatsoever. It is not unreasonable to expect a little common courtesy, even in this day and age. It really puts the bark in the dog, if you take my meaning. Sometimes, in the face of such nonsense, action must be taken."

"You've got no complaints from me." Carson flashed her a thumbs up. "I just wish you'd been here last night. I could've used the backup." He chuckled. "I can see why Granny likes you."

Sister Becky chewed and swallowed the last of her jerky, then sat quietly for a moment, favoring Carson with a thoughtful gaze of her own. "Mr. Dudley... what exactly did Roberta tell you about me?"

"Granny? Ummm... well... that you were a nun, of course. That you two were old friends. And, uh..." he scratched his head. "That you were a... historian or something, I think. A librarian. Right?"

"That is correct, Mr. Dudley. I have been serving both the convent and parish in that capacity for several years now."

"Interesting work?"

"It passes the time."

"Uh-huh."

"Mr. Dudley... I have not *always* been a librarian."

"No?"

"No. As you might have noticed, I have certain... *other* skills."

"Other...?"

"Spiritual warfare, Mr. Dudley. I am speaking of spiritual warfare. Knowledge of supernatural evil and how to combat it. I was trained decades ago by the Catholic Church as a sort of special consultant - a spiritual troubleshooter if you will. My skills were put to good use in various situations and corners of the world that most are blissfully unaware of, but that required urgent and specialized address. Unfortunately, such activity has fallen into disapproval of late. If the truth be known, those with my training are none too popular with the Church at the moment, and I am somewhere near the top of that list. Some of those in high places seem to think that these labors are antiquated and draw negative attention to the church, although I cannot imagine why, and they are not overly fond of that. Organized religion has enough troubles these days, they feel, without stirring more pepper into the pot. The Truth has a way of doing that, sadly. Standing up for something you believe in is a good way to make yourself a target, and there are those who no longer have the stomach for such hardships. At any rate, like it or not, that is the way of the world. And that is also why I am now serving the Lord in the library. I am retired, you see."

"Sounds like a bum rap. Why do you stay with 'em? Can't you... I don't know... church shop... pass around the ol' nun resume or something? I still don't know *exactly* what it is you used to do, but there's got to be someplace out there that doesn't mind if you still do it."

Sister Becky sighed. "I suppose, dear boy, that as much as I vilify our quarry for her weaknesses of pride and tradition, I must admit that, to some extent, I suffer from the same afflictions. You see, it was the

Church that taught me the trade, and it was in her service that I have spent the majority of my life, helping those in need, righting wrongs, facing the forces of darkness and despair. Alas, now I fear that those who lead her have lost their way. I fear they are taking us down a long and treacherous slope, one with a dangerous and uncertain destination. But it is my hope and prayer that they will eventually see the light and that the Church will once again return to her spiritual foundations. If this comes to pass, God willing, I should like to say that I had some small part in it. I do not agree with all of the Church's reasoning, but we do - or at least did - see eye to eye on one thing: the best weapon against *evil* is *good*. Pure good, mind you lad, not the common sort, the purest and best, the kind that is only found rooted in the promises of our Lord and Savior. The traditional methods of fighting spiritual evil may no longer be taught, or in many cases even believed, but if I were to withdraw then they would be losing one of their strongest proponents... and that is precisely what our Adversary wants."

"Adversary? You mean..."

"Satan, Mr. Dudley. The Devil. Lucifer. The Fallen One. Mark my words, he is as real as you or I, although there are many who claim to be Christian who no longer believe that."

"That's lame. How can you have the Big Guy without the Big Red Guy? I mean, I'm no Johnny Bible but aren't they *both* in the Good Book? Seems like a no-brainer to me."

"Pick-and-choose Christianity, Mr. Dudley. Take what you want and leave the rest, that is the mentality of many of the faith these days. And it is a strategy well fostered by the Enemy... spiritual propaganda, pure and simple. Tell me, Mr. Dudley, if you were the Devil and could convince the general population that you did not exist - or better yet that you were some ridiculous fabrication with horns, cloven hooves and a pitchfork - would you do it?"

Carson tugged at his beard. "I guess so. It's just like I learned as a kid on family vacations - y'know, on those loooong car trips when you *really* had to pee and your dad just pulled over at the side of the highway - if no one's watching, you can do whatever you want. Heck, I wish I could convince everyone *I* didn't exist. At this point in my life, I can see a *real* advantage to dropping off the face of the Earth."

"Precisely, Mr. Dudley. Precisely! Well reasoned." She *tsk*-ed disdainfully, shaking her head. "A cowardly path our Enemy has chosen, I may add. Truly deplorable and befitting one of his station. Personally, I have always preferred a more direct approach." Carson, who had seen her direct approach, couldn't argue. "But such is the measure of the beast we face, Mr. Dudley. He is a deceiver - a liar and the Father of Lies, and it is his sole wish to destroy us. Utterly. Body and soul. And he is quite accomplished at the task." She caught the look in his eye. "Ah yes, Mr. Dudley. Our war is not merely against the Living Dead. Make no mistake; the source of a vampire's darkness and power is this same Evil One of whom I speak. I tell you these things because your Vanessa is cut from the same black cloth, stitched in the image and shaped in the tactics of her Master. Know *him*, and you will be that much better equipped to confront *her*."

Carson felt a sudden chill chase its way up his spine. "Okay... I was just getting my head around vampires, and now you're telling me we're taking on *Satan*?! This gets better by the minute..."

"Do not despair, my lad," she gripped his hand reassuringly. "It is highly unlikely that Lucifer himself will appear. In all my years of spiritual warfare, I have only encountered him once, and that was in the guise of a small dog - a chihuahua, I believe - and we were able to evade him without undue incident. He usually prefers to manage things through his underlings."

"That's a comfort."

"Take courage, Mr. Dudley. You have friends to stand beside you, and a God who loves justice... and, I daresay, a fair measure of backbone; otherwise, you would not be sitting here calmly discussing the matter, nor contemplating the task you are. I sense in you, Mr. Dudley, resources that you are as yet unaware of, and a strength beyond your knowing." She peered at him closely then, a sudden interest on her face, her eyes narrow and searching. Inscrutable and unreadable thoughts swam in their green depths. "Yes..." she murmured thoughtfully. "Definitely something..."

Another loud crash shattered her musings. Officer Jackson had returned, his mood showing no improvement. Scowling, he began to rummage through the bulging gear bag he had dropped unceremoniously on the counter.

Sister Becky wrinkled her nose. "Your Mr. Jackson, however, is another matter *entirely*."

Carson couldn't help but smile. Somehow, the fact that Officer Jackson had gotten under Sister Becky's skin made her seem human... at last. For a woman who scarfed five-alarm meat strips and drove stakes through corpses without flinching, this was a good thing.

"Yup... he's one uptight dude, that's for certain sure. But he's okay.

He was a huge help last night - took a royal thrashing and pretty much saved our bacon in the process. Dude's tough as nails. If we find Vanessa in time, I'll be glad to have him."

"*When*, Mr. Dudley. When. Ms. Masterson seems quite resourceful. I have all the faith in her, and am confident that she will track down our quarry before nightfall." She paused. "But just the same, I believe I shall have a word of prayer. 'Water the crops but pray for rain,' as the saying goes. If you will excuse me, Mr. Dudley, I have business to attend to."

Carson watched the nun pick her way through the wreckage toward a quiet corner. She passed dangerously close to Officer Jackson, who was laboring over the contents of his duffel, muttering quietly. Carson noted with some amusement that his words, although clearly provocative, were too soft to pick out with any accuracy. It appeared, amazingly enough, that the big man had backed down. Score one for the nun. Even so, judging by her expression, it appeared that Sister Becky was not entirely satisfied and that not *every* word was unintelligible. She shot a look at the guard as she passed that indicated she would send a few choice prayers his way as well.

Carson glanced out the window. His grin and momentary good humor quickly vanished as he spied the lengthening shadows stretching across the parking lot. There was a familiar squish in his stomach, as if the roller coaster had just started moving again. The day was wearing on. Night was coming. Carson suddenly felt like like both cursing *and* praying, but settled on hoping - fervently - that Sister Becky was right and that Kiki would make it in time. He hated waiting.

* * * * *

As it turned out, he had quite a bit more waiting in store before Kiki finally returned. The shadows had almost covered the lot and Carson had just about given up and was about to head out to look for her when the front door gave its sickly chime and she popped through with a triumphant flourish.

"I think I found it!"

The others gathered eagerly around as she bustled to the front counter and spread out a large aerial map of Las Calamas.

"Okay..." Kiki's eyes darted over the paper as she picked landmarks out of the black and white blobs, getting her bearings. "Here's the Belfry District... this is the old water tower... here's Bellamy

 113

Park..."

"Hey, there's the 24/7..." Carson chimed in. "Sweet. I think that's Jack's truck..."

"Focus, Dudley. Now, it took some doing, but I think I've managed to pinpoint the most likely location for Vanessa's lair."

Carson was poring over the map, his stomach churning with nervous excitement. "Awesome! How'd you do it? Was there triangulation? I *love* triangulation! I bet there was triangulation."

"Uh, no. No triangulation. I just worked the puzzle, used the info and pieced together a pattern - it's obscure, but it's there. See these red dots? These are the sites of the attacks... together they form a sort of hunting grounds. Something the police wouldn't look for, but that makes sense when you look at it in a certain way."

"The scary supernatural way?"

"That's the one. Once I had the general area, I went back to Sister Becky's suggestions. I identified all possible structures within the hunting grounds that met her criteria. From that point, it's just guess work, of course, but after careful consideration and a healthy dose of gut instinct, I'd say the most likely candidate for Vanessa's lair is..."

"Let me guess..." Carson cut in. Struck by a sudden chilling inspiration, he shot a glance out the window and across the street at a dark, brooding structure. "The Curio Shop?"

Kiki looked at him. "Curio Shop? No, not even close. It's an abandoned meat packing plant. Place called The House of Beef." She stabbed a finger at the map, skewering a large, gray blob surrounded by an army of spiky white lines that were probably parking spaces. "It's big, abandoned, and sits all by itself in a rundown neighborhood - the remains of an old industrial development, if you can believe it. Everything Sister Becky said, plus, it's creepy as hell... I figured that was sort of an unspoken qualifier. Even managed to dig up an old photo online." She produced a piece of paper bearing a picture of a towering dilapidated structure. "If that doesn't look like the modern day equivalent of a scary old castle, I don't know what does."

Sister Becky was staring down at the papers, her eyes flicking back and forth intently from the map to the photo. After a moment, a smile of approval bent the wrinkles of her face. "Well done, child. Well done, indeed!"

"What do you think... could that *really* be the place?"

"You said it yourself, Ms. Masterson - it matches every criteria. I

114

could not agree more with your assessment. The House of Beef is most definitely her lair. I feel it in my bones. You have a keen mind and excellent instincts, young lady, and we are well served by both. You are truly a tribute to your upbringing. Your parents must be proud."

Kiki's cheeks suddenly reddened. "Yeah... just got lucky is all," she mumbled, adjusting her stocking cap. She glanced over at Carson, apparently eager to change the subject. "What do you think, Carson... hey, what's wrong?"

"Hmm? Oh... nothing."

"C'mon, you seem... I don't know... disappointed."

"No, no, I'm cool. I just thought..." he shot another glance at the Curio Shop, then tore his eyes away. "Never mind. Nope, not bummed all... in fact I'm stoked. Totally. Awesome job of Sherlocking, woman. Now that we know where she is we can open up a can of the good stuff on this bloodsucker. I, for one, can't wait."

"Damn straight," Officer Jackson rumbled. He was bent over the map, his massive outline throwing shadows over the gray patchwork, studying it carefully, a hard, mercenary light in his eyes. In the excitement of the recent discovery, he seemed to have even forgotten his feud with Sister Becky, standing nearly shoulder to shoulder with her as he reviewed Kiki's discovery with a tactical eye. "Good cover, lots of screening... approach shouldn't be a problem. It's close, too. We could get there by sundown if we hurry. I say we mount up and go bust a cap in this f..."

Sister Becky cleared her throat loudly.

Officer Jackson's face contorted.

"F... f... *freak*." He finished the sentence carefully, deliberately, almost painfully. Carson, who had been holding his breath, was sure that the original choice of words had been vastly different but had been so mangled by the audible grinding of the big man's teeth that it had come out as it had.

"You said it, big man... lock n' load!"

Eager to prevent renewed hostilities and fueled with a sudden surge of adrenaline, Carson ducked behind the counter to retrieve his bat. "Let's get geared up and get this party started! Man... a vampire hunt. Can you *believe* it?! Where's Wesley Snipes when you need him?"

Officer Jackson snorted, breaking off a staring contest with the old nun and turning to stuff gear into his duffel. "Wesley Snipes is a punk. You ever see him punch? No retraction. You wanna *real* fighter, you need Bruce Lee."

"Bruce Lee?! C'mon, Bruce Lee never fought *vampires!* Try again, dude."

"Alright... how 'bout Roddy McDowell."

"*Now* you're talking."

"Or Anthony Hopkins."

"Right on!"

"Or Corey Feldman."

"Corey who?"

"Never mind. Hey..." Officer Jackson eyed Carson's baseball bat critically. "That all you're bringing?"

"Yup," Carson gave the weapon an affectionate pat. "This baby dished out a whoopin' last night. I'm getting attached to it. Besides, it's special."

"Special? What do you mean?"

"Hey, you saw it in action - this is a vampire bat."

Jackson rolled his eyes. "You and your wisecracks."

"Yeah, you shoulda seen that one coming. But Vanessa sure didn't." Carson gave a slow motion replay of his hit from last night. "*Wooosh... pow! Ssssssss...!*"

Officer Jackson frowned, and for a moment, Carson was whisked back to their heated argument of the previous evening. He held his breath, wondering how far his sense of humor had taken him across the line.

Then, abruptly, Jackson's look of irritation melted. In its place was a smile. A genuine smile. "Yeah... she sure didn't, the skanky witch." Apparently the promise of impending violence had cheered the guard somewhat. "It was a nice hit, too. But I got somethin' else for ya..." Jackson turned and rummaged in his rucksack in an uncharacteristic display of generosity. "Not that your stick ain't a good tool and all, but you might wanna up the firepower a little." He drew his hand from the satchel, gripping a businesslike weapon with a docked stock, polished wooden pump and a convincingly large barrel. "You ever handle a gun?"

"Cool! Newb tube!" Carson took the weapon gratefully.

Officer Jackson grinned. "Yeah, you got it. Twelve gauge pump action shotgun, sawed off stock... holds five plus one in the pipe. You ever use one of these?"

"Sure, plenty of times... *Papa Cap II, Gun Knight, Clips of Fury, Lead Rain, Sergeant Machinegun...*"

The security guard squinted, then snorted again good naturedly.

 116

"No, man, not in no *game*... for real. You ever handle a piece?"

"Dude, it's okay, I've got the gun attachment."

"Seriously, bro!"

"Well, if you're restricting me to 'real life,' then no. Never." Carson was squinting down the barrel, taking aim at imaginary bad guys. "How hard can it be?"

Jackson rolled his eyes. "Alright, look... hold it tight, but don't squeeze. Don't worry too much about the sights, just point the hole at the bad thing and pull the trigger... but get close as you can. After that, rack the pump and go again. Just keep shootin' till you're empty. Keep that in mind, you should do okay. Oh, and don't shoot me. Or her." He jerked a thumb at Kiki.

"Gentle but firm, point the hole, pump and shoot, watch the same-siding. Got it."

"And be good to the King," Jackson added. "He's one of my favorites."

Kiki's ears perked up, and she paused as she was stowing her map. "'The King'... you name your guns?"

"Yeah," the guard answered off-handedly. "I name all my weapons." Kiki seemed about to say something else but, after a moment, shut her mouth.

Carson, however, narrowed his eyes and regarded his new acquisition thoughtfully. "'The King'... as in Elvis?"

"The one and only."

"Why?"

Jackson fixed him with a steady gaze.

"Cuz he always knocks 'em dead."

Carson gave a single nod, as if he and the big man had just shared a moment of universal truth that was too powerful to communicate with mere words.

It was Kiki's turn to roll her eyes.

"What about those bad boys?" Carson gestured at a pair of beefy, nickel-plated automatics the guard had just shoved in his belt. "What do you call them?"

"The Wonder Twins," he grinned wickedly. "You oughta see 'em activate."

"Nice. Well, the King is in good hands, my man. Good hands... hey, that reminds me... I got something for you too – it's not *as* sweet, but it's still *sweet*..." Carson reached under the counter and brought out a fresh box of Twinkies. "This'll get you fueled up for the big assault, dude. You'll need all the sugar buzz you can get when the foo hits the fan."

Officer Jackson took the box reverently. "Whoa. Bro." There were tears in the big man's eyes. "I thought you were cleaned out?"

Carson looked sheepish. "Uh... yeah... I sort of had these... stashed. You were going through the Hostess like it was your job and I kind of figured that if we ran out you would... awww, heck. I was just being a jerk. Look... I'm sorry about that stuff I said earlier. I was all wigged out about this Vanessa business and I let it get to me. I was pretty uncool."

Officer Jackson smiled. Carson noticed that he looked a lot nicer and less like he was going to punch you in the face when he did. He liked it a lot more when Officer Jackson smiled.

"No sweat, man. And anyway, you're right... I should lay off the sweets."

"And I should lay off the wisecracks. Apology accepted?" Carson thrust out his hand. The big man engulfed it in his own oversized paw.

"Only if you accept mine."

"Done."

"Hey, tell you what..." Officer Jackson pulled a pair of crinkly yellow treats from the box, passing one to Carson.

"We'll save these two for the victory dance. I usually have a cigar, but..."

"Right on. Victory Twinkie. Officer Jackson, you're starting to grow on me."

"Dex."

"Pardon?"

"Dex. My friends call me Dex."

"Sweet. Dex it is. Oh... and my friends call me..." Carson hesitated, looking thoughtful. "Dud."

Dex's face fell. "Yeah... uh... look, man, I didn't mean..."

"No no..." Carson waved off the apology. "Actually, I kind of like it. I never had a nickname before."

"Beats 'whitebread.' That's what I was gonna call you next." Dex started pulling additional weapons from the duffel, stashing and strapping them about his body. When he was finished, he tossed a quick glance at Kiki. "Well, that's two of us. What do you say, lady? You want a sidearm?"

"Actually, I've got one."

Carson and Dex both stopped, staring. Kiki slid a sleek, dangerous looking semi-automatic out of her back waistband and held it up.

"Hey, what can I say? Look at your window..." She gestured at the wall of missing person posters, looking somewhat defensive and somewhat offensive at the same time. "It's a rough town."

Dex shrugged. "Works for me."

Then he shot Sister Becky a sideways look. A mischievous grin stole across his face. "How 'bout you, grandma? Need a piece?" He pulled one heavy automatic from its holster and held it out to the nun. It looked almost as big as she was.

"Thank you, Mr. Jackson, but I will politely decline." She gave him a stiff look. "Mundane weaponry such as that will avail you little against this type of adversary. Creatures of the Great Darkness such as this one are highly resistant to physical assault, if not entirely impervious, and require an offense of a more spiritual nature. As the Scriptures say: 'The weapons of our warfare are not physical, but mighty before God.'"

Dex smirked and winked at Carson. Before he could stow the weapon, however, Sister Becky reached out and lifted it smoothly and quickly from his hand. She popped the clip with practiced ease, cleared the chamber and squinted down the long nickel-plated barrel at the sights. "Also, the action on the .40 caliber is a bit stiff for my tastes, and I find the feel of these polymer grips does not translate well during rapid firing. Besides..." she pulled the breach open and peered into it critically. "You have cheese in your barrel." Reversing the weapon, she slapped the grips back into Officer Jackson's hand. He could only gape.

Carson threw his hands into the air. "Am I the *only* gun virgin here?!" He sighed, exasperated, then sobered as he glanced out the window. Long shadows from the gas pumps now stretched across the parking lot, painting the storefronts across the street with streaky, sinister smudges. For some reason, it made him mad, as if the shadows were creeping into *his* neighborhood and leaving their dark stain over all that was normal and decent and good. Somewhere inside, he felt gears shifting.

"Okay," He took a breath, steadying himself. "Alright. Looks like it's about time to wrap up show and tell. The sun's almost history - we are officially *out* of time. From this point on, I've got the feeling that life is about to get full-on ape crazy and I want to make sure we're all on board with this whole 'let's bag us a bloodsucker' deal. So let's get one thing straight - there's something nasty in our neighborhood, and we're gonna put the boots to it... agreed?"

He was answered by terse nods. In the twilight shadows of the mini-mart, no one smiled - it was the locker room before the big game and everyone felt it.

"Right. Sister Becky, thanks for all the intel. I'm still not sure exactly how you know what you know, or frankly, why I believe you, but you're about the only thing that makes sense anymore and that's good enough for me. You've been pinch hitting so far, and I don't wanna rope you into something you're not up for... this is our fight, I get that, and I know you're on thin ice with those Church dudes as is... so if you wanna walk, that's cool."

Sister Becky inclined her head graciously. "Such a considerate young man... and such kind thoughts for an old soul. However, while I very much appreciate the sentiment, I could not very well turn my back on you dear hearts, knowing what lies ahead of you. And as for the Church, I am not overly concerned..." she dismissed the notion with a wave. "Excommunication is always a possibility, but then there would be a whole rectory full of 'Church dudes' who would have to put away their own books."

"Sweet!" Carson let his breath out, relieved. "I have to say, that's a *big* load off. If it's one thing I've learned from online games, it's that you *have* to have a leader in every group. Otherwise... chaos. I sure am glad it's you, lady. Okay... so what's the game plan? We're all yours."

"Not so fast, Mr. Dudley," Sister Becky clucked. "I believe you misunderstand my intentions. As I have previously related, I am currently *retired* from my former vocation. My involvement in this matter will be strictly in an advisory capacity. Saint Peter's ghost, I simply haven't the strength or energy left to lead an excursion such as this."

"Retired?! But I thought... well, nuts. Okay, so if it's not you, then who's gonna call the shots?" The question seemed innocent enough. Glancing about, Carson noticed that all three of his co-conspirators were, strangely, now staring at him. The ground suddenly felt slippery. "Uh... hey, breaks on. I can't... I mean... whoa. Uh-unh... you got the wrong guy. I'm not exactly the leader type. I wasn't even in ASB."

"Nonsense, Mr. Dudley," Sister Becky clipped. "You are the night manager here, are you not?"

"Night clerk. Night *clerk*..."

"A mere matter of semantics." Sister Becky's smile warmed, and she patted his hand comfortingly. "I am usually an excellent judge of character, and I can tell that you have what it takes to do this. Whether you see it or not, I believe you are ideally suited for this role."

"How the heck do you figure that?! I've never lead anything in my life. I'm lousy at thinking up plans. I usually don't even know what I'm gonna have for dinner."

"A true leader, Mr. Dudley, does not always say, 'This is the plan...' Rather, he asks, 'What is the plan?', and then listens for the best one."

"Does a true leader want to wet himself whenever he thinks about fighting vampires?"

"Not a deterrent, Mr. Dudley – you must simply remember to relieve yourself before the action begins. Father Jervis always had to do the same, and he made an *excellent* leader. That is, until he... well, let us not concern ourselves with *that* unpleasantness. 'Never show the next horse the bit that broke his brother,' as the saying goes."

"Again, you're a great comfort."

"Now, now, Mr. Dudley, just hear me out, there's a good lad. There are many other reasons to choose you over me. You are younger, stronger, more energetic. This is *your* store, *your* neighborhood, and it has been *your* customers who have borne the brunt of this tragedy - it stands to reason that you, therefore, have the greatest vested interest, and thus, the strongest motivation to see this matter through. There are more practical concerns as well. For example, I doubt that Mr. Jackson would be willing to follow my lead *anywhere*. Is that correct, Mr. Jackson?"

"Damn straight. I ain't taking marching orders from Mother Theresa. B'sides, bro, you're the one signing my checks, so you're already my boss... technically. Hell, you may finally get some work out of me." He grinned.

"There you have it, Mr. Dudley. I believe that settles the matter... as long as Ms. Masterson has no reservations?"

"Don't even ask," Kiki said. "You're the man and I'm in. I finally know what bad hoodoo is and I don't like it. You saw that from the beginning, Carson, even when no one else did." She paused. "And this one's for Pete."

Carson nodded. The ground was feeling a little steadier. "For Pete, then. Alright. I'll do it."

The mini-mart fell silent. Carson stared at the assembled group, and in turn, they stared at him. Everything felt strangely right, although he could hardly explain how tramping off to an abandoned meat-packing plant in the middle of the night armed with a shotgun named "the King" and accompanied by a renegade nun, a trigger happy security guard and a college student with criminal connections to hunt a vampire could ever feel that way.

But then, there it was.

He detected, once again, the curious sensation that he had experienced several nights ago after his conversation with Stinky Pete - not dread, not excitement, but something strangely in between. It was bigger and more powerful and more significant than anything he had ever felt before. It was, he decidedfor lack of a better word, *purpose.* And it was too big to ignore.

Carson cleared his throat. "Alright. As my brother always says, 'Sometimes you get what you need, sometimes you get what you want, but most of the time, you get what you get.' Right now, what we've got is a psycho vampire bimbo who wants to put the permanent hurt on us. We may not like it, but that's the way it is. And it's time we do something about it." He racked the slide on the King, ejecting the unspent shell that was loaded in the chamber and sending it flying harmlessly across the room. It felt good. "Let's go bag us a bloodsucker."

Chapter Seven

Lair of the Vampire Babe

"How far?"

Kiki looked down at a fistful of electronics. The happy blue glow lit up her pretty face, both in stark contrast to the dark, gloomy, rundown industrial forest that hemmed them in. "Not far now. GPS says just a couple of blocks."

"Think we'll make it in time?"

She shrugged slim shoulders. "It should be close. Sister Becky says this bloodsucker's an old one. Apparently that makes her tough but also sleepy - a late riser. It should be close." She shot a sideways glance at the hulking buildings on the far side of the street, watchful and edgy.

Carson could feel her nerves from where he walked a few feet away, but said nothing. He couldn't blame her. The sun had set a short while ago, leaving them in the oppressive darkness of the largely abandoned industrial complex squatting on the Eastern edge of the Belfry district. It had been a worrisome thing, watching the glowing disk disappear beneath the proud, vigorous skyline of Las Calamas, knowing that it was sinking beneath the waters of the Pacific and would not be seen again for what seemed an eternity. Carson had traded his button-down shirt for a black hooded sweatshirt and filled its pockets with loose shotgun shells that Dex had provided. He wore the hood up and carried his bat in his free hand, which made him feel better. The King was slung out of sight on its leather strap under his sweatshirt, which made him feel *much* better. With his free hand, he patted the sleek, dangerous outline of the weapon. It was a constant comfort.

As worrisome as the sunset was, it had nevertheless provided a stunning backdrop for the brief ceremony that preceded Pete's burial a short time ago. The gold and crimson splendor had provided the only color in the somber affair. The proceedings had been short, largely consisting of Sister Becky praying while Carson and Dex dumped a garbage bag filled with Pete's remains into a cement mixer and poured him into the fill of the new construction site. It hadn't exactly been a proper burial, but Carson couldn't help but think that, in some ways, it might have been what Pete had wanted.

But not what he deserved.

He patted the shotgun again and squared his jaw. Tonight was about payback. "How far?"

Kiki checked the blue glow. "Just a few more blocks."

They walked in silence, feeling the night pressing close, ears straining for every little sound. Except for their feet scuffing on the cracked and neglected sidewalk, there was nothing.

Another block passed. Carson felt a poke on his arm.

"Hey... aren't you missing something?"

"Ummm..."

"C'mon..." Kiki grinned at him from the depths of his own shadow, her white teeth a reassuring glint in the gloom. "Just when I got used to you fiddling with that thing, you gave it the toss?"

"I don't..."

"The stick, silly!" She poked him again. "Where's the ol' lucky corndog stick?"

"Oh. Yeah. Right. *That* stick. Sorry, I guess I'm a little distracted with this 'let's go whack us a bloodsucker before she sucks us dry' scenario. Well, I hate to disappoint, but the stick is gone. It got busted when Vanessa was handing out the hurt... poked me pretty good in the side too." He lifted his shirt and showed her a nasty red mark. "I figure a lucky charm that almost punctures your kidney is the kind I can do without. But it's all good - I've got a new one. Something even better."

124

Carson fished under the collar of his sweatshirt and drew out a stitch of cloth. In the darkness, Kiki caught a glimpse of red.

"Pete's bandanna," her face softened. "Carson, that's..." Then she stopped, her mouth pulling down into a grimace as her thoughts turned to Stinky Pete. "Uh..."

"Don't worry, kid. I washed it."

"That's for the best." She brightened. "Well, good choice. I think Pete would be proud."

"Unless we die. I don't think he'd be real impressed by that."

"Let's just make sure we don't, then."

"Deal. By the way, that's a nice little good luck charm you got yourself." He indicated her GPS.

"Thanks. Doesn't look like much, but it gets the job done."

"Yours?"

"Naw... somebody dropped it off at Lucky Earl's, thing was shot. I did some tinkering, got it up and running again."

"You are, like, the Queen of Tech. Is there anything you can't fix, Your Majesty?"

Kiki blushed and looked away.

They walked another block.

"How far now?"

"Right around the corner." Kiki thumbed a switch and the GPS went dark. Its guidance was no longer needed. "We're there."

"Roger that. Hey...!" Carson whispered hoarsely over his shoulder. "This is it!" The faded shadows of Sister Becky and Officer Jackson closed quickly with their own. "Looks like this is Defcon 4. What do you say, Sister B. - got any last minute tips from *The Idiots Guide to Vampire Hunting*?"

The nun inclined her head benevolently, her features as lean, aged and grim as the buildings that towered over them. "Strike hard and fast and with all the strength you can muster. Look to the counsel I have given you, and to each other. And remember what I have instructed you about your earthly weapons - they may knock this creature about, but the real work will be here..." She patted the well-loved shaft of a large wooden cross she held thrown over her shoulder. In the gloom and shadows it looked almost as tall as she was. "Employ such holy devices as I have given you, but know this - it is not the *symbol* that holds power but the *faith* behind it. This, of course, is a matter between you and the Lord Himself. Regardless of your walk, keep them close; they will have some influence over the Dark Ones merely by their own implications."

Sister Becky shifted the weight of the cross, cradling it like a child. The wood was dark and smooth, and gleamed with the wear of years of wielding. Light from a distant street lamp glinted dully from iron caps at its extremities and studs along its shaft and crossbar. The nun had retrieved it before they set out, along with a small bag containing an assortment of crucifix necklaces, vials of water and some wooden stakes. Sister Becky had equipped the group hastily en route, adding a few bits of basic advice about confronting vampires. To Carson, it had been mostly a blur. His newfound sense of purpose held him firmly committed, even though his head was still buzzing with the intensity and unreality of the situation. Still, he had been grateful for *any* assistance and had accepted the offerings eagerly, as had Kiki. The only holdout had been Dex, who stubbornly refused anything from the aging nun. He remained mute on the matter and instead stuck close to his bulging black duffel, which, judging by its size, appeared to Carson to have the approximate contents of a national guard armory.

"Make no mistake," Sister Becky continued. "This is no Sunday afternoon errand. It will be a frightful affair, but if we can weaken the beast sufficiently and get close enough, we should be able to drive a stake through her black heart. And that," she concluded with an air of finality, "will be that. Questions?"

There were none.

"Excellent. Now then... we have discussed the water long enough, as the saying goes, and that won't make it any warmer. It is time to jump in. A quick word of prayer and we shall be off."

She bowed her head and the others followed suit, standing in silence as she murmured softly. When she was done, she crossed herself and lifted her head. There was a sudden gleam in the old nun's eyes and a strange, feverish light that shone from somewhere inside of a younger, more passionate woman. "Now, let's go bust some heads!"

Even her voice sounded different. She set out instantly with a brisk, businesslike pace, hefting her cross to the ready position as the others fell in behind, hard pressed to keep up.

"'Bust some heads?'" Dex scoffed as he trotted behind her. "What do *you* know about bustin' heads, you old goat?! The Good Book teach you that?"

"As a matter of fact, Mr. Jackson, it did. There is a great deal of head-busting that takes place in Scripture, if one bothers to look. In fact, under the appropriate circumstances, our Heavenly Father even recommends it. And I quote: 'Blows and wounds cleanse away evil and beatings purge the inmost being.'"

"'Blows and wounds?' 'Beatings?'" Dex snickered. "Get outta town, old woman! You made that up, just to spite me. That's not in the Bible... is it?"

Sister Becky sighed as if she were speaking with an irritating child. "Proverbs 20:30, Mr. Jackson. Look it up."

"Hey, Dud... that's not in the Bible... is that in the Bible?!"

The nun sighed again, shaking her head.

"Yeah, well... just keep out the way when the fur starts to fly, Grandma. You keep your spiritual mumbo-jumbo clear of my bullets and we'll get along fine. Crosses and prayers might work in the movies, but this is *real* life."

They rounded a corner and the unmistakable silhouette of a towering structure, the biggest they had seen by far, loomed before them. Sister Becky made for it briskly, not slowing the pace of her approach or her dialogue. "I sense great skepticism in you, Mr. Jackson. You are not a man of faith, I take it?"

"Me?" Dex snorted. "Nah... I tried church once. Didn't like it. Just a bunch of hypocrites if you ask me - puttin' on airs with their holier-than-thou smiles and high-and-mighty talk, while the rest of the week they're cheatin' on their taxes and foolin' around on their wives. I don't see the point of it."

"I see. Tell me, Mr. Jackson... do you attend the moving pictures?"

"If you mean *movies,* yeah; I take in a flick from time to time." Dex tried to smirk but was starting to puff trying to keep up with Sister Becky. "Who doesn't?"

"I imagine you meet some distasteful persons there as well... inconsiderate, rude, churlish... yet you continue to go, do you not?"

"Damn straight. I ain't lettin' a few loud-mouth..." He stopped, squinting at her in the darkness. "Wait a minute... I see where you're goin' with this, and you can't. That's totally different!"

"Nonsense, Mr. Jackson - it is, in fact, precisely the same. You go to the movies for the *show*, not the *audience*. You are making excuses for not attending to your spirituality by blaming people instead of addressing the real issues. Frankly, in addition to not being very helpful, this sort of behavior is immature and childish."

"Immature?! Childish?!" Dex was starting to sweat now and his breath was growing short. "You wanna... see childish... old woman?! I'll *show* you *childish*...!"

"Hey... look!" Carson stopped them cold. They had just rounded the corner, and he froze in his tracks, pointing reflexively into the darkness ahead; it wasn't necessary. Together, the four of them stared at the monolithic structure towering above them in the darkness.

They had arrived.

The building was gigantic, dwarfing those around it like a great, bulbous, squatty toad among frogs. Empty blackness stared down at them through broken windows and patchy boards, and a faded sign was just visible, proclaiming "House of Beef" in letters long ravaged by neglect and the elements. A faint breeze scattered several pages of yellowed newspaper across the front lot and wafted the barest hint of a nose-crinkling odor over them. Tendrils of mist crept out from between loose boards in the building's facade, curling about the edges of the monumental warehouse doors that barred the front entrance like the gates of some ancient, foreboding keep.

"Crap," Kiki lifted a hand to her nose. "*This* is where she lives? That's perfect. That's just *perfect*..."

"Yeah... creepy." Carson touched the red bandanna at his throat. "Stud up, guys - we can't stop now. This one's for Pete, remember?" He opened his coat and unlimbered the King.

Beside him, Dex was rummaging through the contents of his overstuffed duffel, his breath wheezing above the rattle and clank. "Man, I'd *love* to be the one to drive a stake through her cold heart..." he muttered.

"Hey, get in line," Carson smiled grimly. "I already got dibs on Vanessa."

Dex stared blankly. "Vanessa? Er... yeah. Vanessa." There was a harsh metallic *snick* as he chambered a round into an assault rifle that looked nearly as large, mean and dark as he did. "Showtime."

"Odin's beard! What do you call that one?"

"Arnie."

"'Nuff said. Let's rock." Carson racked the pump on his shotgun and promptly ejected another unspent shell. Dex frowned, pausing as he stuffed clips into his belt.

"Would you *stop* that?! You're gonna wanna leave some of those *in* the damn thing!"

"Sorry! Nervous."

Carson shuffled his feet, watching absently as the shell rolled off into the darkness and trying to decide in which hand to hold his bat and which the gun. Dex watched a moment, frowning impatiently. Finally, he grabbed the Louisville Slugger and shoved the grip at Carson.

"Just stick the damn thing in your belt and let's get moving! I got the feeling it's wakey-wakey time, and I wanna catch this *&!#$ in her PJ's, not her work clothes."

"I agree with Mr. Jackson," Sister Becky's voice drifted out of the shadows. "At least with his *intent,* if not his choice of words," she added coldly. "'When you come for cause and not for dinner, it is best to enter unannounced,' as the saying goes." Briskly she strode to the warehouse doors and peered through a small crack in the weathered boards. The others clustered close around her.

"It is dark," she whispered, her voice muffled by the musty, age-worn wood. "I see no lights and no reason to seek another means of ingress. Time is of the essence, as we have noted. If she is awake, then she is awake, and there shall be no taking her unawares. She is far too powerful for that. Mr. Jackson, if you would?"

Dex slung his rifle and plied his powerful arms against the door. He strained a moment, and the great slab wavered, creaked, then screeched open a foot or two on rusted tracks, giving them just enough room to slip through.

Without pause, they entered, one by one, stealing into the room and fanning out, eyes straining and ears peeled.

Inside, it was dark. Very dark. Not the kind of absolute dark that left the eyes aching and the soul empty, but almost a worse kind, the kind with half-seen shapes looming out of the shadows, the kind that outlined vague shapes and left the details for the dark uncontrollable parts of the imagination to fill in. Some of the shapes might have been crates, others hulking sections of processing equipment or heavy machinery, others the scattered scraps and detritus left by squatters, hobos and other former tenants. With some, it was just too hard to tell. All in all, it felt as if there were too many places to hide and not enough to hide behind. There were smells, too, at once as unmistakable and yet unplaceable as the shadowed shapes, suggesting ages of death, machinery and cow parts, as well as the hint of fresher bloodshed and fresher aromas - the scents of wax and spice and earth mingled.

With all the vaguery of sights and aromas, one thing was for certain - the place was big. *Very* big. As they shifted and listened nervously, sounds bounced and echoed and were swallowed up by the vast expanse of semi-dark semi-nothingness about them. The faint scuff of a shoe or clink of weapons or the scuttle of some unseen creature sounded alarmingly loud at first, then dissipated almost instantly, as if it had never been.

The last thing they noticed was the chill. It wasn't the temperature so much as the atmosphere, and it stabbed through clothing and skin like a knife, creeping into the joints and prickling the extremities in an unfriendly and uncomfortable way. Every motion felt stiff and sluggish.

To Carson, it seemed like they had stepped through a warehouse door and into a tomb - a big, smelly, echoey, mysterious, frightening tomb that was home only to death. It was a bad place and he felt it. They all felt it. For a moment, there was silence.

At last, Carson's whisper broke the graveside mood. "Did anyone bring a flashlight?"

He was answered by another short period of silence, this one uncomfortable and accompanied by the shuffling of several pairs of feet. Someone swore softly. Finally, something heavy touched the ground with a clink and there was the sound of rummaging.

"Just a sec..." Dex muttered. "I think I might have something..." Then, after a moment, there came a soft *pop* and he handed over a fistful of green glow.

"Here."

Carson looked down at his hand. "A glow stick?" He glanced up at the room, which swallowed the faint luminescence immediately. "Well, at least I can see my *hand* now. How many you got?"

He sensed, rather than saw, Dex's frown in the darkness.

"Great. Awesome. That's just *super.* Welcome to the bowels of death, everyone! Sorry, no one bothered to think it might be *dark* here! Man... in the immortal words of Han Solo: I've got a bad feeling about this."

"You mean Leia," Dex muttered.

"Eh?"

"You said, 'I've got a bad feeling about this.' That's a Leia line."

"Dude... no way. That's a Han line... Han said that."

"Man, they *all* said it... s'just the princess said it first. You can't give *Han* the credit if *Leia* said it first. It's a Leia line. Trust me."

"No, no, no... no way. You got it all wrong. Han says it first. I totally remember - it's in the trash compactor thingy, right before the squeeze kicks in."

"That's sad, bro," Dex shook his head, a vague, negative image in the shadows. "You gotta get your facts straight. Leia pops out with it waaaay before that, right after..."

"Alright! *Enough!*" Kiki hissed. "Congratulations, you can *both*

 130

be King of the Dorks... happy?! Now *stop* trying to out-nerd each other and get your *heads in the game*! We've got this little bloodsucker issue to deal with, in case it's slipped your minds!"

There was a pause.

"'No reward is worth this,'" Dex murmured. Carson stifled a snicker.

"Excuse me?!"

"Look Your Worshipfulness, let's get one thing straight - I take orders from just one person: me!" Carson's voice was strained from choking back laughter. Dex chuckled softly.

"You wanna feel the Force?!" Kiki's whisper was practically venomous. "Make one more crack...!"

The only response was the sudden silence of self-preservation.

"Now listen up, knuckleheads! In case you've forgotten, there's *still* a vampire out there, she *still* wants to violently eradicate us and we *still* have no idea how to freakin' find her!"

"Uh... I don't think that's gonna be a problem..." All traces of mirth were gone from Carson's voice. His face illuminated by the ghostly green of the glowstick; he stared into the darkness above them.

Only, it was no longer dark.

A light had quietly appeared before them, the soft, flickering heat of a single candle, innocent yet ominous. It seemed to float in the air some twenty feet off the floor in the center of the building, mysterious, mesmerizing. It was only after their eyes had adjusted that they noticed it was not suspended in mid air but stood in an ornate iron candelabra. A moment later, a second candle jumped to life to join the first, and the fire hopped quickly from there up a row of candles until the entire candelabra was ablaze. As the four intruders watched, the rush of orange tongues spread to another candle stand, then another and another like a swarm of orderly fireflies. In a moment, there was enough light to illuminate the open second floor platform on which the candelabras stood.

Built on a rusty, tangled web of scaffold and crowded with junk and shadows, the platform appeared to span the entire rear third of the warehouse. A space had been cleared in the center in which had been arranged a comfy, if somewhat archaic and macabre space, that seemed a marriage of boudoir and medieval torture chamber. There were antique divans and lounges decorated with plush throws, thick luxurious area rugs and ornate furnishings in a delicate and tasteful style. All this was mixed cozily with dark iron weapon racks bearing barbed leather whips, hooks, tongs and other tools of sinister delights, as well as faded tapestries on freestanding hangars depicting scenes of human cruelty and bloodthirsty erotica that were simply too horrible to look away from. It was, Carson thought, like looking into the Devil's bedchamber, a rich, opulent and stomach-turning diorama, a bordello of sinister suave.

From the expansive balcony, the ruddy candlelight spilled over onto the floor beneath, illuminating a cluster of squatty offices that stared blankly at them from broken, sightless windows. Perched atop this abandoned shanty town was a large, weathered wooden statue of a Texas longhorn, proudly proclaiming *Hous of eef* in faux-branded letters on one faded side. From there, the candles' glow faded quickly, exposing some of the menacing shapes on the floor as hulking, rusted machinery. Other shapes it only made worse as the cloak of shadows was cast back, piling up in copious folds like a dark sheet thrown over tombstones. Although he could *see* better now, Carson realized, it definitely didn't make him *feel* better.

Before anyone could utter a word, there was a great whoosh*!* and a rush of flame, and the brightest light yet sprang to life on the platform. Pushing back the veil of shadows even further and making them shield their eyes from its sudden intensity, the source of the light became apparent moments later - a huge, ancient, battered cast-iron furnace. It was set in the very center of the dark boudoir, and through the broad grill on its face flickered hungry red flames. The harsh orange light revealed an iron maiden, a small rack and several coffins that had previously escaped their notice.

That, and Vanessa.

Fully revealed by the glare was the Queen Vampiress herself, sprawled lazily on an antique loveseat in the dead center of the platform. The porcelain white of her flesh stood out in stark contrast to the black and crimson patterns of the upholstery and the desperately straining confines of a dominatrix negligee, which left more to the eyes than the imagination. She was relaxed and fully at ease, bathed in the caressing shadows of the firelight, toying with a long strand of raven-black hair.

Watching.

Waiting.

Gloating.

"Steady..." Sister Becky breathed. She shifted grips on her cross.

Vanessa rose with fluid grace, gliding to the edge of the platform, a

 132

smile of regal air and fresh appetites gracing her alabaster features. In one hand, she held an ornate golden goblet to which she placed her perfect ruby lips and supped. They returned more red than before, and she drew her tongue across their full, flawless form as a shiver of delight coursed down her body. She stood there above them, brimming with confidence and naked malediction. She was grim, gorgeous, voluptuous and oozing womanly charm in an intoxicating and almost overwhelming quantity, so that the air seemed warm and cloying and thick. The dark queen stared down at her vassals, helpless beneath the power of her domination. It was her turf and she knew it. The ripple of sinister laughter that flowed down from the platform stirred their souls like a chill wind.

"Good evening, delicious, delectable, succulent morsels of midnight," she drawled lazily. "As I expected, I see zat you have..."

"Blah blah blah..." Dex stepped forward and thumbed off his safety. "A little less conversation, a little more action."

The stuttering thunder of the assault rifle tore through Vanessa's words, and the intervening space and would have carved her neatly up had she not, with reflexes born of Hell itself, suddenly collapsed into a shimmering, spectral cloud of mist. The stream of slugs punched fat mouseholes through the gray mass, but did much more damage to the loveseat and a nearby candelabra than the vampiress, whose misted form was already moving. Before the first of the furniture woodchips touched down, the swirl of living fog flowed over the platform's edge and onto the floor, swooshing through the space like a malevolent, murderous cloud.

Mist met man a second later.

The deafening chop of automatic fire stopped abruptly as the weapon was slapped free from Dex's grip and flew across the room. The stunned security guard followed it a split second later as he was knocked from his feet and sent skidding in the opposite direction on the cold concrete. He was up in a heartbeat, though wobbling, with his nickel-plated .45's clutched in beefy fists, and his eyes wild, hunting for a target.

The mist drew itself up in a ghostly parody of crouched human shape, ready to surge again, a hint of wicked red lips grinning from its depths.

"*Cease!*"

Suddenly the gaunt, imposing form of Sister Becky swept between the two combatants, drawn up to its full height, eyes cold and full of

 133

hard fire. She stabbed a warning glance at Dex, who flinched involuntarily under their naked aggression.

"This is the Lord's work, Mr. Jackson," she clipped. "You have had your outburst. Now, let us try it my way."

Sister Becky turned the green fire of her gaze to the shifting, roiling cloud of mist. Lasers would have had only slightly greater effect. "Come come, my dear. Let us drop this charade. I would see the full measure of the evil that preys on the hapless citizens of this fair city."

The sinister vapor shifted, flickered like an old reel-to-reel film, then suddenly coalesced into the voluptuous form of the vampiress. She stepped out of the mist and onto the cold, hard reality of the slaughterhouse floor, shaking a few clinging wisps of white from her hair and drawing a gasp of shock from three of the vampire hunters.

Vanessa still held the blood-filled goblet in her hand, and this she tipped to her lips for another repulsive sup. Lowering the vessel, she struck a provocative pose, the fingers of her free hand tracing slow, imaginary paths through the no man's land of her ample cleavage.

She pouted. "Zat is the problem vith the Church - zey take all the fun out of things..."

Sister Becky stepped forward brusquely, looking somehow taller and sterner than ever before, the severity of her wardrobe and demeanor a stark contrast to the naked wantonness of the vampiress and her almost-clothing. She drew up mere inches from her foe, facing her eye to eye.

Carson's heart hammered his chest and his numb fingers fumbled for the King's trigger. He had seen first hand the speed and ferocity of Vanessa's attacks and couldn't imagine any scenario in which the nun, at this proximity, could escape anything short of complete destruction. She was doomed.

"So," Sister Becky flicked her eyes coolly up and down, giving her enemy the quick once-over. "*This* is the Spawn of Satan? I am not impressed."

A peal of chilling laughter rippled through the still air, making everyone's neck hair stand and salute. "An entire day to seek assistance and *zis* is vhat you find? Zis shriveled prune?! Vhere is a vorthy foe?! Surely zis... zis... old world *relic* vith her stifling garb and false piety is not your greatest champion? Who vill come and test my strength?!"

"It is not I who come against you, Evil One, but the Lord Himself!" Sister Becky flicked a look heavenward for emphasis, then snapped her eyes back to her opponent.

"If you are going to represent Him, you should ask for a new vardrobe. This garment of yours only inspires ridicule, not passion or fear." Vanessa wriggled her form suggestively.

The nun sniffed. "It is one thing to be evil, but another entirely to be evil *and* a shameless tramp. As the saying goes, 'She who shows the swine her cheek reveals to all her swinely reek.'"

Vanessa shrugged. "*Your* svine does not seem to mind it." She shot a coy glance at Dex.

The big man cursed, but more at himself than the vampiress, tearing his gaze away from her shapely curves and casting it quickly to the floor. "It wasn't like that! I swear...! I was just... deciding where to shoot her, that's all!"

Sister Becky narrowed her eyes and clucked menacingly. "Enough of this banter!" She unlimbered her cross from her shoulder like a soldier would his rifle. "We did not come to trade empty words with you, Spawn of the Lower Gates, but to rid the world of your vile filth!" The cross lifted high. Although massive, it seemed suddenly weightless in her hands. "I come against you in the name of the Lord of Heaven and command you to submit to the fire of His judgment!"

Vanessa smirked. "Foolish old crone. Your faith has no power over me."

For a few moments Sister Becky persisted stubbornly, brandishing the cross even higher and vigorously muttering prayers under her breath. Then, suddenly, she faltered. The fire in her eyes seemed to flicker and fade. As if she suddenly felt its weight, the cross drooped in her gnarled old hands. "Perhaps... perhaps you are correct. It has been so long... perhaps I have been... deceiving myself. I can see it now, so clearly... I have been a fool all these years to trust in... in..." the black hood nodded forward in defeat.

Vanessa beamed, her face reflecting the light of the furnace in a glow that seemed to spring from Hell itself.

"Zere, you see? As I have told you..."

"...*JESUS CHRIST*!"

Sister Becky snapped upright, the cross stabbing skyward and a feverish gleam in her eye.

The golden goblet crashed to the floor, splattering the concrete.

"Ha!" The old nun crowed. "Gotcha! No power over you, eh?"

Vanessa looked suddenly defensive, avoiding the other's gaze as she wiped a spot of blood from her thigh. "I vas startled is all... you startled me!"

Sister Becky's look of triumph slipped slightly, pulling down one corner of her mouth. Her shoulders started to droop again, taking the cross with them. "I see... alright then... I suppose you are correct. It was foolish of an old woman to believe that... *THE POWER OF CHRIST COMPELS YOU*!" Again she snapped ramrod straight, this time surging forward a step to prove her point.

Vanessa jerked visibly as if struck, recoiling involuntarily and falling back several paces. Her mask of haughty disdain slipped.

"*HA*!" Sister Becky spared a hand from her cross to point triumphantly. "You *flinched* that time! I saw it!"

"I did not, you hideous old goat! You merely startled me, as I have said..." There was a wildness in Vanessa's blood red eyes, and her breath was coming quicker.

Sister Becky laughed, a cold sound. "Your tongue is as forked as your Master's, you filthy trollop!" She stepped forward again, pressing. "I saw it as clearly as the sky at dawn... you *flinched* at the Savior's name!"

Vanessa bristled, baring her teeth. There was fire in her eyes now as well. This time she did not back down.

"I did not!"

"You did too!"

Becky stepped closer.

"Did *not*!!"

Vanessa stepped closer.

"Did *too*!!"

Their noses almost touched.

"Did NOT!!"

"Did TOO!!"

"DID *NOT*!!"

"DID *TOO*!!"

With no warning whatsoever, the nun cocked her cross and struck all in one swift motion, catching the unsuspecting vampiress full in the face. There was a *smack!* and a sizzle and Vanessa went down in mid-retort.

Hard.

"Well, you did just a little right there, didn't ya?!" Sister Becky bellowed. At her feet, Vanessa was writhing on the concrete, clutching her smoking face. The nun whirled to regard her companions and brandished her cross like a prized trophy cup. "The Lord will *not* be

 136

mocked!"

Behind her there was a sudden blur of motion, followed by the scream of rending bolts, then the whoosh of air that indicated a massive, metallic object was tearing its way through it. From the shadows where Vanessa had fallen, several hundred pounds of rusty metal bone chipper was hurtling through the air toward the triumphant nun. She was flatfooted in her triumph. There was no time to move.

Then a second blur streaked across the scene, this one catching Sister Becky neatly around the waist and wrenching her clear just as the fearsome missile smashed to earth, shattering the thick concrete to its foundations. Both figures rolled across the floor, carried by the momentum of the diving rescue to a safe stop some dozen feet away. Sister Becky sat up, dazed, and stared at the man who had saved her life.

It was Dex.

For a moment they sat that way, breathing hard, staring at one another in mutual disbelief, Dex's arms still wrapped tightly about the aged nun. In the next heartbeat, they were scrambling to their feet, untangling clothing and weapons and exchanging awkward pleasantries.

"Er... thank you, Mr. Jackson..."

"S'no prob... happy to help... reflex, y'know..."

To their great relief, the exchange was cut short by the arrival of a wickedly enraged vampiress. Lunging from the darkness, her face distorted by fury and a vicious looking burn in the shape of a large cross, Vanessa snapped Sister Becky's head back with a vicious backhand, then seized Dex by the front of his uniform and flung him bodily through the air. A handful of brass buttons skittered and glittered across the concrete in his wake. An instant later, she was on him, and from that point on, she set about making Officer Jackson wish that he had never been born.

A dozen feet away, the brutality of her assault finally snapped Carson out of his freeze. With a shake and a sharp intake of the breath that he realized he'd been holding, life returned. He winced as a tremendous series of body blows shook Dex's frame and knocked handcuffs, spare clips and other equipment from his belt like candy from a piñata. As tough as he was, there was no way he could take that punishment for long. The guard was getting worked. If he didn't do something, Dex was dead.

"Kiki!" Carson barked, racking the pump on his shotgun and ejecting yet another unspent shell. "Help Becky! I'm going after Dex!"

He took a stiff step forward on legs that seemed unaccustomed to movement, forced another, then another as Kiki, visibly shaken, stooped beside Sister Becky's crumpled form. After a moment, he had developed a lurching rhythm and pointed himself toward the fray.

In spite of the poor lighting, it wasn't hard to track the battle. A steady stream of cursing, punctuated by frequent blows, grunts and the occasional clang of bone on metal made it hard to miss. Plus, Dex was bellowing like a runaway elephant.

"*Shoot her*!!" He screamed. "Somebody shoot the *&$%! Shoot her *NOW*!!"

The guard's face was bloodied and bruised, his clothing in shreds as he desperately strove to hold off the enraged vampiress. He swung wildly with the broken stub of a metal pipe, missed and dodged stiffly to the side. Vanessa slashed and spit and leapt, advancing on him like a wildcat as he backpedaled, several slashing blows missing vital organs by a hairsbreadth and others tearing open fresh wounds.

Carson was close. He gritted his teeth and raised the shotgun. It was now or never. He squeezed the trigger.

The first thing Carson realized was that real shotguns were a *lot* louder than virtual ones. They were also much harder to hang onto than your standard console controller, and tended to jump up and kick you in the forehead if you weren't careful. He staggered sideways, ears ringing and stars lighting the way. Colliding with a stack of metal drums, he righted himself and frantically scanned the scene of battle, eager to see the effects of his shot. A dozen feet away, the fury of Vanessa's onslaught continued unabated.

He had missed. By a mile.

Desperately, Carson pumped a fresh shell into the chamber and lurched forward. Dex took a savage claw to the face that tore open his cheek and nearly his jugular. Carson fired. Another wild miss. Vanessa stopped Dex's pipe with her arm as the guard threw a feeble counterattack, vaulted high over a followup backhand and landed neatly on top of a massive bone saw. For a moment, she was stationless, silhouetted in the orange glow of the furnace, head back, hair wild, hissing like a hundred snakes. It was the perfect shot.

Boom!

Miss.

Carson's hearing was gone, his hands throbbing and raw from controlling the recoil of his shotgun, his heart in his shoes. Worst of all was the growing awareness that he was an absolutely terrible shot. He kept on.

Another rack of the pump, another short rush of desperate steps. Vanessa leapt from her perch and kicked Dex in the face. He staggered, blood gushing from his nose, threw a clumsy haymaker, which missed as she ducked and slashed deep into his leg, and he went down. Carson was close enough now that some of the blood hit him. He thrust out the barrel and pulled the trigger, wincing in anticipation of the recoil and nearly out of his skin with desperation.

Click.

He stared down numbly.

Rack the pump, pull the trigger.

Click.

Again.

Click.

Click.

Dimly, above the screams, he realized the weapon was empty. Hands shaking from a massive overload of terror, panic and adrenaline, he froze.

Pocket!! Screamed a tiny voice from somewhere deep in the stunned recesses of his brain. *Shells!!*

"Pocket," he mumbled. "Shells..."

Carson jammed a hand toward his sweatshirt pocket, missed, tried again and hit it on the second try. He fumbled a moment, then yanked free a handful of shells, all of which went spilling and spinning into the darkness as his thumb caught on the edge of the fabric. From somewhere nearby, Dex roared with pain. Carson threw himself to the floor and fumbled frantically among the debris, chasing the faint red reflections of the casings. He came up with three shells and was on his feet and moving, struggling to jam them into the shotgun as the slaughter intensified before his very eyes. Dex was back on his feet but clearly slowing, bloodied, clumsy and darn near finished.

Plastic scrabbled on metal as the shell stubbornly refused to find the opening. Carson's feet pounded on the concrete; his breathing ragged. Dex took a shot to the face, closing one eye. Vanessa screamed in raw animal triumph. Her face was contorted. She was out of control. More scrabbling. The shell still wouldn't go in. Ahead, Vanessa took a fistful of Dex's dreadlocks and seized his throat with her claws, poised to tear out the majority of his critical plumbing in the next instant.

Carson shook the shotgun furiously, desperately. "*Come ON!!* Are you the freakin' King or...!!"

The shell slipped home. He was loaded. Carson looked up, still running, and stared directly into Vanessa's face, her eyes lit with surprise at his sudden arrival. He could touch her if he wanted.

Entirely out of instinct and fear, he raised the gun and fired.

Boom!

Carson caught a glimpse of part of her face being obliterated, and then she was torn away and thrown off into the shadows, headfirst, like a rag doll kicked by a wicked sibling.

"Okay... you *are* the King..."

Carson stood swaying for a moment, absolutely stunned, not even sure if what had just happened had just happened. A moment later, someone was clutching weakly at his pant leg. He stared down into Dex's bloodied face. Quickly, he slung the shotgun and stooped to take an arm.

"Thanks!" The guard gasped, spitting out a mouthful of blood as Carson hauled him to his feet. "You *suck!*"

"Yeah! I know! But I think I've got the hang of it now! When you said, 'close', I thought you meant, y'know, *kinda* close, but you meant *really really* close, so now I got it figured; you just stick the business end *right* in her face and..."

And then her face was back, jumping straight into their midst with an ear-rending screech that tore at their souls and froze their limbs.

Carson lurched back with a strangled yelp, his movements more out of panic than purpose and no more than a slow motion replay in contrast to the vampiress' blinding speed. Vanessa, he noted dimly, was looking much more like road kill than Queen High Mistress of the Bloodsuckers, but the damage didn't seem to be slowing her down at all. She swatted the King away, seized him by the hair and yanked him off his feet, swinging him once around before sending him spinning off through the air. There was a distant crash of splintering wood, too uncomfortably far away for it to have been anything but an unpleasant landing. Without a moment's pause, she whirled on Dex, who had slumped again to the ground, his legs not quite convinced that supporting his own weight would get them anything good in return.

Vanessa closed, hunched and moving fast, flickering firelight from above showing through a ragged hole the shotgun blast had torn in her cheek. Her face, branded by faith and mauled by gunfire, looked grossly out of place attached to the voluptuous, scantily clad female body. Blood red eyes loomed close, full of murder as gleaming fangs and jagged claws reached for flesh.

Dex could only gape, his great arms limp, his strength finally gone. "Oh, *&%$... not again..."

Claws touched his throat.

"Zis time, my darling meat sack, there is no vun to help you..."

"That is not entirely true."

Something wet slapped across Vanessa's face. Instantly, she screamed with the sound of a thousand banshees that ripped at Dex's ears and sanity. Whirling, hissing and spitting, Vanessa leaped and rolled in agony, clawing and clutching at the smoking ruins of her rapidly disappearing face. Appearing suddenly by his side, Sister Becky reached down and took the guard's arm in a firm grip.

"Damn!" Dex gasped, trying not to break her in half as he accepted her help. It was the only word he could get out. Surprisingly, the old nun seemed to bear his weight without undue discomfort.

"You are quite welcome, Mr. Jackson. Simply returning the favor. As the saying goes... we *nailed* her!" A red welt stood out vividly on her cheek and one emerald eye was beginning to darken, but the fevered light shone all the more brightly.

"Damn... straight! What... was that stuff... holy water?"

She sniffed. "Holy water is for amateurs. I use holy lighter fluid. It burns... *and* it burns. *Light her up*!!"

Dex caught movement from the shadows. In answer to the nun's cry, Kiki darted from cover, closed with the enemy and hurled a tight packed ball of flaming rags. The bundle struck the vampiress square on the boustiere and her entire upper body exploded into an inferno of blue flames. The screams were incredible.

"*YES!!*" Kiki punched the air in exultation, then whirled in a start as a shaky hand grabbed her, nearly causing her to drop her mini-torch.

"Whadid I miss?!" Carson slurred, wiping blood and splinters out of his disheveled hair. He clutched his baseball bat clumsily in one hand, the shotgun pointedly absent.

"You're alive!" Kiki squeezed him with an impulsive hug, beaming. "Yikes... you're missing some hair... but you're alive!!" She squeezed him again. "Good news is, you got here just in time for the end!" She jerked a thumb at the vampiress, shielding her eyes from the blaze.

No sooner had Kiki said the words, however, than Vanessa's form contracted and with a rapid *whoosh!* and rush of cold air exploded outward into a giant cloud of fog. Blue flames rolled out in sheets and sucked upward in a plume, illuminating the entire room for a split second before snuffing out against the ceiling.

A split second later, the mist-cloud sucked back in on itself and *poofed!* out of existence, dropping a very bedraggled and no-longer-burning vampiress unceremoniously onto the concrete.

"Sweet Aunt Harriet," Carson gasped. "You gotta admit... *that* was impressive..."

"HA!" Sister Becky crowed. "The beast is weakened! She can no longer hold her Forms of Greater Carnage!"

Vanessa's head snapped up; her mouth twisted into a grim snarl. She was truly a sight to behold, burnt and smoldering, face in ruins and garments, if indeed any remained, mostly indistinguishable from blackened flesh. Gathering herself on all fours, she sprang upward, flickered and was consumed by a flash of dark light, from which emerged a large tattered looking bat. Swooping ghostlike on veiny wings, the bat angled toward the front of the building. There, a sliver of fresh moonlight shone through the crack of the warehouse door.

Carson choked. "Door! *Door!* The door! She's going for the... she's escaping!!!" Desperately, he cast about for something to throw.

"Not on my watch..." Kiki ducked out of her backpack and yanked out a bulky homebrew device that resembled a PDA and $5 worth of miscellaneous electronics duct-taped to a bullhorn. Flipping a toggle switch, she aimed the cone end at the fleeing bat and pulled the trigger.

Instantly a high-pitched electronic whine filled the air, bouncing off the walls in a furious sensory assault and setting everyone's teeth on edge. For the humans, it was uncomfortable. The effect on the bat was extreme. It veered and swooped erratically, like a puppet jerked and yanked by someone who really didn't like puppets very much and who mostly just wanted to see them misused and destroyed. Kiki held the device steady, training it on the fluttering shape until it careened off a metal support beam, scraped along some crates and flew headlong into a wall.

The whine stopped. The others, hands still clamped over ears, stared at Kiki.

"Sonar jammer." She shrugged. "Who knew?"

A second only, he paused then, galvanized, Carson leapt forward with a whoop. "Door!"

Limping and staggering, Dex joined in hot pursuit. The two men charged desperately across the cold concrete, doing their best to forget aches and wounds as they raced to close off the vampiress' escape route.

Banging into the door without slowing, they heaved to with all their weight and muscle. The door screeched, slid, then slammed shut with all the finality of a coffin lid.

Carson whirled, hefting his bat and casting about for their foe. "Where is she?! Anyone got eyes?!"

"Nothin' here..." Dex panted. "Kiki... Sister B... where?!"

"There!" Kiki jabbed a finger into the air, where the ragged, drunkenly swooping figure of the bat glided out of the shadows and dove toward the back of the warehouse.

"She is making for the second floor... back to the very heart of her lair!" Sister Becky hefted her cross along with her skirts. "After her!!"

The chase was on.

Carson and Dex caught the ladies halfway, pausing only to retrieve the King and Dex's Wonder Twins. It took just a moment to locate a set of narrow scaffold stairs leading up to the second level. At the first step, they paused. A flash of dark light and a *thump* from above indicated that something had just touched down. Then they were off; the sound of their feet pounding up the metal steps obliterated all else. As they closed on the top stair, Sister Becky called out a breathless warning.

"Beware! The creature is weakened, but with her back against the wall, she will be at her most deadly! We must proceed with haste but also with caution. Take heart - the end is near!"

Seconds later, they spilled out onto the platform. The space looked bigger than it had from below and more cluttered. It was divided by couches, wardrobes, free-standing tapestries, chests and other elegant trappings into a labyrinth of luxury, providing numerous places to hide. Slowing, they stepped cautiously onto aged, richly woven carpets, picking their way around the wreckage left by Dex's assault rifle and pressing into the vampire's inner sanctum. The only light now came from a handful of flickering candles in a single iron holder. The others, along with the great furnace, had gone strangely dark. Lit by a handful of red embers, the furnace's malevolent grill grinned at them out of the shadows like a hungry dragon.

Dex, in the lead, suddenly thrust up his hand. "Stop!"

"What... you see something?!" Carson gripped his shotgun, ready for anything.

"No... can't... breathe..." Dex sucked in great lungfuls of air, sweat pouring down his face. "Why can't... she just... stand and fight... I *hate*... runnin'!"

They paused, regrouping, waiting for the big man to catch his breath. After a few moments, he nodded wearily and they moved out, picking their way cautiously through the clutter. Carson swept the shadows, wary and cautious.

"What's with all the furniture?" He whispered. "Judging from what I've seen, it's not like her clothes take up a lot of room."

"Hmph," Sister Becky snorted softly. "It is decadence, Mr. Dudley. Pure hedonism. Just because she does not wear them, does not mean she does not possess them. The Old Worlders grow more and more self-absorbed by the century, preening and prissing in their selfish desires and base vanity. 'Immortality breeds immorality' as we say in the business. Well, as for myself, I would rather have graceful aging than eternal damnation any day. 'Shriveled prune' indeed! She may be able to withstand automatic weapons fire, this bloodsucking tart, but I should like to see how well she managed growing old."

"Hey..." Carson drew up short and pointed. "Is that supposed to happen?" A layer of fog had seeped up from the floorboards and was pooling around the feet of the furniture. "I thought you said... you know... Stuff of Greater Things and whatnot..."

Sister Becky's eyes narrowed. "That is not a Form of Greater Carnage, lad. Merely a parlor trick. Stay alert. Things are about to happen."

Carson swallowed and adjusted his grip on the shotgun. Dex's hand clamped on the pump before he could rack it.

"Save the ammo, bro. I got the feeling you're gonna need it."

The mist was growing, writhing, moving, despite the absence of a breeze or any movement of air. The candles cast an eery orange glow on its thick gauzy billows, and it seemed that strange shapes and half-seen faces formed, faded and swirled within it, just on the edge of vision.

"This ain't good. Circle up." At Dex's bidding, the four turned their backs to each other, forming a tight knot in the center of the loft. Within moments, furnishings, tapestries, furnace and all were obscured by thick sheets of chilly, clinging mist.

"I've been here before," Carson rasped. "She's coming."

"Steady, Mr. Dudley. We shall be ready for her."

"Yeah. Let her come, I say," Dex murmured. There was a quiet *tink* from his direction.

For some reason, the sound raised the short hairs on the back of Carson's neck. There was something undeniably ominous about it.

"Uh... Dex? What was that?"

"Nuthin'. Just stay frosty."

"Dude... I've played enough shooters to know that the littlest sounds come just before the biggest booms. It sounded like *tink*. What was the tink?! The tink is making Carson nervous."

"Just a little insurance."

"Define 'insurance.'"

"The kind that says, if we get ganked by a vampire witch, she gets ganked too." The big man flashed a glimpse of an object he held carefully concealed in his giant palm.

"Um... Dex... is that a live grenade?"

"Damn straight."

There was the general shuffle of feet as the circle expanded.

"Chill, people! It's cool. Got my hand on the thingy."

Carson made a noise in the back of his throat.

Kiki stared, eyes wide and fixed on the tiny round shape. "Uh... I... uh... oh my... can you... can you put it back?"

"The pin? What?! Put it... no way, sister! This here is my ace in the hole! Besides, the pin's down there somewhere. I chucked it."

Dex glanced back and caught the panicked expressions on his companion's faces. He sighed and rolled his eyes. "Sheesh. Civilians. Alright, look, I'll get rid of it, okay? If it'll make you pantywaist's feel better... I'll just flush her out instead." He lifted the grenade over his head in a motion just fast enough to cause the others to cringe. "Heeeeeeere kitty kitty kitty..." He cocked his arm to throw. "Heeeeeeere ki..."

And suddenly she was there. Without so much as a rustle of leather or a whisper of mist, Vanessa simply appeared in their midst, fangs bared, splitting the air with a bloodcurdling shriek. The hunters froze, slammed with fear and horror, unable to grasp for the moment the sheer intensity of the nightmare she had become, burnt and battered and smoking and furious and disheveled and beautiful and terrible all at once. In shock, Dex dropped the grenade. It disappeared into the pool of fog at their feet with an ominous *clank*.

They were dead.

Or would have been, if not for one thing:

Carson.

Carson alone, of all the group, had not been frozen in fear. A split second after the grenade dropped, he lifted his shotgun and fired. The roaring blast caught her full in the torso and flung her off into the mist.

"Fire in the hole! *Fire in the hole*!!" Shoving Kiki, Carson spun and grabbed for Sister Becky's habit as he dove for a shape that loomed out of the shadows and which he hoped was something large, heavy and able to stop shrapnel. Dex was already moving. A split second after they hit cover, the grenade exploded.

Up to this point, Carson had thought the King was the loudest thing he had ever heard. He was wrong. The noise and concussion from the grenade were violent and disturbing, and he could feel both through their cover as if it weren't even there. The floor bucked beneath him, and the sound of shrapnel striking wood stabbed faintly through a sudden case of deafness like hailstones on a tin roof. Something fell over. Then there was silence - the deepest, most unnatural silence he had ever not heard.

Beside him, Dex struggled to his elbows. He mumbled something, his eyes vague and dullish. It sounded something like, "*Bold you hide plush her...*", but Carson couldn't be sure through the monotone buzz that filled his head. He gave it a few seconds, then tried to speak in what he hoped was a quiet voice but which he was certain was shouting.

"Everyone okay?! Dex?!"

"Yeah, I'm good..." The words filtered faintly through stuffed cotton. "Lost the Twins, but didn't take any hits."

"Sister B.?!"

The nun nodded tersely from behind a shredded davenport a few feet away. "I am unharmed... but likewise disarmed." She showed empty hands.

"Yeah, me too... I dropped everything when I bolted." Carson shook his head ruefully. "I think I've got permanent hearing damage, but at least we're... wait a sec... where's Kiki?!" He glanced around frantically, craning his neck to see around furniture and the few straggling patches of mist that had survived the blast. There was no sign of her. "Uh-oh. Not good. Guys, we gotta..."

A peal of maniacal laughter cut him off. Peering cautiously through a large shrapnel hole in the wardrobe that was uncomfortably close to his head, he caught a glimpse of tattered black nightie and wild, frazzled hair. His face went white. "*Oh man...*"

"Vere are you, my troublesome blood bags?!" Vanessa's voice had lost its silky tones and taken on a hard, rasping edge, like a file on a steel girder. All semblance of polish and posturing was shattered and her accent was spilling thickly through the cracks. "Do you still live? Is your blood still coursing, vaiting to join my own, or is she spilled on

 146

the floor of my boudoir... if so, for shame! For how I so now desire to sup of it!"

"What's the sitrep, Dud?" Dex arched his neck, straining for a glimpse, but couldn't risk moving too much for fear of exposing himself.

"She's got her," Carson whispered, his voice strained. "Got her by the throat. She looks okay for now... a little roughed up, but okay... thank you God! Looks like Vanessa took a hit from that pineapple, though... wow. She lost some hide on that one."

"If still you live, my savory little *prutschkas*, you had best come forth! *Come forth,* I command you! You have left somethink behind ven you run away... somethink pretty..." There was a stifled squeal. Carson tensed, made to stand, but was held back by Dex's heavy hand.

"Not yet, bro... chill..."

"But she's got her! She's got Kiki! And she's gonna kill her, I know she'll do it. Dude, this is bad... this is just all *bad*..."

"I telling you again, darlink fleshling *voolborgs*, cast down your veapons and show yourselves! If not, I vill have no reasons to spare zis young pretty! After all... you have made spill my drink... and all of the exertions you have put upon me cause me to feel great thirst..." There was a solid yelp, followed by thrashing and struggling which trailed into a soft whimper.

Carson tried to rise again but was restrained. He looked sick. "She made a cut... claw... her neck! She's draining Kiki's blood into her goblet! We gotta...!"

"We will, Mr. Dudley," Sister Becky's firm tone cut through his panic and held him rooted. "We will." Carson spared her a glance, his eyes wild. The nun's black hood had slipped off, showing iron gray hair pulled back in a severe bun that was now halfway to undone. Tufts of wiry silver poked out in all directions, making her look more fierce than usual. "But whatever is to be done, we must do it together and with care. Alone or in haste, we shall perish."

Out on the floor, Vanessa continued her rant.

"Come out, come out vherever you are, you tasty *butschkins* filled vith your life-juice!" Her rasping, sinister singsong sent chills down Carson's spine and filled his mind with terrible images of what would happen to whoever went out. "You have *nothink*, succulent meat folk... no *hope*, no *future*, no *choice*. Come forth, now, like good little bloodlings. Come see your dear, dear Vanessa... she who goes by so many names... Vanessa the Butcher, Vanessa the Darkheart, Vanessa the Devourer! Come see the merciful death I may choose to bestow on those who submit before me..."

"Man, she can talk," Dex muttered.

Carson willed his body to relax, forcing the images of Kiki's torment out of his head and focusing on Sister Becky's words. They made sense. Slowly, he turned and sank to the floor, following his heart. His eyes were still leaning toward wild, but he knew it would take more than brute force to save his friend. "Alright..." Breathe in, breathe out. "Well... this sounds like a good time to ask 'What's the plan?'"

"I hate to say it, man but the *&$#! is right. We got nothin'!"

"Incorrect, Mr. Jackson," Sister Becky wagged a finger. "We have precisely what we entered with: our courage, our wits and our sacred duty. We have a holy mission to fulfill, and if we stand by it, the Lord will not abandon us! Our task is clear - we must *save* Ms. Masterson and *destroy* this creature!"

"But how?!" Carson could feel the wildness creeping back. "She's gonna kill Kiki! *Now*! We can't just sit here on our thumbs and wait for that to happen!"

"One thing's for sure, we can't just surrender," Dex shook his head grimly. "We do that, she'll wipe us all, and you know it."

"Well, if we don't give up we have to *fight*, and how're we gonna do that?! We've got no weapons!!"

"Actually..."

"Ahem..."

Dex and Becky reached into their clothes and promptly produced holdouts, the big man a compact, snub-nosed automatic and the nun a small, gleaming vial of holy water. Carson looked back and forth, surprised; by this time, though, he knew he shouldn't be.

"Okay... so we've got weapons. That's something. Anybody got a plan to go with 'em?"

"Well," Dex's voice was steady and lethal. "It ain't fancy, but I say we just up and give her hell. Just plain throw down. She's on the ropes, who knows... could be just enough to push her over." He gave Sister Becky a hard look. "Unless you got a problem with that?"

"On the contrary, Mr. Jackson. The idea has definite merits." She hitched up her robes and met his gaze, ounce for ounce with aggressive intent. "Do continue."

"She doesn't know where we are... we got surprise and all that. If we hit her now, while she's yakkin', we might be able to knock her off balance... might give someone a chance to get the girl clear."

"Excellent!" Sister Becky's eyes practically sizzled. "We go *straight* at her. Full frontal assault, right up the middle, give her everything we've got, and buy as big a distraction as we can for Mr. Dudley to effect a rescue."

"Wait a sec... what was that 'Mr. Dudley effect a rescue' part?'"

"The first order of business, Mr. Dudley, is to secure Ms. Masterson's safety, a fact on which I think you would agree. Mr. Jackson and I will create a distraction... a diversion if you will. We are appropriately armed and should be able to take her attention off the young lady. It will then fall to you, Mr. Dudley, to pull her clear. You will steal around behind the creature, if you are able, and be ready to extract her when we strike."

Carson digested, trying to tune out the increasingly heated ranting of the vampiress and not having much luck. "Alright... alright! Assuming that works, what then?"

Sister Becky shrugged. "If we survive? One obstacle at a time, Mr. Dudley. One obstacle at a time."

From beyond the wardrobe there came another yelp and a stifled scream. Carson hopped into a crouch. "Not exactly what I wanted to hear, but I'm in. Let's do this!"

Sister Becky crossed herself and whispered a quick prayer as Dex checked the clip on his automatic.

"...black-hearted hussy back to the pit where she belongs. Amen! Well, lads, let us be about it."

"Think you can make your way around?" Dex whispered at Carson.

The clerk nodded tersely. "Yeah. Looked like Vanessa was missing an ear. I should be good."

"Roger that. Showtime!"

The big man snatched a metal urn from nearby and gave it a heft, sending it over to the far side of the loft where it clanged loudly. Out on the floor, the raging monologue stopped. Without a word, Carson stole off silently into the shadows. Becky used the distraction to cross to Dex.

"This is nuts, y'know." The guard was grinning broadly.

"It certainly is, Mr. Jackson." The nun was grinning too. "It certainly is."

They waited, counting breathless seconds. Vanessa started to speak again, this time in a high-pitched shriek, the words fast and nearly unintelligible.

"How long should we give the kid?"

"A touch longer, Mr. Jackson. Just a few more moments."

Another pause, broken only by the constant drone of Vanessa's diatribe, which was rapidly working itself into a rambling, psychotic tirade. They made out a few phrases, including "swimming in entrails" and "unholy supping on the blood of the damned," but most of the rest was lost. Dex wriggled, put his eye to the hole and watched.

"So... you got anymore of that Bible talk?"

"I have Jeremiah 50:25: 'The Lord has opened his arsenal and brought forth the weapons of his wrath.'"

"Wrath... yeah. Wrath is good."

A harsh shriek from Vanessa tore through the loft, followed by a scream from Kiki and a crash.

Dex was on his feet. "Well, I think that's just about long enough. She's about to go vampire supernova out there. How you wanna play this?"

"Up close. We go in like lambs and come out like lions, as the saying goes... but only once we have a clear target." Sister Becky stashed her vial behind her, tucking it loosely under her belt.

"I'm down with that. It'll be dicey, though... Kiki's in the line of fire."

"You shall have your shot, Mr. Jackson."

"You can gimme that?"

She nodded, once and with confidence.

"Fair enough," Dex tucked the automatic out of sight behind his wasteband. "You're on point. I got your back."

Sister Becky checked her vial, making sure it was quick to hand. Satisfied, she stood abruptly and stepped out of cover, hands held high above her head. Dex was close on her heels.

"Enough, hellspawn!" The nun fixed a look of fierce resignation on her face and locked eyes with the vampiress across the loft. A peal of venomous laughter tore loose from Vanessa's throat, and she involuntarily tightened her grip. Blood leaked in a nasty red ribbon from Kiki's throat, dotting the floor and dripping into the golden goblet. Cautiously, slowly, Sister Becky made her way forward.

"*Ahaaaaaa*!! *Zabor strud*! Excellent, my precious sack-like succulents! You have chosen the vise vay... the *only* vay... the vay zat leads the quickest to death's embrace for all of you!" Vanessa's eyes were wild, the light of madness dancing in their crimson depths.

Evidence of the grenade blast was quite apparent, having done some rearranging on her face. A piece of shrapnel was lodged above one eye, causing it to bulge out and pull the eyebrow up in a quizzical fashion. Another had stuck in the side of her face, stretching the skin back from the corner of her mouth and giving her a garish clown smile that exposed most of her teeth. If she noticed this or Carson's absence, she gave no sign. She continued her rant.

"I shall savor zis dispatch, as I vatch the life's blood drain from your bodies, writhing and vhimpering and screaming! Come to me, beloved vessels of unholy ambrosia, come to Vanessa and know the embrace of the final dark!"

"Kinda reminds me of my ex..." Dex muttered under his breath. Sister Becky kept moving, deliberately and slowly, eyes locked with her enemy, willing herself not to look for Carson in the shadows behind Vanessa.

They had covered half the distance. It would be close.

"We shan't be the last to hunt you, you insufferable vixen. Others shall arise to continue the fight." Sister Becky paced off a few more cautious steps, judging distance.

Vanessa crowed, throwing back her head and wrenching Kiki's neck painfully. Blood sloshed from the goblet. *Let them come!!* If they are as clumsy and pitiful as you, I shall enjoy the sport, as I have our own!"

"I am pleased that we could entertain you. As clumsy and pitiful as we were, it appears as if we have left you with reminders of our night together that you shall long remember." Becky looked her ravaged form up and down disdainfully.

A few more steps. She was close now. Almost close enough.

"Indeed you have, you foul, vorthless, bitter old *drogmatika*..." Vanessa dragged a tongue across the ragged remains of her lips. "But it is *I*, Vanessa, who am the victor! And you shall more than repay me vith the varm, sweet syrup of your life! Even one as aged and decrepit as you still has some vorth in her tired old veins..."

Green eyes narrowed to slits. Close enough. "Well then, if you have thirst, wicked one... by all means let me slake it!"

In one deft motion, Sister Becky yanked the vial, unstoppered it and hurled its contents. The blessed liquid struck Vanessa full in the face and, for the second time that day, she knew the searing agony of its judgment Shrieking, she recoiled as her flesh boiled and smoked, exposing a patch of torso that was instantly slammed by three hollowpoints from Dex's .44. The crashing booms of its report sundered the air, wrenching the vampiress back and jarring loose her hold on her victim.

"Booyah!!"

With a wild shout, a crash of toppling furniture and a wide flung tapestry Carson hurtled from the shadows and snagged Kiki with a full-on flying tackle. Yanked clear of the vampiress' clutches, rescued followed rescuer on a quick and painful trip to the floor, skidding and bouncing in a flurry of arms, legs and flying antiques.

They rolled to a halt in a tangle, several yards away. Carson struggled to orient himself in the semi-darkness, removing his elbow from Kiki's solar plexus. She gasped for air.

"Sorry! You okay?!"

She nodded weakly, clutching at her bloody neck. "Yeah... thanks...!"

"No prob... hey, if you could move your leg...?"

Kiki shifted, drawing her knee out of his crotch. "Sorry..."

"It's cool... just let me breath a sec..."

"Hey, your bat!"

"Yes!!"

Still wincing, he rolled a few feet and reached out awkwardly for the handle of his Louisville Slugger. Hope blossomed at the smooth, familiar feel of the leather-wrapped grip. They had rescued Kiki, but there was still a fight to finish, and he wanted to get a few licks in before Becky and Dex finished off their foe. He made to rise, lifting the bat.

That was as far as he got.

A stiletto-heeled boot jammed down on the weapon, pinning it and his fingers to the floor. He yelped in pain. A second boot kicked hard into his belly, lifting him clear off his knees and driving all the breath from his body. He was in the air for what seemed like an eternity. Crashing down hard, gasping, he willed his crushed diaphragm to suck in air but got no response. Lights flickered in his head, vision spinning and strobing like an urban dancefloor. Through the flashes he saw the boots coming at him again. He curled. They struck with rapid-fire precision, hard, merciless blows, raining on his arms, chest and back as he was kicked and kicked. Carson knew they were legs, but they felt like two-by-fours. He curled tighter and tried to shield his head, struggling to cling to consciousness.

Worse than the pain was the crushing knowledge that something had gone wrong.

Horribly wrong.

Then he was being lifted as if he were a child. He was flying again, and he wondered vaguely whether this landing would hurt worse than the previous one.

It did.

Smashing through an ornate table, he rolled to a stop, blacked out for a moment, then came to. Before he could get his bearings, Vanessa was on him again, catching the front of his shirt and yanking him off the floor and into the air with one hand.

Fighting desperately to focus his eyes, Carson stared down into the remains of her face, a wildly contorted and barely recognizable mess of fury, like a rubber Halloween mask that had been left on a hot stove. He clutched the hand that clutched his throat, kicking his feet feebly in the air.

"You...!" He choked. "What...!" His mind spun, unable to comprehend the sudden wicked reversal of fortune.

"They are *dead!*" Vanessa shrieked, a bit of bloody froth speckling Carson's face. "And now *you* shall follow!" She let him fall, hard. His legs slammed awkwardly into the floor, and he pitched sideways, but she caught him tightly before he toppled, crushing him to her breast. Clamped in her iron embrace, Carson was helpless to move or act. Blackened skin scraped against him and a terrible odor, much like burnt cat, filled his nostrils. His head swam.

Vanessa hissed as she arched her neck to strike, her stagnant breath washing Carson's face and causing him to gag. Her eyes lit upon the red kerchief knotted about his throat. It was the last line of defense between fangs and flesh, pathetic and ineffective... and she knew it. "Ahhh...! I have tasted *zis* before! And now, I shall taste it again!"

Carson twisted his head with a violent effort and locked eyes with her, his voice wheezing but filled with all the defiance he could muster. "Choke on it!"

The black mouth parted, needle-pointed fangs gleaming. A soft moan of anticipation escaped her throat.

She struck.

...and instantly recoiled, mouth boiling and smoking, lips sizzling. Carson hit the floor in a daze, sucking air like a drowning man. He rolled to his side, feeling his throat clumsily for puncture marks. There were none. His elbow bumped something hard that rolled on the wooden floor - his bat. Seizing it, he twisted and lashed out in a vicious stroke, catching the gagging vampiress across the knees. He felt them buckle, struck again, then again and was rewarded by a crash as she collapsed.

Surging to his knees, he proceeded to pummel her with a series of frenzied blows, filled with a wild fury and savage satisfaction as the solid hardwood pounded into her arms, ribs, head, face. He kept hammering madly until, with a savage hiss, Vanessa snatched the bat and jerked it from his hands, nearly gutting him with a savage claw as he lunged backwards and rolled stiffly to his feet. She was hurt and slow to rise.

Carson, however, had risen too quickly and wobbled. His legs suddenly faltered, unable to take his weight and he staggered backward, going down... until something massive stopped him. Twin pythons caught him gently, keeping him upright.

"Easy, bro..."

"Dex!" Carson gaped, staring up into a mess of blood and dreadlocks. "She said... but you... but she... you were dead!"

"She exaggerated."

Dex propped him back on his feet, wincing at some fresh gashes on his chest. Behind the big man Sister Becky limped into view, giving her oversized cross a warm-up swing. Her habit was shredded and he could see blood, but there was a spark in her green eyes that meant payback was coming.

Kiki appeared as well, passing him his shotgun. She had her sonar jammer in one hand and drew her automatic with the other, looking pale but determined. She flashed a weary grin and nodded at his kerchief.

"What exactly did you wash that thing in?"

"Holy water. Turns out it's great for stains."

Carson yanked the remaining shells from his pocket and crammed them into the King. He had no idea how his comrades had survived Vanessa's assault, but right now, he didn't care. The fact that they had was enough. They had a job to finish.

Behind him, he heard the comforting rasp of a pair of .45 automatic slides racking home. Dex stepped up, Wonder Twins in hand. He flashed a tiny smile. "You're all clear, kid. Now, let's blow this thing and go home."

Weapons bristled. Shoulders squared. Teeth clenched. Somewhere in the bowels of the vast, shadowy plant, a rusty old timeclock struck midnight.

It was go time.

Before them, crouched at the very edge of the platform, Vanessa rose, a gaunt, battered, lingerie-clad specter of death.

"*Fools!*" She shrieked. "*Sticks and stones*!! *Belanik... bielgo!! Nuthink*?! *Immortal!! Invincible!!! You cannot harm me!!!*"

Carson racked the slide on his shotgun. For the first time that night, no unspent cartridge was ejected.

"Maybe not... but it's sure gonna feel good to try."

And they tried.

At first, Carson was dimly aware of sounds: Sister Becky shouting as she fired off spiritual blows, the rasp of Dex ejecting clips and slamming fresh ones home, the high-pitched whine of Kiki's sonar jammer. Then, even that was gone, masked by the droning, white-noise hum as his eardrums simply gave up. His shotgun kicked like a mule, over and over, but this time he was ready and leaned into it, gritting his teeth and working the pump. The air was filled with shells, casings, holy epithets and a pungent cloud of gunsmoke as the fury of their onslaught poured into the vampiress. Vanessa's body shook and jerked like a freakshow marionette, momentarily overwhelmed by the suddenness and violence of the attack and unable to do anything more than take it. Shoved and hammered by the relentless punishment, she stumbled backwards until she teetered on the very edge of the platform. She hung there a moment, suspended, clawing at the air... then pitched over and was gone.

Carson stopped pulling the trigger, dimly aware that he had been out of ammo for several seconds. He was breathing heavily, the sound of inhale-exhale rushing through his head like a wind tunnel, waiting for the nightmare to start again, preparing himself for the worst.

Nothing moved.

After a few moments he became aware of a muffled thumping, which he realized was a voice - Dex's voice. The big man was gesturing with his pistol and saying something, or rather shouting something, judging by his expression. Carson squinted through the smoky haze at Dex's lips and made out a single word: *Reload.* He hastened to comply and the others followed suit. They waited, tense, tired, hurt and too much of all three to do anything more. After a few more moments, the ringing had subsided enough for a shouted conversation. Dex lead off.

"What the hell?!"

"Dude... what he said!"

"Okay... what now?"

"This is either a clever ruse, my friends, or she has found some means of escape. In either case, there is only one way to know the truth."

Led by Sister Becky, they crept toward the edge, senses alert, weapons ready. Still, nothing stirred.

Reaching the threshold, they steeled themselves and peered over.

"Dude..."

"Wow..."

"Blessed Father..."

"Sonofa..."

Below them lay the still, tattered wreckage of the Great Vampire Queen, seemingly suspended in mid-air. After a moment, it became clear that she wasn't, however, but was rather sprawled upon the broad back of the wooden bull statue mounted atop the offices beneath the platform. From their vantage point, they could clearly see what kept her there: Vanessa was neatly impaled on the the tip of one of the wooden steer horns. Several inches of its keen point sprouted through the wreckage of her chest, streaked with red. Her eyes were fixed and staring, sightless, a bizarre mixture of unstoppable rage and complete surprise decorating her features.

"What are the odds of *that*..."

"Jinkees..."

"By all that is holy..."

"There's somethin' you don't see every day..."

They stood in silence, letting it all sink in.

After a moment, Carson lowered his weapon wearily. "Well... looks like it's time for that victory Twinkie."

"Damn straight!" Dex reached for his breast pocket and pulled out a pulpy yellow mess. Cream filling smeared his fingers and the front of his tattered uniform. "Aw, crap..."

Kiki was still staring, awestruck. "Well. Wow. I... I don't even know what to say."

"I do." Carson laid the King across his shoulder and fixed the corpse with a steely gaze. "Scratch one bloodsucker. Cause of death..."

Dex grimaced. "Don't you say it..."

"Wooden steak. Right through the heart."

Chapter Eight

Beginnings and Endings

"Thanks, but I've already got one."

Carson glanced down at the business card, then up into the long, careworn features of Detective Patch Parsons, Las Calamas Police Department, Homicide Division. The officer frowned down at him from his superior height and authority. Greying brows bunched, dark brown eyes probing Carson's face with all the subtlety and guile of a bare bulb. Today, his close-cropped gray hair and dour expression made him look more like a drill sergeant than a college professor.

"Keep it. I have the feeling you may need it."

Carson kept it. He stuffed it into his jeans pocket, forcing what he hoped was a disarming, unassuming and completely innocent smile. "Sure thing, Detective... you bet! Always happy to help the good ol' LCPD."

Detective Parsons drilled a few more inches into Carson's face with his gaze. Abruptly his eyes softened. A ghost of a smile played across his lips, and he seemed about to say something. It made Carson uneasy, but he stuck to his lame grin.

Then, without another word, the detective turned on his heel and shuffled for the exit. The chime gave its sickly warble as he pulled the door open, stepping aside to allow Kiki to enter. She flashed a disarming smile and thanked him with a wave, grabbing conspicuously for the first product within reach, as if she were merely dashing in for a quick errand. With a polite nod, Parsons was gone.

Carson gave her a plastic smile across the counter. "Just the electric nose hair trimmer, Miss?"

"Yes... and could you wrap it, please? It's a gift."

"Suuuuuure..."

Carson craned his neck nonchalantly to see around the red of her stocking cap, stabbing buttons randomly on the cash register.

"Is he gone?" Kiki muttered.

"Close enough...!"

Carson vaulted the counter with a whoop and scooped up the petite blond, spinning her through the air as he laughed out loud. "*Hallelujah*, girl... it's good to see you!" He plopped her back on the floor, where she blushed furiously and grabbed a bread rack to steady herself. "We gotta celebrate!" Carson smacked his hands together, struck by sudden inspiration. "Freezie!" Vaulting back over the counter, he snatched a pair of cups from the dispenser and went to work with a practiced hand. "Yellow okay?! It just seems to say 'yahooooo!'"

"Er... sure!" Kiki straightened her cap. "Yellow is great."

"Man!" Carson's elation mingled with the cheery *splop* of the Freezie machine. "It has been a loooooooong five days! I been *bustin'* to talk to you guys... it has been absolutely *killing* me keeping my lips zipped!"

"Hey, it was your idea," Kiki chuckled, playfully holding a paper napkin across her face like a mini-mart Matahari. "And I quote: '*No one must know we were involved...*'"

"Yeah, yeah, rub it in! I stand behind the decision, but that didn't make it easy. It's like ordering the 4-star spicy from the Taj Palace... sounds good at the time, but you pay for it the next couple of days." Carson plunked a pair of brimming Freezie cups on the counter and stabbed a spoon straw through both lids at once. "At any rate, I don't think you'll be needing *this* any more..." He whisked away her paper mask with a flourish and took up his cup. "Here's to us – the fearless vampire hunters!"

Kiki met his toast, smiling. She took a long pull, savoring the cool sweetness of both the drink and the victory. They stood silently a

 158

moment. Life was good.

"Well, I'd have to agree," Kiki spoke at last. "It was hard, but it looks like a little time and distance was a good idea." She nodded in the direction Detective Parsons had disappeared. "Looks like you're Mr. Popular these days."

"Wait a sec, brain freeze..." Carson clapped a hand to his forehead, eyes screwed shut. He breathed in a rapid, shallow succession until the delicious agony faded. "Man, no matter how many times... so, yeah! I've really been making some new friends lately. That was my third and - hopefully - *final* visit from the good ol' LCPD."

"Glad I missed it. How'd it go?"

"Let's just say that Detective Patch Parsons of the Las Calamas Police Department, Homicide Division, is not entirely convinced that we were not somehow involved in recent events that occurred in an abandoned meat packing plant in the glamorous Belfry District."

"Does Detective Patch Parsons of the Las Calamas Police Department, Homicide Division, have any *evidence* of this alleged involvement?"

"Not a lick."

"Then, I guess it didn't happen." Kiki winked. "Besides, with all the repairs in here lately, I don't know how you would've found time to fight vampires... or whatever is alleged to have happened at said meat packing plant." Her sharp blue eyes swept the interior of the shop and she whistled. "Wow. You guys *have* been busy, haven't you?"

The store had changed dramatically since her last visit. All evidence of the battle with Vanessa was gone. Fresh drywall, new glass, shiny new metal racks and the smell of fresh paint gave the store a feeling of newness and fresh beginnings. Best of all, the forest of "missing" posters in the front window was gone.

"I approve."

Carson adopted a humble air. "What can I say? I've had sort of a new zest for life this past week. And Jack didn't blink an eye - just said he was glad I was alive and sprung for the whole fix-it job. Said he'd been planning on remodeling the place anyway."

"So I have to know... what did you tell him?"

"That a vampire dominatrix busted the place up, murdered a local homeless dude who was one of my best buds, then tried to do the same to us, forcing us to tear the mini-mart to shreds in self-defense."

"Yeah?"

"Yeah. Except for the whole vampire-dominatrix-murder-tear-up-the-mini-mart-self-defense part. During the retelling it *might* have come across more like 'gang-of-street-punks-looking-for-a-quick-score-so-I-ran-for-my-life'. I hate lying to the old dude; he's been like a father to me. But, I figured under the circumstances, it would be better than giving him the mind-bending details."

Kiki smiled warmly, but there were ghosts behind it. "Yeah. Mind-bending. Sometimes, I'm not even sure I believe it myself. How 'bout you?"

"I'm ready to believe a lot more than I used to."

"I hear you there." She rolled her eyes and took another pull on her Freezie. "So, that takes care of Jack. How about your new buddy the Detective - did you hand him the same line?"

"Pretty much. The only difference was I didn't mind lying to him. I'd just as soon avoid as many questions as possible."

"Think he bought it?"

Carson shrugged. "Heck if I know. I think he suspects something, but he wasn't about to say so. Kept asking about this place called the 'House of *Cow*' or something..." he paused for an exaggerated wink, "...that was supposedly the scene of some pretty grisly discoveries last week. Cops only found out thanks to an anonymous tip. They found some bodies in an old meat locker, evidence of abductions and torture, and apparently plenty of indications that a totally *bodacious* throwdown had taken place there recently."

"Bodacious, hunh? Those were his exact words?"

"I'm paraphrasing. But you could see the dude was impressed. Said they hadn't seen that kind of destruction at a crime scene for years. *Years!* Anyone walking away from that intense a ruckus has to be one bad mutha, according to Parsons."

"Another paraphrase?"

"Not that time. 'One bad mutha,' his exact words, cross my heart. I told you the dude was impressed. Kinda makes you feel warm inside, doesn't it?"

"Kinda. But more like the sort of warm you feel right after you puke. Did he tell you what the going theory is?"

"He let slip a few tidbits, but overall he was pretty tight-lipped. The important thing is they think whoever was living there was responsible for all the missing persons. And there hasn't been a disappearance for a week... go figure. They're keeping the case open for now, but Parsons says if they don't have any new leads by the end of the month, they're tossing it into the unsolved file. And that, woman, is

 160

a wrap."

"He didn't look like he was too happy with that."

"Not in the slightest. But what the hey... it might not sit well with the lawman, but I think it'll give the rest of Las Calamas some peace."

Kiki glanced at the empty front window. "Amen to that. So how about you, Carson... you finding some peace?"

"Still sleeping with the lights on. You?"

"I'm doing alright."

"Hail Xena! You mean to say, it doesn't give you the willies? Not even a little?"

"Nah. It was pretty hairy, that's for sure, but it's over. What do you think, she's coming back?" Kiki was smiling, but Carson couldn't tell how much of the question was genuine and how much jest.

"No. Absolutely not. No way. I mean... what do *you* mean?" His own happy smile faltered. "You're not telling me... you don't think..."

Kiki's white tanktop inched as she shrugged.

"You know how it is in the movies. Something *this* big... there's bound to be a sequel."

Carson squinted at her, then threw back his head and waved dismissively.

"Uh-uh... no way, woman... forget it! Stop yanking ol' Carson's chain. We got her. Plain and simple. Fair and square. Sister B. even said so."

"And you believe her?"

"Like I said, I'm willing to believe a lot more than I used to."

This time Kiki's grin looked genuine - or at least that's how he decided to take it.

"Alright, then," she giggled. "Gone is gone. So... how's business?"

"Better," Carson was happy to change the subject. "Customers are coming back, sales are improving... 'trending up' as Jack puts it. Seems that not having a psychotic, megalomaniacal bloodsucker in the neighborhood is great for business." He took another pull on his Freezie and glanced around the room. "I just wish Pete was here to see it."

"Yeah... I... I think he'd be proud."

"Yeah?"

"Yeah." She reached out gently and folded back Carson's rumpled collar, exposing a patch of faded red bandanna "I do." They smiled at each other. "It looks good on you."

Carson struck a pose of mock heroism, favoring her with his best Indiana Jones grin. "Thanks, doll... you think red's my color?"

"It's you alright. And it makes a lot better lucky charm than a crusty old corn dog stick."

"You can say that again. Good ol' Pete. Even though he's gone, he still had my back. Or at least my neck, which as it turns out was much more to my advantage." He toyed with the bandanna a moment. "Been wearing it just in case. But, heck... it's been a week, I guess we're out of the danger zone now. I suppose I won't be needing my lucky charm any more." He slipped the knot and pulled the kerchief free. It lay in his hand, the weight of memories making it solid and reassuring against his palm. "Feels weird to take it off."

"What are you gonna do with it?"

"I'm giving it back to Pete," he said with a firmness that indicated he had given the matter much consideration. "Thought I'd take it out to his... er... 'grave,' I guess... and return it to its rightful owner. Maybe there's some more fresh construction or a fill spot I can slip it in. Y'know, just to make final peace, say good-bye again, tell him thanks, all that stuff. I'm done with it, I figured he should have it back."

Kiki's smile was sad. "That's nice."

Carson answered with a nod. "I sure miss him."

"Me too." Kiki's gaze drifted and Carson caught another glimpse of ghosts. "I *really* do. Funny. I know I didn't... I mean at first he..." she faltered, tried again. "I guess I didn't realize until too late what it... what it was that... Aw, heck, I just wish I hadn't been so..."

Carson frowned. "You okay?"

"Yeah... sure. Let's just say... let's just say he brought back some old memories. The not-so-good kind." She forced a sunny smile, chasing the ghosts away with her sparkling blue eyes. "But that's *my* baggage. Pete was a good man. Big heart. Heck, he saved my life. You don't forget that."

"And we won't. To Pete."

"I'll drink to that."

They toasted again, and both took a long pull on their Freezies.

"Dang!" Carson clapped a hand to his forehead. "I *hate* that!"

Kiki giggled. As she waited for Carson's brain freeze to subside, she stared out the window at the rays of the lowering sun. Her face grew sober. "I still can't believe he's gone. Sort of makes you think, doesn't it."

"Howzat?"

"You know... mortality and all that - here one minute, gone the next. Things can happen so fast." She considered a moment, weighing some internal matter, then dug into her back pocket and pulled out her battered yellow second-hand GPS unit. Its cracked screen caught the light and seemed to wink. She slid it across the counter. "Here."

"Your GPS?"

"Yeah... only, it's not mine. It's yours."

Carson's brow arched. "Whoa there, little lady... I can't take your thingy."

"It's alright, I've got another one," She flashed a second device, equally distressed but just as serviceable. "I scrounged it up at Lucky Earl's and got it running - got it linked with that one. Figured we could, y'know... sort of... keep tabs on each other. Just in case."

"I don't know what to say. No one's ever given me a personal locater device before."

"Just keep it. I've got the feeling you might need it."

"For the sequel?"

"Yeah... for the sequel."

He smiled. "Alrighty, then - you're awesome. Thanks. But if anyone calls me a geek, I'm telling them it's part of my Halloween costume."

"Watch it."

"Sheesh! Sensitive."

From outside, the faint sound of violent arguing reached their ears.

"That has a familiar ring to it."

"And what a sweet, sweet ring it is... never thought I'd miss the sound of that."

The door banged open and loud voices rushed into the room, ruthlessly trampling the door chime.

"Certainly you do not maintain that her end was a mere *coincidence*, do you?!"

"Hell no! It was *brute force* and *head-bustin'*, that's what it was! If you're gonna chalk it all up to some act of the Almighty, then I expect to at *least* see a bolt of lightning or somebody's face appear on a tortilla. Don't you give me that *Touched By An Angel* bull – only thing we got touched by was a freakin' *vampire!*"

Sister Becky snorted, straightening her habit and turning away with a disdainful frown. "I prayed; it happened. Try as you might to explain them away, Mr. Jackson, those are the facts, plain and simple."

"Oh, I see how it is - you're just trying to take all the credit." The bickering had reached the counter now and Dex flashed Carson a sly look. "I suppose you coulda taken that bloodsucker all by yourself, eh?"

"It certainly would have been a lot simpler without you crashing about like a deranged walrus, that much is for certain."

"I *must've* been deranged to save your withered old backside!"

Sister Becky stiffened even more, a feat which Carson would have assumed impossible had he not seen it with his own eyes.

"An act," she said in a voice as cold and barren as the Arctic wastes, "for which I have already thanked you, Mr. Jackson. Repeatedly. And one which you seem intent on calling attention to at *every* possibility - *hardly* the behavior of a gentleman, I might add."

"Yeah... you got me there. I ain't no gentleman. But I really kicked *&%$!, didn't I?! C'mon, admit it!"

"I shall not even dignify that with a comment, *Mister* Jackson."

She shifted her attention to the others and, without warning, a warm smile lit her face. "Ms. Masterson! Mr. Dudley! So good to see you, dears...!"

Sister Becky dispensed with handshakes and came at her friends with fierce hugs, embracing them with warmth and affection. Carson pulled back with a smile, dabbing at a slight spot of wetness on the back of his neck.

"C'mon, Sister B. - you doused me with holy water six times on the way back from the House of Beef. Do I pass yet?"

"It never hurts to be cautious, lad." She patted his hand, smiling disarmingly.

The next few minutes were filled with the sounds of happy reunion; after which, Carson flipped the *Closed* sign on the front door and served up a celebration feast of fresh, ice-cold Freezies and his finest mini-mart fare. Kiki and Sister Becky settled in at the counter, chatting amiably, while Carson gave Officer Jackson the grand tour.

"Place looks great!" Dex stuffed three fingers of gooey yellow nachos into his mouth. "S'like a bran' new store, man! Mmmm... thes're *great*... yeah, she cleaned up real nice. Real nice. Loo's like y'even got th' dent outta th' freezer door."

"Actually that's a new one. When you crashed into the old one, the impact bent the frame and sheared some of the bolts. We had to replace it. That head of yours is like a cannonball."

"You're tellin' me," Dex chuckled, fishing about in his plastic nacho tray for a fresh payload. "By the way, I dig the reader board out front. 'Thnks Pete - We'll Mis Yu - Yu Rock - Red Freezies Half-Price'. Nice."

"Thanks. It's not much of a memorial, having your name splashed on a mini-mart sign board... plus, I sort of ran out of letters. Jack had me put 'Please Pardon our Progress' on the backside. But, somehow I think Pete would have approved."

"Nothin' fancy but just right for an old soldier." Dex stuffed in another bite and crunched contentedly. "Oooh, *baby*... Yup, lookin' good, alright. You can hardly tell this place went through a major rumble a week ago."

"I could say the same about you." Carson had been idly scanning his friend for signs of injury but had found little more than a few fading bruises and some fresh scars. "How are you feeling?"

Dex grinned his broad white smile. "Solid, Dud, solid. Ribs are still a little tender, but they'll mend. How 'bout you?"

"Well, my hearing is back, the double vision cleared up, and I stopped peeing blood - I'm taking that as a good sign. But dude, *you*...!" He shook his head in wonder. "You got *worked*! You should be eating through a straw, not standing here in my store wolfing down nachos! How come you're not in a hospital?"

Big shoulders shrugged dismissively. "It's the training, I guess. You take enough shots, you get used to it. Ain't nuthin' but a thing. Little Super Glue in the deep cuts and some extra time in the rack, and I'm good as new. Hey..." Dex paused to dispense with the last of his snack, eyes closing momentarily as he licked his fingers, a glow of ecstasy lighting his face. "Oh man... yeah, that's the stuff... *mmmmm!* Anyway, you oughtta come down to the gym with me sometime... take a few falls, do some reps... maybe even hit the shooting range and tear up some paper. Who knows... you might even learn to shoot." He showed his teeth and much of his recent meal in a mischievous grin.

"You do that for me, and I'll teach you how to eat like a human being, Gargantua."

"Just for that, double reps." Dex laughed and took a playful tap at Carson's arm that almost sent him through the cooler doors.

Carson chuckled. "Okay, what gives? I never saw you so much as *smile* before - unless you were hurting somebody, about to hurt somebody or finding new ways to insult me - and now you're actually *laughing!* Last week you were the poster boy for social defective disorder and now, after a near death experience and absorbing more punishment than the mechanical bull at fat camp, you're almost... I don't know... *bubbly.*"

Dex shrugged. "I dunno... we just popped a cap in a bloodsucker; maybe that has something to do with it. If that don't put a spring in your step, I don't know what will."

"It really makes you appreciate the little things, that's for sure."

"I can't remember the last time I was ever part of something *that* big - if ever. Can't put my finger on it, but it felt like... like..."

"Purpose?"

Dex looked at the ceiling, considering. "Maybe... I guess... but who can say, hunh? Hell, maybe I was just in a rut."

"That was some rut."

"*&*#$! Grand Canyon, man."

"Language, Mr. Jackson," a distant reprimand reached their ears.

"Damn..." Dex muttered. "The old goat has ears like a..."

"And I'll thank you *not* to refer to me as 'the old goat!'"

He rolled his eyes. "I may start drinkin' again."

"Good idea. Then you two would *finally* have something to argue about."

"You think this is bad, you shoulda heard us in the car."

Carson blinked. "Car? You mean you... you rode together? You *drove* her here?! On purpose?!"

"Weird, ain't it? Guess that's just me being bubbly again. Hadn't fought with a woman for almost a week - guess I was startin' to miss it."

"Personally I'm not ruling out brain damage. You took some pretty good shots that night - that can change a man."

"I don't know which one is scarier, bro. Vanessa had the vampire juice, but the Sister... well, the old go... 'lady'... has spunk; I'll give her that. I say we keep her."

"Why not. I don't know anyone else who knows the Greater Forms of Carnage and carries blessed lighter fluid."

Dex laughed again, his great belly shaking with mirth. It still sounded strange to his ears, but Carson found that he was quickly growing accustomed to it. He also realized, quite on impulse, that he would miss it.

They had completed their circuit of the mini-mart by this time and returned to the front counter. Dex checked his watch with a critical eye. "Look, I hate to break up the party, but I gotta split in a few." His laughter faded into a grin. "I got a job waitin' across town. It's good to see y'all again, but I'm guessing you didn't just call us here to admire the new coat of paint, Dud. You got anything else on the schedule, you

 166

better get on with it."

"Well, now that you mention it..." Carson cleared his throat and waited as the room fell silent. "As my large friend here so eloquently pointed out, it's not every day you 'pop a cap in a bloodsucker.' Tends to be a life-changing experience. And since we all had our lives changed together, I thought we should do a little debrief."

"Debrief?" Dex looked amused.

"Yup. You know: recap, compare notes, get closure, brag about how awesome we were... put this whole thing to rest. And, as your completely unwilling and totally railroaded team leader, let me finish up my dubious term of service by saying something that simply *has* to be said: *you guys ROCKED!* I mean, Great Caesar's bathtub!! The guns, the running, the shooting, Dex taking the big bumps, Sister Becky dropping the J-Bomb, Kiki busting out the tech... we *spanked* that freaky chica, six ways from Sunday!"

"Prayer, preparation and perseverance, Mr. Dudley."

"We had the tools, we had the talent."

"No one died... that was good."

"Good?! It was *awesome!!* Don't be so humble, guys! I mean, I never fought a vampire before, but I couldn't imagine it going any better than that. I wouldn't change a thing..." Carson paused. "Except for the hand grenade. That was just a little too 'Semper Fi' if you ask me."

Dex snorted. "Don't blame me, blame her," he jerked a thumb at Sister Becky, who suddenly became engrossed in a nearby collection of Pez dispensers.

Kiki's eyes narrowed. "Wait a sec... you don't mean..."

Sister Becky flushed a slight shade of pink.

Carson gaped. "It was *YOU*?! *You* gave officer trigger-happy a *live grenade?!*"

"Yup," Dex's grin answered the question before Sister Becky could attempt to avoid it. "She slipped it to me on the way up the stairs, just before the final throwdown. I told you the old goat has spunk."

Carson's jaw continued to sag. "But... but all that talk about 'physical weaponry has no effect,' 'waste of time,' blah blah blah..."

"I said *limited* effect, if you will recall, Mr. Dudley," the old nun broke her silence. "I did not say *no* effect. Besides," she sniffed, "I thought, with his military background and training, Mr. Jackson would be able to handle the device with some measure of responsibility. I had no idea he would almost blow the four of us into St. Peter's pocket."

Dex let her barb fall flat, enjoying seeing her on the spot too much to take the bait. He shook his head, looking thoughtful. "You gotta ask yourself - what kinda nun keeps *grenades* lyin' around?!"

Sister Becky dismissed the comment with a toss of her hood. "You have shown no special fondness for thinking up to this point, Mr. Jackson - I see no need to wear yourself out upon the task now. The device was merely a hand-me-down - a knickknack. Just a leftover from a time long past."

"Hand-me-down? Knickknack?!" Dex rolled his eyes. "Back in the Army, we had a another way of describing 'em: high explosives. And they're damn hard to come by, that's for sure. Makes me wonder what else you're hiding under them robes. You got deep pockets, Granny B. Deeeeeeeep pockets..."

Sister Becky folded her hands inside her sleeves and adopted an air of supreme indifference. She offered no further defense. Carson figured it was about time to step in.

"Speaking of deep pockets, how about a homemade sonar jammer? I've seen you bust out some tech before, Kiki, but this blows them all away. That was one way cool gadget."

It was Kiki's turn to blush. "Just a last-minute thing, really... thought it might come in handy."

"Handy?! I'd say it saved the freakin' day!"

"I must add, my dear," Sister Becky added. "In all my years of making war with the Undead, I have never seen an Aerial Transfiguration Escape thwarted. I can guarantee you that it quite opened the eyes of our recently departed adversary."

"Yeah - can you say 'bat guano?'"

Dex chuckled. "It was sweet alright. But it wasn't the only wrinkle in her game plan - she got a *lotta* surprises that night. Bet she thought she had us cold."

"She definitely thought she had *me*," Kiki agreed heartily. "Which made two of us. After that grenade went off and she nabbed me, I didn't know whether you guys were alive or dead. There's nothing quite like being slowly bled out into a golden cup after being nearly blown up to make you miss your friends."

"Yeah, I was on the pucker list too," Carson put in. "More than once. There was no shortage of narrow escapes that night - even Sister B. Man, I thought you were nun pancakes for sure. And you would've been if it hadn't been for your friendly neighborhood Ho-Ho scarfing security guard. I tell ya, dude... that was one heroic rescue. You two must've flown 25 feet."

For once, Dex made no attempt to rub in the details. He merely smiled. "We all did our part, man. We had each other's backs." His eyes flicked to Sister Becky, then back to Carson. "And while we're handin' out kudos, how 'bout *you?* When that monster babe jumped us at the end, we all froze... *all* of us, man... except for you. Me, I just about loaded my polyester pants. But not ol' Dud, nosiree - you didn't flinch, didn't even blink an eye. Just cut loose with the King and yanked us outta harm's way. You saved our bacon, man. Now I gotta know... how the Hell did you hold it together?!"

"Well... the way I see it, we all played to our strengths that night. I knew *something* was coming, but I didn't know what. I didn't have Kiki's brains, or Sister Becky's faith or your mad soldier skills, so I just went with what I knew."

"And what's that?"

"I closed my eyes. Scary stuff isn't scary if you can't see it."

Dex stared for a moment, then tossed his head back and roared with laughter. "Damn! Ignorance is bliss, eh?"

They all joined in then, laughing. It was the good, honest, cathartic laughter of those who had recently survived a train wreck or tornado, the kind that cleared out the basement of such stressful leftovers as fear, pain, worry or intimidation. When it had run its course, the worst of their ordeal seemed, at last, to be behind them.

"Well, I guess that about wraps things up." Dex finished his Freezie with a final juicy rattle of his straw and slid the empty to Carson. "I'm on duty 'cross town in about 15, gotta move out." He paused, sweeping the place with a final glance. "Never thought I'd say this, but I think I'm actually gonna miss this place."

"Well, don't go getting all teary-eyed just yet. Jack says he's thinking about renewing your contract. Word on this street is this is a tough neighborhood. He seems to think we could use a little extra protection."

"Sweet! That's good news, bro... cuz your cakes are the freshest!"

"I can honestly say you're the first person to ever say that to me. I find it disturbing but also flattering. Oh, and hey, it reminds me..." He reached under the counter. "Got a little something I've been saving for you. I believe I owe you a replacement victory Twinkie."

Carson tossed him a packet of golden snack cakes which the guard caught nimbly with one hand.

"Thanks, bro! Tell you what... I'll save these for later." Dex tucked them into his breast pocket.

Carson quirked an eyebrow. "Those are Twinkies. You realize that, don't you? Delicious yellow sponge cake, irresistible creamy filling - most of what gives meaning to your life here on Earth. Twinkies. Did I hear you say, 'save them for later?'"

Dex shrugged. "Recent events, y'know. Thought I'd lay off the sweets a little and see about trimming this down." He patted his girth. "After all, I gotta be back for the sequel."

Carson groaned. "Again with the sequel! What *is* it with you people?!"

"You've seen the movies, bro, you know how it is - they *always* come back. Word on the street is they never found a body..."

"That's because it turned into black powder and blew away on a light breeze. You saw it same as me! Vanessa is gone, dude, g - o - n - e... she is *not* coming back, there is *no* sequel... right?"

"Whatever helps you sleep at night."

"Great... thanks for that. That's super. You're a *real* pal. Just for that, I might not give you back your gun." Carson reached under the counter again and came up with the chopped-stock shotgun that had saved his life. "But, then I guess I couldn't say, 'the King has left the building,' which I've been dying to say ever since you gave it to me. So, I'll forgive you this time." He held the weapon out to Dex. "Thanks for the loaner."

Dex glanced at it, then back at Carson. He held his gaze a moment. "Keep it. I got the feelin' you might need it."

Carson opened his mouth, hesitated, then closed it. "Thanks. No one's ever given me a shotgun named after a dead, overweight 70's rock icon before. I'll treasure it. And I really really really *really* hope you're wrong."

"Me too, Dud. Me too." Dex turned to go

"Oh, crap!" Kiki glanced at her watch and quickly snatched up her backpack. "Can I catch a lift? I've got a class starting like *now*. LCC is only a couple blocks away...?"

"Sure, lady. Grab your gear. The Gold Shield Express is at your service." Dex gave a mock bow which threatened to burst the buttons on his shirt. "How 'bout you, Granny B.? It's a long walk home, and I'd hate for you to break a hip between here and there. I don't see a Med-Alert bracelet on you."

Sister Becky smiled warmly. "Thank you kindly, Mr. Jackson, but I believe I shall decline. It is shaping up to be a very lovely evening, and I would prefer to spend it under a glorious spring sunset of the

Lord's creation and not a dark cloud of insufferable vulgarity of yours."

"You just broke my heart, old woman. I ain't forgettin' it." Dex winked at Carson again. A moment later, he and Kiki were gone, already laughing and chatting as they were swallowed by the growing shadows.

Sister Becky adjusted her habit and whispered a short prayer. "There. I owe the Lord a few dozen more Hail Mary's, but I shall settle accounts with Him on the way home." She clucked. "Our friend, Mr. Jackson, is quite the Hittite... but a good man to have at your back in a scrap," she added grudgingly. "You were quite correct in your assessment, Mr. Dudley - we were blessed to have him. Now then, I must confess, dear lad, that there is more to my remaining behind than the avoidance of a certain trigger-happy security guard or the promise of an evening walk. I have been looking forward very much to speaking with you privately, if I may be so bold."

Carson was mildly surprised. "Oh? What uh... what for?"

She watched him a moment, emerald eyes inscrutable. "I am curious, Mr. Dudley - now that you have survived it, what have you learned from your first encounter with the supernatural?"

"It hurts. A lot. Altogether, it reminds me of the last time I fell down the stairs - a bunch of things were happening all at once, all of which were incredibly painful, and I couldn't wait for it to stop."

"A fairly accurate description, Mr. Dudley. Confrontations with great evil most often follow a similar pattern. And yet, in spite of it all, you persevered. You rose to the occasion most admirably and led us to a resounding victory. If I may say so, young man, you made an excellent leader."

Carson gave her a wry smile. "You may indeed, but you'll probably be the only one. I never really felt like I was leading anything but the way down the drain. If you ask me, it's a miracle things turned out the way they did."

Sister Becky's eyes glittered. "Ah yes, Mr. Dudley. I would heartily agree with you in that assessment. It was a miracle indeed. Most definitely."

"Okay, but when I say 'miracle' I mean... and when you say 'miracle' you mean..."

"Come come, Mr. Dudley. You were there. You saw the end with your own eyes."

The image of Vanessa's broken body speared on the giant steer horns swam vividly through his recollection. "The eye don't lie."

"A fair statement."

"Alrighty then. That's a tough one to argue with. But you've gotta take a little credit too, Sister. Without all your advice and help and such, we'd be empty vampire drink boxes by now."

"As I have stated previously, Mr. Dudley, it was my pleasure to serve in an advisory capacity."

"Yeah, about that... 'advisory capacity.' Something *else* I've learned from this little experience is *never* tick off a nun. Man, what carnage. If that was 'advisory capacity', I'd hate to see what happens when you're calling the shots."

Sister Becky tilted her gaze heavenward with pious humility. "One does what one can, Mr. Dudley. As the saying goes, 'An old wolf's bite can still hurt the foot, not by it's strength but by where it's put.'"

"That may be so... but why do I get the feeling you could've taken her all by yourself?"

Sister Becky laughed, suddenly, and it was as if an Irish band had suddenly struck up a tune. "In my youth, Mr. Dudley... in my youth."

"So how about you? Did you get anything out of all this?"

She paused, reflecting, genuinely pleased by the question. "Perspective, Mr. Dudley," she answered finally. "I won't call it *fresh* perspective, at my age, but perspective nonetheless. I confess that I had all but hung up my holy water, as it were, and resigned myself to more mundane service to the Church. And the world. But perhaps I was a bit... premature in my retirement. No, I suppose I shan't put the crucifix in mothballs just yet and shall keep my eyes open awhile longer. Not that I will post a sign, mind you - I wouldn't want to rile up the priests... or would I? At any rate, the bottom line is that I shall be at your service, Mr. Dudley. Do not hesitate to call on me again should the situation require it."

Carson threw up his hands. "*Again* with the sequel?! What is it with you guys? It's done... over and done! I thought of all people, *you* at least..." His voice trailed off as he peered into unreadable green pools.

"If there is one thing in this life I have learned, Mr. Dudley," Sister Becky said softly. "It is this: there are very few matters that are ever truly *done*." She paused a moment, considering her next words carefully. "Mr. Dudley - has it ever occurred to you that God has a plan for you?"

"Eh?"

"Your encounter with Vanessa... your struggles, your experiences, your pain, your miracle and eventually your victory... *all* of it. Ponder, Mr. Dudley. Ruminate. Certainly these things have made an impression on you? Can you say that you are the same person you were a week ago? No, I daresay you cannot. The simple fact is that you are *changed*. Different. A new creation, as it were. How, perhaps not even *you* can say. But I daresay that it was not mere luck that led us safely through our encounter nor brought the four of us together." Her expression remained enigmatic as she studied his face.

Dipping a hand into her sleeve, she produced a small, battered iron cross on a short chain. It looked as old and weathered as Sister Becky herself, and somehow, just as strong and comforting and full of dangerous stories. She extended her hand and the bit of metal swung slowly, filling the space between them. Carson reached for it without hesitation, feeling its smooth, cool weight in his hand.

"Keep it. I have the feeling you might need it."

Carson accepted the gift without a word. Sister Becky smiled and turned for the door. As she put her hand on it, she paused and looked back.

"The path of faith takes us *through* dark places, Mr. Dudley - not *around* them."

With that, she was gone.

* * * * * * *

"You know, that floor'll get a lot cleaner if you move the mop from time to time."

"Hm? Oh, hey Jack!" Carson shook himself from his thoughts. "I was uh... just spacing out. Long week, I guess."

Jack smiled, glancing at the large pool of mop water that had gathered around his feet. "Don't sweat it, kid - you've earned it. Been working your tail off. What kinda boss would I be if I made a fuss over a little handle nap?"

"Thanks, Jack. You're the best."

"You sure you don't wanna reconsider my offer and take a few days off? I bet you could use the rest."

"Naw... no way. I'm good. Besides, this place is nicer than mine now. If it had cable, I'd sleep here."

Jack beamed at the mini-mart, like a father admiring his daughter in her best Sunday dress. He was well past middle age, short and squatty with a faded Hawaiian shirt stretched tight over a body crafted by years of bean burritos and soda. His face and hands were well tanned by exposure to heat lamps, and he wore the casual, easygoing expression of a man who loved his job and didn't sweat the small stuff. He pulled off a pair of black vintage sunglasses, rubbed his comb over and stood admiring his store, oblivious of the mop water soaking through his flipflops. "Sure turned out fine, didn't she?"

"Yup. Sometimes I even forget I'm at work." Carson leaned on the mop handle again, sharing the moment of reverie. They stared, blissful, taking it all in.

"I could look at her all day..." Jack murmured. "But hey, I got business. Put that thing down a minute, kid. I have somethin' to talk to you about."

"Sure, Chief. What's up?"

"First pour us a couple of Freezies... purple. That's my favorite, y'know."

"I'm on it."

Carson moved to oblige. Jack stood a moment longer, basking in the glory of his store. He breathed deeply, exhaled, a slow smile creeping across his face. "Ahh... mop water. Is there any more comforting smell?"

"It's the ammonia... my secret ingredient," Carson called from the front counter. "Just a hint, though - too much makes the walls spin."

"I remember the first time I set foot in this store," Jack brushed his fingertips across a wall, tenderly, reverently. "Just a snot-nosed kid with no money, no class and no one to tell me I couldn't live out my dreams. Used to come in here for gumballs." He glanced at Carson. "Do we still carry gumballs?"

"Aisle 2."

"Yeah, yeah... 2." Jack nodded vaguely. "Anyway... never thought I'd end up workin' here, much less owning the place. It's been my home... my friend... my life."

Carson joined him, handing over a brimming Freezie. "Good news - now we can bury you here too, if you like. I had the boys build a special little place for you in the freezer when they were doing the remodel. I think you'll like it - it's right between the pizza sticks and the hot pockets."

"I love hot pockets." Jack's gaze grew distant and his tone dreamy. He took a long pull on his Freezie. "Love 'em."

The store was silent except for the occasional squeak of their straws.

"So what's on your mind, Jack?"

"Oh... yeah. That. Well, here's the deal, Carson: I'm leaving."

The comment fell with a thud that shook the plastic packages on nearby shelves. The mini-mart itself seemed to flinch.

"Sassafras... you are not!"

"It's true, Carson. Swear on a mop handle. I'm retiring. Callin' it quits. Sayin' sayonara. Hangin' up the neoprene gloves... you know the drill."

"What... what..." Carson floundered. "What happened?! It's not all this..." He gestured at the store, fearing that recent events had some bearing on Jack's decision.

"No, no... no worries there, kid. This deal was in the works awhile ago. Before all this mess. It's part of the reason for the remodel, actually. I didn't want to hand my beauty off lookin' anything but her best." He ran a hand fondly over the gleaming stainless steel of a shelf. "Nope, I saw my chance and I took it. I'm not getting any younger, kid. I'm selling out to Seven Corps."

"Seven Corps... the parent company?"

"That's right. They called me out of the blue a few weeks ago, made me an offer I couldn't refuse."

"Just like that?" Carson whistled. "There's a lucky break. What are you gonna do?"

"Well, for starters, I'm finally gonna put this shirt to good use." He plucked at the faded flowers on his lapel. "Gonna check out the action over on the islands. Look me up if you're ever over there. I'll be the only 60-something old fart hangin' ten."

"I'll bring a life preserver."

"I'd appreciate that."

Straws squeaked again while Carson let the news soak in and Jack stored a few last memories.

"Good luck, Jack." Carson stuck out his hand and the older man took it fondly.

"Thanks, kid. Thanks for everything. You keep your nose clean, keep working hard, who knows? You may do as well as me someday."

"I can dream. Say..." Carson frowned slightly. "Corporate's never taken an interest in us before. Why the sudden change?"

Jack shrugged. "Dunno. Our numbers are good, no problems on record... except for recent events, and that was all *after* the fact, like I said. Couldn't have had any influence. Happens from time to time, I guess." He grunted. "Hell, they're probably spooked about Super Maxi-Pad moving in. You ask me, a little healthy competition is good for stirring things up, but you know how it is with corporate types - probably see it as a turf war, enemy invasion and whatnot. Those suits play by their own rules, and as far as I'm concerned, they're welcome to 'em. All I know is they made me a sweet offer and I took it." Jack beamed like the neon 24/7 sign behind him. Then, his grin flickered slightly. "Hey, uh... one word of advice, though. Just watch out for those guys, kid. They're sharks. They won't understand this kind of stuff like I do." He waved a hand to indicate the general sense of disaster and horror of the last few weeks. "But, you're a good kid. You stop dippin' into the till and close down the illegal poker in the back room, and you should do alright."

"I'll see what I can do, Pops, but I've got some big spenders lined up for next week. Who knows, maybe corporate will want in on the action."

Jack laughed. "Yeah... you'll do alright, kid. You'll do just fine. Oh, by the by... I put your name in for night manager. Stanley will buck for it, but that's his tough. You always were my number 1."

"Thanks, Jack. That means a lot."

Jack nodded, then looked around with a sigh. "I'm gonna miss this place. Take care of her for me, willya kid?"

"Sure thing, Jack. She's in good hands."

Carson followed his mentor out into the cool, fresh spring air. Around them, the Belfry district was once more abuzz with lights, cars and people; the thrum of the city streets pulsing and pumping. Life had returned to Las Calamas. Together, they stood at the edge of the front sidewalk, staring out at the lights of the city and up at the stars.

Carson found his thoughts drifting back over the last few weeks, and it struck him how much had changed in such a short time. He still remembered, plain as day, how he felt, standing in almost this same spot on that fateful evening, fear and adrenaline, and a strange sense of something else flooding through him that he couldn't quite describe but that made every inch of his skin tingle and his insides feel warm. He felt it then, and also when he stood over Vanessa's body.

And here it was again.

Purpose.

His eyes roamed the scene, flicking over pedestrians, passing cars, the dim outline of the Curio Shop across the street, a couple walking hand in hand... then back to the Curio Shop. He felt the tingle again, running up his spine like a low voltage current.

"Hey, kid - what's that?"

Carson looked down at the red bandanna in his hand. "Oh, this? Just something that belonged to a friend of mine. I was just going to return it."

"You headed that way now? I'll walk with ya. The store'll keep."

Carson paused, weighing the cloth in his hand. The fabric seemed to carry more weight tonight than it had on days past. He glanced across the street at the dark, empty windows of the Curio Shop. On impulse, he stuffed the worn kerchief into his back pocket.

"Thanks, Jack, but I'll pass. Think I'll keep it awhile. I've got the feeling I might need it."

About the Author

Chris Weedin was born in 1970 and grew up with a healthy dislike for horror stories and movies. After graduating from the University of Washington with a Bachelor's Degree in History, everything went wonky - now he absolutely loves the stuff. He has worked as a furniture deliveryman, professional tutor, youth minister and computer system administrator. He is the creator and developer of *Horror Rules, the Simply Horrible Roleplaying Game* and has written or co-written seven books for the game. He lives in Selah, WA with his lovely wife and two lovely and obedient children, all three of whom are almost never scary.

Get the Game That Started It All...
Before It Gets YOU!

A fun, quirky little horror-comedy RPG that's guaranteed to make you DIE laughing! The core rulebook for the 5-star roleplaying game contains everything you need to play, including complete rules, character sheets and a sample adventure script. Based on your favorite movies (like *Shaun of the Dead, Slither, Drag Me To Hell*), *Horror Rules* is great for beginners, hard-core gamers and anyone who likes a little screaming and dying to brighten their day. Go ahead - we dare ya...

Available now at gaming stores, bookstores, Amazon.com and other retailers that aren't too chicken.

Now... You Can Own the Adventure Script That Inspired the Novel!

Why just read about it when you can live it... or die it... or whatever. Just get the thing!

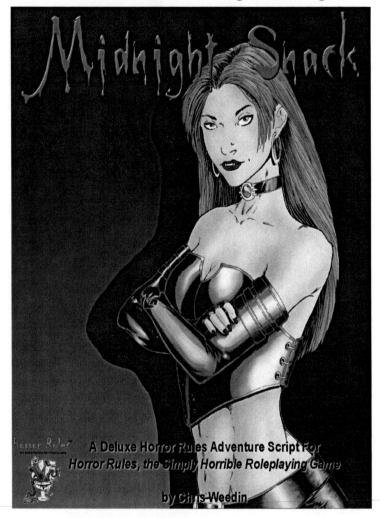

A Deluxe Horror Rules Adventure Script For
Horror Rules, the Simply Horrible Roleplaying Game

by Chris Weedin

Available in standalone electronic format at www.RPGnow.com

Hey, You! More Stuff!!

Available now at gaming stores, bookstores, Amazon.com and other retailers that aren't too chicken.

Script Crypt Vol 1 - Psychos and Sickos
Four complete Horror Rules adventure scripts featuring the best (and worst) of your favorite psycho maniacs, bloodthirsty sociopaths and other charming folks. It's all the axe-wielding homicidal fun you can handle!

Script Crypt Vol 2 - Four Damned Scripts
As promised, this damned supplement gives you four damned adventure scripts packed with more damned Bad Guys than you can shake a damned stick at!

Script Crypt Vol 3 – The Better To Eat You With
This supplement contains four adventure scripts featuring some of the hairiest, hungriest and most vicious beasties who've ever crossed your path. Guess who's on the menu...

Script Crypt Vol 4 – Very Bad Places
What do a perfectly ordinary insane asylum, a subterranean cavern infested by evil spirits and the gateway to Hell have in common? They're all in this book! Open the door to four complete Scripts and take your game to some very bad places...

Ghostowns & Gunsmoke
Take your Horror Rules action to the Wild, Wild, Wicked West with this brand new rules expansion for the basic game! Strap on your sixguns, saddle up your horse and get ready to slap leather with the forces of darkness. It's the Good, the Bad and the Ugly... the REALLY Ugly!

Crucifiction Games
NO PAIN, NO GAME

Even MORE Crucifiction Games Products
Now Available at RPGNow.com!

Check out these killer PDF and electronic downloads at www.RPGNow.com! Pump up your gaming, print what you need and save a buck with these nifty supplements for *Horror Rules, the Simply Horrible Roleplaying Game.*

Horror Rules Ready-to-Die Characters (PDF)
Fifty pre-generated *Horror Rules* Characters, complete with Stats, Skills, pictures and all the rest, all in convenient PDF format... just print and play! Perfect for those particularly brutal HR Scripts or anytime you need a quick Second String Character.

Horror Rules Mini-Games (PDF):
"Rotten Wood" and "Bad Blood "
Take all the hard-hitting, pant-wetting action and chills of your favorite horror-comedy RPG to the tabletop! These miniature rules adaptations are presented in PDF format and include Character and Bad Guy minis, full color maps, Horror Markers, weapon markers and more. Fully compatible with the RPG, the counters and minis sport actual game stats and can also be used in standard HR. Quick and hard-hitting, Mini-Games are *Horror Rules* with an attitude. Let the battle begin!

Had enough? NO?! Then check out
www.crucifictiongames.com

Free Adventure Scripts, Horror Rules Music, Games, Stories, Online Character Creator and more!

Just when you thought it was safe to go back on the Web...

Breinigsville, PA USA
03 May 2010
237252BV00001BB/1/P